THE
WIVES
WE PLAY

THE
WIVES
WE PLAY

An Unconditional Novel

Briana Cole

KENSINGTON PUBLISHING CORP.
www.kensingtonbooks.com

DAFINA BOOKS are published by

Kensington Publishing Corp.
119 West 40th Street
New York, NY 10018

All Kensington titles, imprints, and distributed lines are available at special quantity discounts for bulk purchases for sales promotion, premiums, fund-raising, and educational or institutional use.

Special book excerpts or customized printings can also be created to fit specific needs. For details, write or phone the office of the Kensington Sales Manager: Kensington Publishing Corp., 119 West 40th Street, New York, NY 10018. Attn. Sales Department. Phone: 1-800-221-2647.

Dafina and the Dafina logo Reg. U.S. Pat. & TM Off.

ISBN-13: 978-1-4967-2196-9
ISBN-10: 1-4967-2196-9
First Kensington Trade Paperback Printing: January 2019

ISBN-13: 978-1-4967-2199-0 (ebook)
ISBN-10: 1-4967-2199-3 (ebook)
First Kensington Electronic Edition: January 2019

10 9 8 7 6 5 4 3 2 1

Printed in the United States of America

I want to dedicate this book to my parents, Tequila and Anthony. Every encouraging word, every loving smile, every supportive moment in my life made me feel like I could conquer the world. Without your love, I would not have had the courage to try. Thank you both for being my inspiration, my role models, and my best friends. I can finally put this creative writing degree to use, huh?

Acknowledgments

First and foremost, I have to thank God for His many blessings in my life. Without His love, mercy, and favor, I know I wouldn't be where I am today.

I am so thankful for all of my family for supporting me through my writing career, from talking about new story ideas and marketing strategies to my venting about writer's block. Tequila, Anthony, Lindsey, Grandma Sallie, Grandma Linda, Papa, Auntie, my sisters Paige and River, and all of my aunts, uncles, cousins, and friends (because I have way too many to name). Thank you so much for being there for me and serving as my personal street team, because you believed in me more than I believed in myself. Even if you did lose one of my first stories by misplacing the floppy disk *cough, cough* Auntie. ;-) Also, for those of my family who are not here but still made such a huge impact on my life: my grandfather Lenwood and my great-grandmother Ann. Love and miss you both. Thank you for watching over me and helping guide me into my purpose.

Special thanks to my boys, Sean and Eli, who put up with Mommy's long writing hours and even offered to help me with my stories on several occasions. It is because of you two I pushed myself as much as I did. I always wanted to make you proud of me. I want to lead you both by example, showing you that you can accomplish anything you set your little minds to. Dream big, live bigger, and pursue everything that is placed on your hearts, babies.

On the publishing side, I am forever in debt to my phenomenal agent, N'Tyse. After just one conversation, you saw something in me, and I am glad you have so much faith in my career. I can't wait to see what is in store for us. Thank you to the entire team at Kensington Books, especially Selena James. There are no words to express how much I appreciate the opportunity and your bringing this story to the market.

Last but not least, my sincerest gratitude to my readers and supporters. You hung in there with me, sharing, posting, encouraging, recommending, and I am thrilled to continue sharing this journey with you all. Enjoy, and thank you for allowing my stories into your homes and hearts. I'm so excited about what's to come!

All my love,
Briana Cole

THE
WIVES
WE PLAY

Chapter 1

Something told me tonight was going to be special.

I could hardly contain my excitement as I followed the host through the maze of linen-draped tables, each topped with a single candle and surrounded by overdressed patrons. The ambiance was certainly set for romance and luxury, and I blended right in with my Tom Ford copper-toned sequined dress, which hugged each and every petite curve of mine. A gift from my man, of course. Lord knows I couldn't afford a $6,000 dress like this if I had to make the money myself.

Another thing I couldn't help but notice was my brown face was one of only a few in the entire restaurant. A crowd of crystal blue eyes against porcelain white skin turned curious gazes in my direction, no doubt wondering who the hell I had to screw to even be allowed in the building. I had become used to the questioning looks when alongside Leo. He was a man of power and great wealth, and me, well, I was just the arm candy. The trophy. And that was just fine with me. Especially considering my boyfriend already had a wife. Just let me look good and spend his money, and I was content with keeping my face made up, my body in the gym, and my legs spread in exchange.

The host showed me through a sheer curtain to a round booth.

It was dimly lit and entirely too large for a party of two, but I knew Leo didn't mind paying extra for privacy and comfort.

"My love." He rose to greet me and, as customary, I held out my hand. Leo turned it over and planted a gentle kiss on my palm. I loved when he did that. His eyes swiped over my body with an approving nod. "You look like a masterpiece."

I grinned at his words. The man could charm me clean out of my panties. "I know," I gushed, placing my hands on my hips. The gesture had the already mid-thigh hemline rising just a bit. "And, my oh my, don't you look completely edible." The cream linen suit seemed to radiate against the stark contrast of his black skin. His locs were fresh, and he had taken care to have them braided to the back. It had been a minute since I'd seen them down, so I didn't realize they reached past the middle of his back. Leo usually kept his locs piled high in a man bun on top of his head and out of his way. He smiled, his dimples creasing his cheeks and barely noticeable underneath the fine hairs of his well-trimmed goatee.

"So," I prompted as soon as I slid into the plump leather cushion of the booth. "You certainly went all out this evening."

"It's a special occasion."

My nose wrinkled in a curious frown. We usually didn't do the anniversary shit. That was for serious couples. Not us.

Before I could open my mouth and ask what he was referring to, our waiter appeared at the side of our table, a linen cloth slung over his arm, a bottle of wine in his hand. He greeted us and began to pour the rich red liquid into our glasses. No need to ask what kind of wine it was. Knowing Leo, it was delicious and expensive and that was all that mattered to me.

I hadn't even bothered to look at the menu. Leo ordered the same thing for both of us, some fancy dish I couldn't pronounce. We handed over our menus, and I waited until we were alone again before I spoke up.

"Special occasion?" I reiterated. "For us?"

"Just period." Leo reached across the table and grabbed my hand in his. He used his thumb to caress my knuckles. The excitement was all but twinkling in his chocolate irises and I felt my own anxiousness beginning to bubble up right along with this silky wine. My mind began to hum with possible scenarios of where this was going. But for some reason, my thoughts kept settling on him handing over the keys to either a house or a car. Hell, maybe both.

"How long have we been together, my love?"

"Few months."

"How many? Do you know?"

I didn't. I hoped that the question was rhetorical, but he waited patiently while I fumbled through the previous months and events we had shared. "Like around three or four, right?" I guessed.

"Eight," he corrected with a gentle smile. "Eight months, two weeks, and five days, to be exact."

I strained against the smile on my face, hopefully masking my apathy. What was he getting at? Was that too soon for him to buy me a house?

"It has been probably the best eight months of my life," Leo went on, almost to himself. "I hope you know just how special you are to me."

My smile widened. "Of course I know, sweetie."

"Well then, you should know me well enough to know I don't make rash decisions. I'm very strategic, calculated, and usually once I set my mind to something, I just go for it. No questions. No hesitations."

I nodded as my heart quickened. If it was a car, I hoped he had gotten it in red. Something sporty and flashy. I liked flashy. And I hoped he'd paid the insurance up. He knew damn well I couldn't afford insurance on any vehicle after a 1995.

Leo blew me a kiss before rising to his feet. He still held my hand in his and pulled me up out of the booth with him. His eyes slid past mine and nodded in greeting to someone behind me. Confused, I turned and eyed the woman who approached.

We had the same taste, apparently. She too wore Tom Ford, but her dress was black, ankle-length with a sheer side panel that revealed just the right amount of skin to be classy. A high weave ponytail cascaded down to touch the small of her back. She was taller than I am, a little more curvaceous, and chocolate skin as rich and as smooth as a piece of black clay pottery like you could find on a vendor table at some art festival.

She held out her hand in my direction. "Kimera," she greeted with a huge smile. "I'm Tina Owusu."

Owusu? I glanced to Leo and back to Tina, my head reeling with the strange yet familiar visitor. I ignored her outstretched hand, instead turning my back on the woman to narrow my eyes at Leo.

"This is your *wife?*" I snapped, jutting the manicured nail of my thumb in her direction. "Did you really invite your wife to dinner?"

"My love, let me explain."

"Explain what?" I pulled on my hand to release it from his grasp, but he tightened his grip.

"It's not what you think."

"It's not? Well, what the hell is going on, Leo? Care to explain this shit to me? Because I'm not understanding."

Leo, still clutching my hand, dropped to one knee. And my heart dropped just as fast. I didn't even see him reach for the velvet box. Before I knew it, it was in his hand, the marquise-cut diamond glistening from the white cushion. I couldn't do anything but stand there speechless. Not because he was proposing. Hell, I had been proposed to a number of times, and usually I knew it was coming. But, no, I was shocked as hell because Leo's wife was still standing right there, waiting for my answer just as patiently as the man kneeling in front of me.

I took a step backward, bumping my hip against the nearby restaurant table. Somewhere, the jazz music had died down, and I felt as if all eyes were focused on me and Leo, still on one knee in his crisp linen slacks. I wanted to slap him. Slap him for putting me in this awkward situation. For making a mockery out of this whole thing.

Sure, I knew he had a wife. Well, let me correct that. I knew *now* he had a wife. When Leo first strolled up to my line at the bank where I worked, I didn't know he was married. I just saw a sexy-ass man with a complexion that looked like something fresh off an African culture oil canvas. His smile was slow and deliberate underneath the mustache as he made no move to hide his eyes wandering up and down my body. I felt the blush warm my cheeks and, smirking, I averted my eyes and busied myself with the Post-it notes on my counter.

"You shouldn't do that," he said, his accent seeming to caress each syllable.

"Do what?"

"Look away," he said. "Most pretty ladies like it when they see a man appreciating."

"Well, most men don't make it so obvious that they are appreciating," I said with a flirtatious grin.

"Well, I'm not most men." He held out his hand across the counter. "I'm Leo."

I paused before placing my hand in his. He took his time lifting it to his face. To my surprise, he turned it over and placed his lips gingerly against the tender flesh of my palm.

That had been all it took. The sexy Leo Owusu had plenty of charm and family money, and he hadn't been shy about lavishing both on me. I wouldn't say I was the kind of girl that would go weak at the knees over material shit. Well, let me stop lying. Yes, I was. The pot was damn lovely.

So when Leo finally revealed the truth, that he indeed had a wife, I had to say I really wasn't shocked. To tell you the truth, I knew my attitude was more of nonchalance. It didn't concern me. What he did in the confines of his own vows wasn't my business. He claimed they had an open marriage and that she knew about me. I'm not going to lie; that did seem awkward, but I quickly swallowed that pill too. The way I saw it, at least we didn't have to sneak around and shit. And after he assured me and reassured me I wouldn't have to worry about no bitch trying to catch me outside with fists and Vaseline, I was actually relieved.

"Kimmy." Leo pulled me back to the present and I again looked from him to the ring box he held in his outstretched hand. His wife, Tina, watched me closely, and it made me nervous as hell when she remained quiet and expressionless. She had drawn back the privacy curtain and now the entire ordeal was on public display like a Lifetime movie. I could feel a multitude of eyes from the restaurant patrons zeroed in on our little "romantic" scene. Anxious smiles and even a few phones were pointed in our direction to capture this moment. And here I was, frozen in embarrassment with a collection of curse words already gathered on my tongue. *What the hell did he think he was doing?*

"I want you to be in my life forever," Leo poured on the charm at my continued silence. "Marry me, Kimmy."

I knew my next move was about to be on some classic Cinderella shit, but I no longer cared about the audience. Or the appearance. Unable to do anything else, I turned on my heel and half ran toward the exit. I was slowed down by having to dart and weave through the maze of occupied tables and nearly stumbling in my six-inch stilettos. Anger propelled me forward, and I pushed through the glass door and inhaled the crisp night air.

The vibrant roar of downtown Atlanta traffic greeted me, and I welcomed the noisy relief. After the stunned silence, I needed the chaos to drown the confusion. What the hell was Leo thinking? First, he invites me and his wife to dinner tonight, only to propose with her standing right there? Looking on like this was completely normal. Who the hell proposes to the side chick?

"Kimmy."

Shocked, I turned back toward the building. I surely hadn't expected Tina to come after me. But there she was, seemingly gliding in my direction like she was in New York Fashion Week. I had noticed before that she was just average looking. The kind of Plain Jane face that didn't really give definition toward the pretty side or the ugly side but teeter-tottered somewhere in the middle, despite the makeup. Yet the diamonds that glittered from her fingers, ears, and neck had her moving with cocky arrogance like she was above any and everybody. I didn't like the bitch.

"Kimmy," she called again as if I weren't looking right at her.

I rolled my eyes. "Kimera," I corrected with a frown. "You don't know me like that."

She smirked, and her warm chocolate complexion appeared to glow with the attitude. "You have been sleeping with my husband for about eight months now. Trust me. I do know you like that." She took a step in my direction, apparently trying to see if I was going to storm off, but curiosity had me planted on the pavement. She closed the distance between us, and I could smell her Flower Bomb perfume permeating in the air. Well, to be honest, I couldn't tell if it was hers or mine, because Leo had bought me the exact same fragrance. *What were these people into?*

"What do you want?" I asked when she made no move to speak.

"I just want you to come back inside," she said. "Accept the proposal. Leo is serious."

"Did he send you out here to come get me? Seriously? His wife to come beg another woman to marry her husband? What kind of shit is that?"

Tina blew out a frustrated breath. "He was afraid that I may have been the reason you declined his offer."

"You think?"

"That's why I wanted you to hear it from me. You both have my blessing. I don't want to stand in your way."

I was so confused. I felt the beginnings of a headache throbbing at my temples. Shit was baffling me.

"So wait. Are you two divorcing or something? And why the hell are you so cool with this?"

"Divorcing? Who? Me and Leo?" Tina let out a snarky chuckle. "Girl, no. 'Til death do us part. I will always be Mrs. Owusu. But I am willing to share with you."

"Share? Your husband? Haven't you been doing that for the past few months?"

Now Tina's smile was genuinely humorous. "Touché. But now I'm offering you a chance to make it official. Because at the end of the day, what do you have to show for it? Some jewelry and some furniture in that raggedy-ass room in your parents' house?"

A fresh swell of anger had me tightening my fist; the urge to punch this smartass bitch in the jaw was overwhelming. Tina clearly sensed my intentions and held up her hands in mock surrender. "No offense," she said, though her tone was clearly one of an offensive nature. "I just mean that being the woman on the side only gets you so many benefits. You want to be the temp all your life, or you trying to actually get hired permanently?"

I was fed up. The bullshit she was spewing was absurd, not to mention unbelievable. How did they really expect to pull this off? And why? Where was Leo, and why had he sent his wife to handle this ridiculous sales pitch?

"Y'all idiots are crazy and deserve each other," I mumbled. "Leave me the fuck alone." I was already turning and marching up the sidewalk.

"No, you're the idiot if you don't take him up on this offer," she called to my back. "I suggest you think about it and we'll be in touch with the details."

I kept walking. Since when did logic make me an idiot? And what the hell was there to think about? The certainty in her voice had me quickening my steps, even as her words continued to reverberate.

Chapter 2

"So wait, this chick ran after you?" Adria was laughing so hard she could barely get the words out.

"She was hardly running," I mused, shaking my head at the memory. "It was more like a Beyoncé walk. On some 'world-stop-and-look-at-me' mess."

Adria apparently found more humor in the situation than I did as she gripped the side of the doorframe to keep from falling over.

"Wait. Like literally following you and damn near begging you to marry her husband? How does that even sound? How can you even part your lips to let words like that come out?"

I shrugged. I had just relayed the events from last night's dinner, much to my best friend's amusement. It sounded even more ridiculous hearing it out loud.

I lay sprawled across my queen-size bed as she busied herself sifting through my closet, her laughter echoing throughout my tiny bedroom.

"I'm glad you find this shit so funny," I said, struggling to hide a smirk of my own. "I'm still in shock."

"Girl, I can't believe he even asked that. You must have that golden 'stairway to heaven' poom-poom for him to be wanting to marry you after eight months with a wife at home. You got that joker sprung in love, huh?" Adria stepped out of the closet, holding a flimsy red sundress to her body.

"You out your mind if you think you about to stuff your fat ass in my dress," I teased, and I chuckled as Adria flipped up her middle finger in my direction.

A decade-long friendship had established this kind of rapport between us. But even though Adria was a curvaceous size twelve to my petite size six frame, her sexy ass was far from fat and we both knew it. Funny how Adria and I were polar opposites but blood couldn't have made us any closer. My girl couldn't stay out of twenty-two-inch Peruvian bundles to save her life, while I was faithful with my pixie cut. I had gotten so many compliments since I'd chopped off my long tresses in college that I had forgotten what hair looked like on me. Plus the jet black against my bronzed complexion made me look so much older, in my opinion. Older in an attracting-older-rich-men kind of way. So the look had stuck with me.

Adria disappeared into my closet once more, and I leaned back against my headboard.

The conversation between Tina and me kept replaying over and over, and I would be lying if I said it wasn't bugging me. Especially about me living at home with my parents. Hell yeah, it was weird and downright embarrassing. But after trying the college thing and realizing my love for parties outweighed the way too lenient class expectations, I dropped out. The temporary jobs I landed were really just enough to cover my gas and give my dad a few dollars on the light bill. No way could I afford to live on my own. So, pride aside, I had shacked back up in the bedroom I'd had since middle school and made do with the basic essentials. I lucked out with my job at the bank, thanks to Adria's aunt, truth be told. It was great working alongside my best friend, and at least I was making more than minimum wage, but I was bored out of my mind at work. Numbers were Adria's area of expertise, not mine. My love was makeup. That's why I would be glad when we opened our own retail cosmetic store, Melanin Mystique, like we had been talking about for years now. At the rate we were going, however, that dream was looking more and more unrealistic. Every extra coin I had from work, and Leo, was going toward getting my own place. Still living at home at twenty-four? I was way too good for that shit.

"And who said anything about love?" I added as Adria reemerged from the closet, this time empty-handed. "Leo never told me he loved me. That's why the whole thing is so crazy. I mean, it's not even legal."

"Exactly. Picture you, your husband, and his wife strolling around Centennial Park like one big, happy family."

She was right. No matter how hard I tried, I couldn't make sense of the foolery. What would people say? What would my parents think? I couldn't even bring myself to mention it to them. I had been very skimpy on the details of my relationship with Leo, of course. They knew I was seeing someone, but nothing else was their damn business. Especially considering my dad was the founding pastor at Word of Truth Christian Center. And my mom was on every board and ministry committee in the community. The last thing they needed to know was their daughter was fucking and sucking a married man. I was grown, but Mr. and Mrs. Davis were purebred black folks, and both would've been on my ass before God himself got the news.

"So, how is your brother?"

I rolled my eyes at how casually Adria had attempted to propose the question. Casually obvious.

"Fine. I talked to him yesterday, and he says he wants to bring some chick by soon to meet us. I guess he is pretty serious about her because you know Keon ain't never had a relationship longer than three weeks."

Adria dismissed the comment with a wave of her hand. "That

doesn't matter. Until he walks down the aisle, men think they are fair game. Apparently even after is fair game for some of us."

I didn't bother responding to the shady joke. I didn't pride myself on dating married men, and it wasn't like that's what I sought out. But sometimes that was what was available. And, hell, I wasn't the one who was married, and if the husband didn't care about his wife or her feelings, why should I?

"So are you nervous?" All humor had faded from Adria's voice.

"About?" I feigned ignorance, though I knew exactly what, or *who,* rather, she was referencing. My brother's best friend, Jahmad, was as much a part of this family as any of us. And with him just moving back to town, he was bound to show up some time soon. Which wouldn't be so bad if we hadn't crossed that line and started dating a few years ago.

I don't even know if you could call it dating, considering we rarely went out and all we did was sleep together. Which is one reason why we kept the little fling a secret from my family. That, and out of respect for my brother Keon. Lord knows we didn't want to hear his mouth trying to protect his baby sister.

My dad always told me, "You can lie to anybody. But you certainly can't lie to yourself." And, boy, I had tried my damnedest to lie to myself. Tried to convince myself I was only attracted to this man because he was so fine. I had tried to downplay it because if I had to be honest with myself for a bit, for just a small moment, I would have had to admit that I had been in love with Jahmad since I was fourteen when my brother brought him and their wild-ass friends home from a basketball game one evening. At the time, I'm sure I was on some puppy love shit, but that was still enough for me to jump on our little sexual arrangement as soon as he did a double take in my direction. The feelings only deepened the more he showed me the slightest bit of attention. Of course, I wanted more. But, hell, he didn't seem to see me any more than what was between my thighs. And at that point, I would take whatever I could get. As long as it was Jahmad.

Eventually the little friend-with-benefits deal fizzled out. Oh, I had tried, trust me, I had tried my best to salvage it, because I wanted him in my life, and I spread my legs for him every chance I got to prove it. Then I changed tactics.

My messages were more and more frequent, and I was slowly trying to steer clear of sex with him altogether, substituting instead with "Good morning, handsome" and "just thinking of you." Surely he would take the hint, right? I wanted more. Dammit, my heart deserved more. I was ready to give it all to him. But apparently that shit was one-sided, because by the time I saw him in the grocery store with some light-skinned girl with a short haircut ironically similar to how I wear mine, I'd had to dilute my feelings and pretend not to care to keep from sobbing all up and down aisle three. So the little interaction had been a simple wave, and we'd gone on about our business. Well, he had. I didn't seem to bother him at all. And that was probably what hurt the most.

So when Keon told me Jahmad had accepted some IT position in Houston a year ago, it was more sweet than bitter. At least I wouldn't have to deal with him anymore. Until now.

Adria grinned at my prolonged silence. "I take it you are nervous," she answered her own question.

"Girl, please," I answered. "Jahmad ain't nobody to be nervous about. Sure, we have history but that has been over."

"Uh huh." Adria's comment was laced with doubt. "If you say so. But no point in adding to your already complicated situation anyway."

"Hardly complicated. Leo and his wife are crazy as hell if they think I'm going through with this." Okay, maybe that was somewhat of a lie. Truth was, as much as I didn't want to admit it, the strange proposal had piqued my curiosity. And part of me—granted, a small part, but a part of me nonetheless—was considering the pros and cons of calling Leo to get more information on what this marriage would entail. But I needed to keep all of those thoughts to myself for now. Adria wasn't judgmental or anything, but even I had to question my own sanity at the bizarre situation.

As if on cue, my phone vibrated on the nightstand for what had to be the twentieth time. Adria and I exchanged glances. "Is that Leo again?" she asked, though we both knew the answer.

I leaned over and swiped the screen to reject the call once more. I couldn't decide if Leo was being persistent, stubborn, or stupid. "He didn't bother me this damn much when we were actually dating," I said, my face creasing into a frown.

Not even two minutes later, the text message notification chimed. Before I could react, Adria snatched up the phone and read it herself. *"Call me now please. It's an emergency. Leo."* She handed the phone to me. "You believe him?"

I rolled my eyes. Emergency, my ass. "He's just acting desperate," I murmured. The question now, though, was, why?

After I walked Adria out, I crossed into the formal dining room to find my mom scribbling something on her whiteboard. The room had become her makeshift office, the antique table buried under a spread of papers, manila folders, and a laptop and printer. She had appointments and reminders on the wall for every kind of committee meeting, fundraiser, or function within a twenty-mile radius. I once told her she did more work now than before she retired.

I stood in the doorway until I was satisfied she had completed whatever she was jotting on the board. She finally looked up at me, a slightly aged mirror image of my coconut-brown skin and wide-set doe eyes. "You look like you got something heavy on your mind," she said, her eyes narrowing in mock scrutiny.

I feigned a smile, though I knew it was useless. My mama knew me better than I knew myself sometimes. And I was sure my stress was written all over my face. Sure, it was easy to *say* I was going to forget about Leo altogether. To pretend I was fine without seeing him another day or dealing with any of the drama (because it sounded like nothing but drama already). Sure, I could do it. In theory. But still . . .

"How do you know if you're ready to get married?" I asked.

"Well, for starters, you wouldn't need to ask that question," my mother responded with a smirk. I nodded. *Touché.* "Where did that come from?"

I shrugged. "Just curious."

"Is it that man you've been sneaking off to be with so much? The Bible does say it is better to marry than to live in sin . . ." She trailed off and gave me a pointed look.

If she hadn't been staring at me, I would've rolled my eyes. Yet another reason why I needed to get the hell out from under their roof. Every day living here was like being at Bible study.

"But you need to be happy," she went on at my continued silence. "Don't just get married for the sake of getting married or because you think it's time, Kimmy. It isn't easy, and if you get into it under the wrong pretenses, you and your husband will end up unhappy and perhaps even seeking happiness in other people."

I nodded in acknowledgment, but that bit of wisdom wasn't enough satisfaction to make me completely disregard the idea altogether. But why? Why was I even letting this ridiculous notion linger as a possibility? It didn't take me long to answer my own question. Money and sex. That's why I had been so amicable with his situation for as long as I had anyway. A montage of images from the past few months flipped through my mind: a shopping spree on Rodeo Drive, jet-skiing in the British Virgin Islands, sampling authentic Italian dishes up and down the cobbled streets of Venice. That's the kind of life I desired. The kind I deserved. And the sex, well, it wasn't earth-shattering, but it damn sure seemed like it when it was on the fiftieth-floor penthouse suite overlooking panoramic views of the New York City skyline. So, yes, I heard my mother, I heard Adria, hell, I even heard my own common sense. But I needed more details to make as informed a decision as possible. Which meant I needed to talk to Leo.

As soon as I got upstairs, I kicked my door closed and snatched up my phone. Seven more missed calls from Leo since I had walked downstairs. Unbelievable.

Exasperated, I dialed his number, not surprised when the call was answered before the first ring finished. "Hey, Leo. We need to talk."

There was a pause before the voice chuckled. "Honey, Leo is busy."

I pulled the phone away from my ear to check the number. Sure enough, it was Tina on the other end of Leo's phone. "Busy? He told me to call him—"

"Have you given any more thought to his proposition?" she interrupted.

"First off, what difference does it make to you?" I snapped, agitated at Tina's curt attitude. "Let me speak to Leo."

"I told you. He's busy."

"Well, have him call me when he gets *un*busy." I clicked off the phone and frowned, replaying the conversation in my head. Since when did Tina get so much authority? Why the hell was she so intrusive? It wasn't like I would be marrying her, but she was sure acting like it.

Chapter 3

It already felt like a mistake.

I glanced at the text message once more before lifting my eyes to the shoppers peppering the sidewalks of Atlantic Station. A break in the Spring cold front had finally brought out some sun, thus drawing a larger crowd carting everything from bags to children. But still no Leo.

I hadn't really expected to hear his voice when I had picked up the night before. Tina's cocky ass had me suspicious as soon as his number flashed across my telephone. But, to my surprise and delight, it was indeed him. He had wanted to meet up to discuss everything, and I readily agreed. There was a lot I needed to say but even more I needed to hear.

The tug of guilt had pulled me even more strongly when I woke up that morning and had to express to my dad, yet again, that I wouldn't be attending church. His disappointment had been so heavy I could almost feel it in the air. My dad was a simple man, so it was hard to disappoint him. But somehow I managed to do it more often than not. He had been asking me to go to church for the past several Sundays. And as the pastor's daughter, I'm sure there were numerous whispers about my absence from my mother's side in the front pew. But usually, my Sundays were reserved for Leo, and after last night's call, today was no exception.

The crisp smell of a Cuban cigar hit my nose before I saw him. I turned just as he rounded the corner and made his way between iron bistro tables that cluttered the walkway. He was still fine as hell in his slacks and loafers, his solid blue button-up hanging off his massive frame.

"Looking for me, my love?"

I swear I tried not to smile but that damn charm of his and the way his accent licked those words had me thankful I was already seated on one of the benches.

"Thanks for meeting me," I responded, not bothering to hide my icy tone. Leo didn't seem fazed.

"Anything for you." He leaned down, and I turned just in time to allow those luscious lips to graze my cheek. His eyebrows drew together in a surprised frown. "So cold, Kimmy?"

"Stop, Leo. You know why I'm here."

Leo lowered his body to the seat beside me, intentionally too close, when I felt his thigh bump mine. "Yes, I know," he agreed. "But why so formal? I thought you would be happy about accepting my offer."

"First of all, I haven't accepted anything," I said quickly. He was really not going to make this easy.

"Then why are you here, my love?" Leo leaned down to kiss my shoulder and I shuddered under the contact. Shutting my eyes, I released a shallow breath. Good question. Why was I here? "Listen, I'm not trying to make this difficult," he said when I made no further move to speak. "I just want to be with you. Officially. Why is that so bad?"

"It's not bad, but you are acting really stupid if you don't see how this will complicate my life. What am I supposed to tell my parents? My friends?"

Leo shrugged. "That we make each other happy and want to be together."

"Leo, be serious. You know it's not that simple. My dad is a pastor at a very large church here. How can I bring you around? Not to mention the legal aspect. Is it even legal to have more than one wife?"

"No. That's why I'm not talking about making you my wife legally."

Now I was surely confused. "What do you mean?"

"Polygamy is illegal here, yes," Leo explained. "That's why we don't consider it polygamy but polyamory, which just means having multiple, consenting, loving relationships. Many lovers. And there is nothing wrong with that. Tina is my one and only wife, legally on paper. You will be my wife in every other sense of the word. We'll have a ceremony, small or big, up to you. Everything you've dreamed in a wedding. You'll move in with me, sleep with me, and act as my wife while I act as your husband. It'll be no different than any other marriage in that sense."

I sighed, not objecting when he pulled my face in for a kiss. He made it sound so easy and so complicated at the same time.

"No, it won't be like any other marriage," I murmured. "Tina will be there."

"Tina has always been there."

He was right, and it damn sure hadn't mattered for the majority of our relationship. But still, the idea sounded so . . . permanent. "Why can't we just stay like we are?"

Now it was Leo's turn to sigh, and I listened to the heavy lace of frustration in the breath he released. "Kimera, don't you see I'm trying to give you everything you have now, plus more? We'll still do everything we've been doing, but now you can reap the benefits. Don't you want money? You'll have a monthly allowance to do whatever you want. Don't you want to move out of your folks' place? You'll have your own room in my house. Eight bedrooms, movie theater, gym, pool, a maid, a cook, and a driver.

And all you have to do is to keep being you. Keep doing what you're doing. Why is that so hard?"

The more he spoke, the more sense he was making. Which was damn sure what I was afraid of. Why did something so wrong sound so right? So logical?

He remained quiet as I watched the people pass by but didn't really look at them. It was as if he was giving me the opportunity to process his words. Letting them sit on my mind and heart. My heart. That's one thing that kept nagging at me. I had always dreamed of getting married, eventually. My ultimate fairy tale with the man I loved. But I didn't love Leo. I hadn't even cared to. Jahmad's ass left my heart broken in pieces, so the way I saw it, that love shit was for the birds. But here was Leo, everything I had pictured for myself. Not to mention what he could and would do for me. Stuff I wasn't able to do for myself.

As if on cue, my eyes landed on an empty storefront and the words *Melanin Mystique* seemed to materialize right there on the building. A line of eager customers wrapped out the door and the vision had my lips curving. If I could get the money for the store . . .

"Don't you want that?" Leo's voice interrupted my thoughts as he turned my face to his. "Don't you want that happily ever after, my love?"

"Marriage is about love, Leo," I whispered, my eyes level with his. "And you don't love me." To this day, I don't even know what compelled me to make that bold statement.

Maybe I wanted him to. Maybe I yearned for that love that was absent with Jahmad, even though I knew I couldn't give any in return. But even then, it would make this situation a little more . . . what? Justified? Tolerable? Wouldn't that be reason enough to go through with this?

I wasn't actually expecting a response and Leo didn't bother with one. He let the question hang in the heavy silence between us, cloaked in awkward tension at the admission of what was missing. Why this faux marriage idea was really causing a kind of inner conflict between my head and my heart. Then, as if in apology, he took my hand and lifted it to his lips, turning it over and gingerly kissing my palm.

"I'm not ready to admit that," he murmured, his words muffled against my hand. "That part is complicated. But, my love, do you really think you can find a better husband than me? I want to be with you. Isn't that what matters right now?" Leo dropped my hand and leaned in to kiss my cheek next, standing with the gesture. "Call me when you're ready to make this happen," he said.

I caught that. *When*. Not *if*. He disappeared in the crowd and left me to ponder his words. The conversation left a bad taste in my mouth and I clearly read the obvious ultimatum. It was all or nothing. Either move forward with this . . . what was it? A situationship? Business arrangement? Or leave him alone altogether. And was I really prepared to do that? Hell, I was no better off than I was when I graduated high school, honestly. Barely at that. Financially, I was surviving but nowhere near comfortable and I had nowhere near what I needed for myself.

My eyes caught my reflection in a nearby storefront. My thigh-length black Givenchy jacket and Louis Vuitton booties stood out against the fogged glass. All from Leo. Even down to the Coach purse that rested on my lap and the matching perfume that I smelled emitting from my pores. All Leo. Would it get better? Hadn't I tried to look for love in Jahmad? And look how that shit had ended up. I sulked at the familiar memory. And here I was with a man offering me the world. Maybe it wouldn't be so bad that I had to share it temporarily. And it damn sure would be temporary. Maybe in his country that shit worked out, but this was the United States, and Leo was sick in the head if he even remotely thought "happily ever after" really meant forever.

I saw Jahmad before I even heard what he was saying. Speak of the damn devil.

He had changed. Significantly. Oh, don't get me wrong, the man was delicious before, but age and time had merely enhanced his already attractive features. Taller, bulkier, his chiseled face more defined. He had grown his hair out a bit, a clean-shaven fade on the sides that led up to soft sponge twists at the top of his head. And, damn, he had let that beard grow long and thick to the point I had to wonder how soft it would feel between my thighs. Mercy!

When I didn't respond to whatever he had said, his lips curled into a knowing smirk and an easy laugh caught my ear.

"What?" I said, though I knew it would make the situation even more amusing.

"I said, 'When I left you had that same ugly frown on your face. I see some things haven't changed.'" My mind flipped back to the last moment I had seen him, and he was right. I had been frowning to mask the hurt. I crossed my arms and gave him a pointed look.

"Funny. I was coincidentally thinking about the same person both times."

This time, Jahmad did laugh. "I've been known to have that effect on people."

Before I could object, he snatched my wrist and pulled me into his arms for a hug. I felt my tense muscles relaxing as I leaned against his body. Damn, he felt good. He felt comfortable. He was right. He did have that effect on people. Especially me. And I hated him for it.

I pulled from his grasp and took a step back, shielding my eyes from the glaring sun so I could meet his gaze. "Long time no see," I said, struggling to keep my voice cordial. "How was Texas?"

Jahmad shrugged and stuffed his hands in the pockets of his jeans. "It was good. Not home, though. I missed Atlanta."

I nodded, suddenly feeling awkward. "Well, I bet you're glad to be back."

"Kimmy, why you acting like you don't know me?"

Shit. I had considered myself a great actress but the man could read my heart on my sleeve. I sure as hell hadn't expected to run into Jahmad. Let me stop lying. Of course I had, eventually. Just not now. Not while my mind was still fresh on my conversation with Leo. While I had so much going on, and that, combined with the shock of seeing him again, had me completely frazzled. Not to mention I felt the first few prickles of my annoyance that I could only attribute to his calm and normal demeanor. Of course I didn't have the same effect on him as he did on me. I was just another woman on the hit list. He had been able to bounce back too quickly after our little . . . what was it? Fling? He had moved on like I hadn't even mattered. Honestly, the shit still hurt. And here I was thinking I was healed.

Jahmad glanced behind him into the crowd. "So who was ole boy I saw you with?"

I paused for a moment. I hadn't even known he had seen me with Leo. "A friend."

He grinned, seeing right through the lie, but he didn't speak on it. "You want to grab something to eat?"

I didn't realize I was smiling until my cheeks tightened. *Damn, calm down, Kimmy*. I scolded myself. Could I be any more obvious? I debated declining the offer, but my desire outweighed the strength to formulate a rejection or excuse.

"Sure. I was—" I stopped short when the woman approached us. I knew, even before she flounced up and stopped short at Jahmad's side. Even before she wrapped her arm around his and nudged him playfully like they shared some secret greeting. Even before her eyes turned to me and narrowed as if she could read the lustful thoughts filling my mind. I knew she was all his because she was just Jahmad's type.

Mixed to a beautiful light complexion that tinted red at even the slight hint of a sun ray. Large curly weave that accented her small face. And petite. He had always liked them slim and tiny-framed, and this one barely came to his shoulders. The tight maxi dress she wore was entirely too overdressed for a day out in Atlantic Station, and though she didn't really have curves, it did accent her body in all the right places. I hated her.

"Baby, who's this?" she asked, leaning into Jahmad even more to stake her claim.

I recoiled in jealous disgust. Did the bitch have to rub it in my face?

"This is my homegirl." Jahmad tossed a friendly smile in my direction. "CeeCee, this is Kimmy. Kimmy, my girl CeeCee."

"Soon to be fiancée," she added with a wide grin. "Jahmad and I were just ring shopping. Did you want to join us?"

It felt like the wind had been knocked from me. Just when I thought . . . hell, what did I think? That Jahmad and I would just pick up where we left off? That he would admit he loved me all along?

"I've got to get going," I said, keeping my voice light. I wasn't going to give this bitch the satisfaction that she had rattled me.

"I thought you said we could go get something to eat." Jahmad frowned at my weak escape tactic but I was already backing up.

"Rain check," I said. "Maybe when you're not so busy. Good seeing you again."

I felt his eyes on my back as I turned and quickly bent a corner. I hated myself for still letting Jahmad get to me. For having these feelings that didn't go away. They clearly had just been lying dormant, only to be reignited by the first glimpse of him. But it was obvious he wasn't thinking of me in that way. Never had. Was Leo right? Would I find better than him?

"Kimmy, wait." I hadn't realized Jahmad had followed me until I felt him grab my arm. Surprise, rather than his grip, had me turning to face him, snatching my arm back from his fingers.

"Jahmad, please. I need to—"

"What is up with you?" He was angry. Good. So was I.

I crossed my arms over my chest. "What the hell are you talking about?"

Jahmad gestured in annoyance. "This. You. What's with this li'l stank-ass attitude, Kimmy? I mean what's up? I thought we were cool."

"Did you really, Jahmad? Was that before or after your engagement?" I bit off the words, immediately regretting them as they left my lips.

"Oh, I see. You mad about CeeCee." Jahmad shook his head, and I couldn't tell if he was still annoyed or amused. "Damn, Kimmy, you are really something. Listen, we need to talk." His tone had softened and for an instant, I considered taking him up on that. A brief instant.

"No. I'm busy." I turned and headed up the walk. I'm not going to lie. I was disappointed as hell when he didn't bother following me this time. But by the time I reached my car, I knew it was for the best. I didn't need to hear whatever the hell he had to say. He had a wedding to plan. And so did I.

Chapter 4

"Dag, chick. You been looking at that thing every chance you get."

I glanced up from my phone as Adria leaned against the counter. On a sigh, I slid the device back into the pocket of my crisp navy work slacks. She was right. It had been damn near a week since I'd initially tried to reach back out to Leo about his proposition. Three voicemails and seven text messages later, I still hadn't heard from him and honestly, the silence was making me worry. Had he changed his mind? Had I pissed him off that bad? Hell, it wasn't like Leo to go more than a couple days without communication, and it sure as hell wasn't like him not to return my phone calls.

I glanced around at the empty bank. A few customers were either at the customer service desks or completing deposit slips at the large marble table in the center of the room. But no one appeared to require my immediate attention.

Adria frowned at my continued silence and nudged my arm. "Girl, what is your problem? You walking around here looking pitiful."

I forced a smile. "No reason."

"Please don't tell me it's over that Leo shit."

"No," I lied quickly. I couldn't tell my best friend what I had decided. Whether it was embarrassment or fear of her judgment, I knew to keep my mouth shut about the whole ordeal. "It's Jahmad," I went on, feeling better because that, at least, wasn't a complete lie. "I met up with him the other day. Him and his *fiancée*."

Adria's mouth flew open. "You're kidding! Fiancée since when?"

I shrugged. "No idea. Now he wants to talk, but honestly, Adria, I ain't got shit to say. He's called me a few times." Three to be exact, but I refused to acknowledge the bullshit I knew he was about to feed me. I had my own problems.

I resisted the urge to check my phone once more and instead turned back to my cash drawer. It was about time for me to get ready to go anyway.

"Ms. Davis." I turned at my name and spotted Adria's aunt, Pam, waving me over. She resembled Adria in that she had that same turn of her lips where you didn't know if she was amused or irritated.

I tossed a questioning glance at Adria, who shrugged her shoulders. "She's been on some kind of power trip lately," she murmured. "You probably forgot to turn off a light when you closed."

The humor was weak, but it did make me chuckle. I sure hoped it was something that minor.

Pam gestured for me to follow her into her office and, quickly locking up my drawer, I followed. She stood by the door and waited for me to enter before shutting it behind me.

"Please have a seat, Ms. Davis," she said, her voice stoic. I tensed. Not Kimera, not Kimmy, but *Ms. Davis*. As if this woman had never bathed or potty-trained me. As if she hadn't whooped my ass right along with her niece when she caught us sneaking in after curfew from the homecoming dance. So much for this being a minor issue.

I lowered myself into the guest chair in front of her massive desk and waited while she seemed to try to collect her thoughts.

"Let me just cut right to it," she started, looking in my direction. I say that because it was more than obvious she wasn't looking at me but more like off to my right ear. I frowned but kept my mouth shut.

"You know we value your work here. But after an informal audit, we have noticed your drawer has come up short on numerous occasions."

The hell? My frown deepened at the statement, and I jumped up before she had a chance to finish. "That can't be right. What occasions? What audit? I make sure my drawer is counted down to the penny every time I close out. There must be a mistake."

Pam opened a folder on her desk and sifted through what appeared to be some kind of ledger. "April eighth, transaction history shows your drawer should have had $886.43. Actual count was $739.43. April twenty-third, transaction history shows your drawer should have had $1,427.00. Actual count shows $1,182.00. May eleventh—"

"Aunt Pam, that's bullshit!" I didn't bother to hide the elevation in my voice. Fuck professionalism. None of this was true. "You know me. You know I wouldn't do this. I didn't steal any money."

Pam closed the folder and sighed. Still, she averted her eyes. She glanced to the large window, exposing her view of the parking lot, to the computer screen where she had minimized the Internet browser on her Amazon shopping cart. She brushed invisible dust off of her desk; she did everything but look at me. "I'm so sorry," she murmured. "We are going to have to let you go."

"Aunt Pam—"

"Don't worry about the money. I'll take care of it," she rushed on. "I just need you to gather your belongings and leave."

I opened my mouth again but no sound came out. Shocked confusion had me planted to the floor, and I hadn't realized she had prompted security to escort me until I felt Jerry's big burly-ass hand touch my shoulder. Fuming, I shrugged it off. "That's fucked up," I snapped, and I was all out of things to stay. All out of objections. Where the hell had they gotten this information, because it certainly wasn't true.

Embarrassment had me hurrying through the bank to snatch my purse from under my counter. I felt the questioning stares from my co-workers. Especially since Jerry had to make a pro-duction out of this little task, walking just as fast as me, his steps in sync with mine so it was obvious he was escorting me to the door. I heard Adria call my name but I ignored her too. Just needed to get out of there. I needed some air because with every-thing that had just taken place, I felt like I was being suffocated.

I squinted as I emerged into the afternoon sun. Because we were nearing closing, only a few cars sprinkled the parking lot. I saw my little beat-up Toyota Corolla parked under the shade tree, my usual position. Damn, I had lost my job. What the hell was I supposed to do for money? My little car had well over 200,000 miles and was due for more repairs than I could afford. But with no more income coming in, what was I supposed to do?

I felt my phone vibrate in my pocket, and I immediately knew it was Adria. I couldn't talk to her right now. What was I even going to say?

Damn. I hissed as I turned the car over and it merely spurted a few noises in response but didn't crank. *Please not now.* I tried again, but sure enough, she didn't start, and I angrily hit the steer-ing wheel. *Shit.* I glanced in the rearview mirror back at the build-ing. I was going to have to face Adria anyway. I needed a ride home. I would have to sort out everything else later.

I had just stepped back onto the curb when a clean black limo eased into the parking lot and stopped entirely too close right in front of me. The back tinted window rolled down, and I groaned as Tina's grinning face shown through. I saw my scowl reflected in the black sunglasses she wore. She had changed her hair, this time a dramatic bob that fell to her shoulders.

"Good afternoon," she greeted brightly. "Do you need a ride?"

I paused and I attempted to glance behind her but, of course, nothing but darkness. "What are you doing here? Where is Leo?"

"He's busy at the moment. He sent me to get you. Get in." By then the driver had circled the car and pulled open the door. I saw Tina scoot over on the leather seat and pat the area beside her. "Come on," she said, her voice a little more forceful. "We have shit to do."

I bit my tongue against a snappy comment. This chick was too bossy for my liking. But I did as I was told. I caught sight of Adria coming outside just as the driver closed the door. She continued to peer at me strangely through the tinted glass and I shrugged, then, remembering she couldn't see me, I rolled the window down.

"Kimmy, what the hell—"

"I'll call you later."

"Why—"

"Later." I repeated as we pulled away from the curb. I rolled the window up and sat back on the seat.

"You're really going to have to cut off that friendship," Tina was mumbling as if to herself as she poured herself a glass of wine. "She's way too nosy."

She's my friend, I wanted to say but instead remained quiet. I didn't owe this chick an explanation and I would be damned if she thought she could tell me about who I was going to be friends with.

"Where is Leo?" I asked again. "Why is he always sending you to talk to me?"

Tina took a leisurely sip from her glass and crossed her legs, the Giuseppe pumps she wore angled in my direction. No doubt to rub in my face. Especially considering I was dressed so homely in my slacks, kitten heels, and bank-issued monogrammed button-up faded to a light blue from entirely too many washes. "Like I said, he's busy. He's going out of town soon and needed to take care of some things. But trust me. I know how to handle this without him. After all, you're coming into *our* marriage. Not just his. Don't you think we should get better acquainted?"

"I think this is already uncomfortable as it is."

Tina wasn't bothered by the comment, or at least she didn't let on to be. She smiled into her glass as she knocked the rest of the drink back before setting it in a nearby cup holder. She then lifted a briefcase onto her lap and popped it open. "I need you to sign these papers," she said, passing a folder to me. "Just basic stuff. I'm sure you understand."

I opened the folder, already frowning at the legal jargon contained in the document.

"Just a basic nondisclosure agreement and terms," Tina offered as I studied the papers.

"Leo told me this wasn't official since he's already married."

"Right," she agreed. "But as you know, Leo is a very wealthy man and we have to protect him and his assets. Plus, we have to establish some boundaries."

I nodded. It made sense, but still. I forced myself to read through the information instead of just skimming. Legal words about his finances and something about marital property. The agreement was for ten years and basically if I were to ever leave prior to that, I was leaving exactly with what I came in with, which was shit. I accepted the pen she handed me, but the tip of the pen froze on the signature line. It was temporary, I reassured myself. I had gone back and forth about how long I was actually going to stay in this thing before I needed out, and I gave myself a year. That seemed fair. One year to sift all I could from him, enjoy the luxury, get that business started, and find a way to terminate the contract without losing everything. He sure as hell wasn't getting ten years out of me. Tina was watching me closely so I hid my hesitancy by pretending to reread the document. I sucked in a breath and scribbled my name at the bottom.

The next few pages went into details about the arrangements while in the relationship. I would sleep in the residence and he may, or may not, sleep with me. I was responsible for making myself accessible, basically at his beck and call. I would receive a credit card with a $50,000 limit plus, and this part had me smiling, a monthly stipend of $10,000 for "essentials," it read. I would possibly have access to sensitive information regarding Leo and his finances and I was to keep all of that confidential.

At the bottom of the page it kind of left everything open-ended by saying I would need to do other wifely duties as requested but I would receive additional perks. Not sure what other wifely duties would be requested, but the money amounts jumped from the page and were enough to have me salivating.

"What kind of other perks?" I asked anxiously.

"Oh, you know. Trips, vehicles, expensive restaurants, pretty much anything you want," Tina said with a wink. "Leo is a very, very generous man."

I flipped some more to see some kind of terms and conditions. As his wife I wouldn't be able to have a relationship or sex, protected or unprotected, with anyone else. That seemed like a given. Though a hypocritical given, since here he was able to have multiple relationships. But then again, he was the one paying. Not me. This was his little arrangement, not mine. So I really didn't have a place to say what the hell he did. As long as I did my part.

On the next page, more terms about how I would love, trust,

commit myself to growing and changing and creating a future with him, all that other bullshit. I signed my name, initialed where appropriate, and closed the folder.

"Great." Tina took the folder from me and sat it back in the briefcase. "I knew you would come around, Kimera, and it's really for the best." This time, she poured me a glass of wine and handed it to me before pouring herself another. "Welcome to the family, Ms. Davis," she said and clicked her glass against mine. "From here on out, we'll refer to each other as wives. 'Other lover' just doesn't have the same ring to it, don't you agree? Or would you prefer side chick?" The little glint in her eye let me know she had, indeed, thrown the shade I'd caught.

I didn't respond. Instead, I took a sip of the warm, red liquid of my wine. Her words should have aggravated me, but I was more focused on the sudden swell of excitement that had my heart thumping in my chest. Or was it nervousness? What the hell had I just done?

We rode in silence for a moment. We had long since pulled off the interstate and had now wheeled into some kind of office district. Rows of unmarked brick buildings lined the plaza, and I craned my neck to catch a glimpse of a name or some indication of where we were headed.

We stopped in front of one building. I waited as the driver got out and opened the door for me.

"We need to check you," Tina said when I made no move to get out. "This is one of Leo's friends. A doctor . . . He says you're clean, but we just want to be sure. I'm sure you understand. I'll wait out here."

Obediently, I slid from the seat and walked up the stone walkway toward the building.

The lobby was quaint, with minimalistic décor in modern hues of pastel blue accenting the walls and furnishings. It was empty except for a pregnant woman at the reception desk who spared me an absent glance as I entered the area. Because it was so small, I suddenly felt I was intruding. Luckily, I didn't have time to sit down. A young nurse in lime green scrubs opened the only other door in the room and grinned in my direction. "Come on back," she said with a smile and I, like an idiot, glanced around to make sure she was talking to me. "She called ahead." The nurse explained, and I really felt stupid. I was going to have to get used to all the accommodations that came with being Leo's wife.

Forty-five minutes later, I had pissed in the cup, given enough blood to have my arm bandaged and weakened from being sucked dry, and I was now laid out on the procedure table with my legs elevated and the top of a bald head peeking up from between my thighs.

I couldn't help but shift uncomfortably as he poked and prodded and took swabs of my walls.

"Leo is a lucky man."

I glanced down with a frown as if the man could see me. The comment was surprising but the man spoke perfect English with barely a hint of an accent.

"Excuse me?"

Dr. Lin and his nurse took turns swapping equipment before he sat back to remove his gloves. "Oh, not about that," he said with a grin and a wave in the direction of my still exposed vajay-jay. "I mean to have a woman as beautiful as you."

I forced a smile and sat up on my elbows. "Thanks, I guess. Are we done here?"

"We are."

"When can I expect my results?"

"You'll hear from us only if something turns up positive."

I nodded and waited for them to exit. His nurse left, but Dr. Lin seemed to be taking his time. As if he had something else to say.

"Is something wrong, Doctor?" I prompted.

His smile was thin and he made his way to the door. "You just take care of yourself," he said before leaving me alone.

For some reason his words unnerved me. What the hell was that supposed to mean? If I had been thinking, I would have probed him some about Leo. Tina said they were friends. So he probably had a bunch of information I needed to know. Not that it mattered now, though. The papers were signed, the deed was done. But I would've felt more secure if I had . . . what? Ammo? Something I could save for a rainy day?

I dressed quickly and made my way back to the front. The receptionist greeted me with a grin and some paperwork. "Please sign these general consent and release forms," she said, sliding a clipboard in my direction.

"Anyway, I could see Dr. Lin again for just a quick moment?" I asked as I signed my name to the papers.

"Aw, I apologize. Unfortunately he's going to be a minute. He's in with another patient. Do you want to wait or have him call you?"

I shook my head. "No, don't worry about it. Thanks." I would have to maybe catch him if and when I spoke to him again. I'm sure Tina was eyeing her watch at the length of time it had already taken.

The driver was waiting as I emerged from the building, and he immediately opened the door to the limo. I got in and damn near jumped off the seat when I saw the pregnant woman from earlier sitting across the back seat, quietly rubbing her protruding belly from underneath her cotton ankle-length dress. She glanced in my direction but didn't smile, nor did she make eye contact. In fact, she kept her head bowed, instead focusing intently on her stomach.

Tina was wrapping up a call, and after a small laugh and a casual "Talk to you later," she hung up and smiled at me.

"We all set?" she asked.

I shrugged. "I guess. I'll know for sure in a few weeks."

"Oh I'm sure everything is good." Tina noticed my eyes on the mystery woman. "Oh, sorry. Kimmy, this is Lena. Lena, Kimmy, Leo's new wife."

"Hi," she murmured, not bothering to look up.

"Lena is quite shy," Tina explained. "You damn near forget she's around. Don't worry, you'll get used to it."

"Used to it?"

"Yeah. Lena is Leo's other wife. She's number two."

Chapter 5

Unlike most girls, I never had a recurring fantasy about my wedding. Never gave much thought to the frills and froufrou because, frankly, I was never a frills and froufrou type chick. Which was weird considering how much of a divaesque debutante my mother was. But I was her daughter in looks and name only. All that other knight in shining armor, 'til death do us part, happily ever after Disney shit left with Jahmad.

But if I had stopped long enough to actually think about my future and the little details that would make up such a significant decision in my life, I know what I was going through, what I was agreeing to would not have even been a factor. So why was I sitting in the changing room of some elaborate bridal store in Buckhead, a plush white robe concealing my naked frame, downing my third glass of complementary champagne, and eyeing yet another hideous bridal gown picked out by my "doting" fiancé and his wives?

Wives. Plural. I was still processing that little latest bit of news. Here I was wondering how I would handle Tina, and now in waddles wife number two, and sickeningly pregnant at that. I know I shouldn't be so mean. Hell, the Lena wife seemed quiet and shy enough to stay to herself. She hadn't so much as looked my way as we rode to the bridal store. Even after we had made a pit stop to pick up Leo so he could accompany us and he took turns giving each of us a passionate kiss on the lips. Of course Tina had to make the biggest production of her kiss. Moaning and carrying on like the contact was making her cream right there in the limo. I turned my nose up in disgust and church mouse Lena just stared out the window, rubbing her bulging belly. So it wasn't so much her as it was the whole plot had thickened. And I didn't like being caught off guard.

I curled my toes in the plush carpet and scanned the row of gown selections that hung in front of me. It was like they got progressively worse. Lace, florals, long sleeves, and overly dramatic skirts that hung like Victorian-style chaos. I didn't know if they were purposely trying to pick the most unflattering dresses or if it was just a coincidence the last eight looked like this. *This is Leo's style,* Tina had assured me as I stood in front of them on the stage. I turned in front of a three-way mirror, and every angle had been just as ugly; my obvious dislike showed on my face. But Leo had been beaming, Lena had been quiet, and Tina, well, Tina had stood on the stage with me, using my shoulders to twirl my body this way and that as if it was the position I disapproved of. No, bitch. It was the dress.

Melanie, a petite young woman with entirely too much cheerfulness to be doing anything other than what she was doing, sailed back into the room with another dress draped over her arm. "Here we go," she sang, holding it up for me to see. "This one was your husband's pick."

I was unimpressed. More lace, with a high turtleneck-looking neckline and cap sleeves. This one was an ivory color but at least it didn't have the huge ball gown skirt. The A-line was simple with a slight cinch at the waist before it fell straight to graze the ankles. I shrugged. "I'll take it."

Melanie's eyes ballooned at the hasty decision, and she glanced from me to the gown. "You don't want to try it on?"

"No, it's perfect."

I could tell she was confused by my words coupled with my un-enthusiastic voice, but frankly I was tired and would rather shoot myself than spend another minute being stuffed in dress after de-pressingly ugly dress. But to my surprise and relief, Melanie's smile bloomed, and she hung it up on an available hook. I caught sight of the price tag and immediately knew why. The damn thing was $26,000. Her commission off this sale was about to bust her purse. She couldn't care less whether I liked the dress or not. As long as I bought it.

"So are those your bridesmaids?" she asked as she began the task of measuring me.

I paused. How was I supposed to answer that? I mean from this point forward, what do I say when someone asks me about the others? Lie?

"They are my bridesmaids," I answered quietly because techni-cally that was the truth too. Leo had wanted them in the cere-mony, and I guess I was in no place to argue.

"That's beautiful," Melanie continued. "You two getting mar-ried. In my line of work, you see a lot of happily-ever-afters and it's so nice to find your one and only, one true love." She sounded like some Cinderellaesque commercial, and it was nauseating. Es-pecially because it was all bullshit. He wasn't my one true love and I sure as hell wasn't his one and only. But I smiled and nod-ded because that was easier than explaining that part.

Melanie made more small talk, most of which I just mumbled in agreement with before she left me to dress alone. I slipped back on my work clothes and left the stuffy dressing room, happy to be done with the whole process.

Tina stood as I made my way back to the central floor, her face wrinkled in a frown. "Where is the dress?" she all but scolded. "Leo wanted to see the dress."

My eyes slid to Leo, who also had a questioning pout on his lips. Of course I couldn't tell them the truth, that the damn thing was just the lesser of the dress evils that revolved around back there, so I feigned a polite smile.

"Oh it's gorgeous. Thanks, sweetie. I just wanted it to be a surprise."

Tina looked as if she wanted to say more but bit her tongue when Leo rose and crossed to pull me into his arms. He planted a tender kiss on my lips, Tina's rank perfume wafting from his pores. "That's my love," he said and nuzzled my neck. "I can't wait to see how beautiful you are in it."

Tina cleared her throat, and Leo turned to her and pulled her in for a hug. A hug, I knew as Melanie came from the back, that was too intimate for a simple bridesmaid and groom exchange.

Leo didn't seem to care as he kept his arm around Tina's waist. "How long will it take for the alterations?" he asked.

"Uh." Melanie was clearly taken aback by the public display of affection. "About four to six weeks."

"Too long." Leo used his free hand, the one that wasn't nestled on Tina's ass, to reach into his pocket and grab his wallet. "How much to have it back in a week?"

It hadn't even occurred to me to ask more about the actual ceremony. Damn, he wanted to get married in a week?

Melanie eyed the wallet he dangled in front of her face, and just that easy, she was refocused on her job and not the strange interaction between the members of her five-thirty appointment. "I'll go talk to my supervisor." She beckoned him to follow her with a nod of her head and a wink. "I'm sure we can work something out to accommodate your requests."

The comment wasn't flirtatious at all, clearly fueled by greed, but the suggestion and the way Leo followed sent a pang of jealousy through me. Damn, what the hell was my problem?

They disappeared to the back and Tina took my arm and steered me back to the circular couch. "Well, good. One more thing off the to-do list." She sighed and collapsed next to Lena and I did as well.

Not nearly as relieved for the same reasons but equally relieved it was over.

"Lena, how you feel? How is he?" Tina turned her attention to the woman. The corner of Lena's lips turned up in a small smile and she nodded.

"Good." Her voice was small and barely above a whisper.

Tina seemed satisfied by the short answer and she turned back to me. "She doesn't speak much," she explained as if reading my mind. "Leo married her for kids since I can't have any. We all have a purpose."

Purpose? Hell, I couldn't help but wonder what mine was. Tina didn't elaborate, and it wasn't until much later I realized I should have prompted her to.

———⋙•⋘———

I wasn't surprised to see Adria sitting in my parents' driveway when the limo pulled up to the curb.

"Pack up," Leo had instructed as I slid from the car. "Just the necessary stuff. We have everything you need at the house. We'll be back Tuesday to get you moved in."

I didn't respond as I shut the door behind me and listened to the gravel crunch under the tire as the car pulled away. I started up the driveway as Adria hopped out of the driver's seat, her feet echoing on the pavement as she stomped in my direction.

"Kimmy, what the hell is going on?" she fumed. "What happened earlier? You know everyone was talking about how you stole money and my aunt had to fire you. Please tell me that's not true. And who was that?" She gestured widely in the direction of the limo that had long since vanished down the street.

I decided to tackle the easy part first. Lord knows I still needed to prepare myself for the latter inquiry. "First off, I don't know why the hell she fired me. I haven't stolen any money. I wouldn't do that."

That seemed to calm Adria down about seventy-five degrees, and she leaned against the trunk of her car, crossing her arms over her breasts. "Well, that's good to know," she said. "I'll talk to her. See where she got her information from. Tapes or logs or whatever. I'm sure once we get the truth she'll give you your job back."

For a moment it crossed my mind. A brief moment. "That's okay. I don't need it anyway."

Adria lifted a curious brow. "Oh? Does this have anything to do with Richie Rich in the limo? Who was that anyway?"

Now see, here was my dilemma. I loved Adria. I really did. That girl was a sister to me. We didn't keep secrets, never have. When Adria got shit-faced at some party, that I hadn't been invited to, I may add, and her dumb ass messed around and tried Ecstasy, she had come running to me the next day about it, as soon as she could. And I had been mad she had dipped out on me for some friends she had just met, but I had listened and she had shared. No secrets. No holding back. I was the only one who knew she had had that abortion, I had accompanied her for moral support, and she knew how I had lost my virginity to my high school teacher's son Devon, a jerk twelve years older than me. The experience had been awful and the sex even worse, but she'd listened and I shared. No secrets, no holding back. I wanted to convince myself I wasn't blabbing, because I didn't want her to feel some kind of way I had lucked up on such a cushy deal. But that was a lie, even as the thought crossed my mind. Adria wasn't the envious type. I tried to remember the terms of the contract and if I could actually be open regarding this relationship. But it wasn't like that shit mattered to me either way. Not enough to keep me from telling my best friend. If I could be honest with myself, I was ashamed. No, she wouldn't judge me, but I would still feel convicted and, frankly, I didn't want to re-evaluate the decision. I didn't want to walk on eggshells any time I mentioned Leo. I didn't want to have to judge myself.

"A guy I met." The lie came simply, and I rushed on before she could read through the visage. "He was kind enough to give me a ride. You know my shitty car was acting up again."

"Where did you meet him?"

"He came to the bank."

"Well, at least you gave up that Leo bullshit. Oh, speaking of bullshit." Her lips peeled back in a sneer. "Jahmad came here looking for you."

I rolled my eyes, suddenly irritated. "Looking for me?"

"Yeah, he came up with your brother. They went out somewhere a minute ago but he asked me had I seen you and said to call him."

"Whatever. Did he have his fiancée with him?"

The snappy comment had Adria laughing, and she held up her hands as if in surrender. "Whoa. This is the second time you've mentioned him getting married. Sounds like someone isn't too happy about it. Care to share with the class?"

I didn't want it to bother me. It shouldn't. But it did. It was. I shouldn't have been hurt. Jahmad had always been a smooth talker and I should have expected all the right words before, during, and after he was sexing me down. So the fact it was bothering me made me that much more angry.

Or maybe I was upset because it was bothering me and it wasn't bothering him. That just showed how much he cared. So why did it matter now? What was so urgent that he needed to speak to me now?

Adria nudged my arm when I didn't answer, and I shook my head. "I'm not mad," I lied. I was clearly mad. "I just don't care. There is a difference." But I did care. Too damn much. "Come help me pack."

"Pack? Where you going?"

"I found a place."

"Girl, that's great. Where?"

I never realized until now how true the saying goes: The more you lie, the more you need to lie. How the hell was I going to keep my best friend out of the loop on something this important? I was already feeling it strain our relationship.

"Oh, they're back," Adria announced before I had a chance to answer, and I turned as my brother's gunmetal grey Jeep Cherokee wheeled into the driveway.

My mother's genes were hella strong, because Keon and I were the exact replica of her. He too shared the same honey nut complexion, doe eyes, deep-set dimples that combined with those long-ass eyelashes that gave him that boyish baby doll face that weakened many a woman. We could have passed for twins, especially because he was only two years older than me and he really thought he was my daddy because I came to his shoulders. He called himself growing out his hair, and he kept it nice and lined up so the rugged look appeared intentional, not like he just didn't know how to groom himself. And he definitely used all of his looks and charm to bed every woman in the city.

Yes, he was the epitome of a ladies' man. I didn't judge because it wasn't like I was an angel myself. But he took bodies to a whole 'nother level. Every female friend, co-worker, congregation member it seemed like he had gotten a piece of. He told me once he was a sex addict and I just laughed it off but, honestly, the more and more women I saw revolve through his sheets, the more and more I believed it. But being the coach for the high school basketball team seemed a bit of a conflict if all the mothers just had to fuck him so he would let their sons play. Word got around so everyone, including my religious parents, knew their son was a hoe's hoe. I think they had long since given up trying to dispel the rumors. So, honestly, my little plural marriage paled in comparison to my brother. Well, at least I thought it did, so it made me feel better.

Keon got out of the truck, still dressed in his usual work attire, a jersey shirt and some basketball shorts. Fresh Jordans completed his outfit, no doubt a gift from some chick or another.

"Where you been, KayKay?" It was more of a greeting than a

question and just as quickly, he turned his attention to Adria, who smacked her lips. "What's up, sexy," he said, pulling her against him.

"Keon, go on somewhere," she snapped, shoving his chest. He exaggerated a grind of his pelvis against her leg and she pulled back, though it was obvious she liked the attention. Adria had been spreading her legs for my brother since they were in middle school. Everyone and their mama knew it, because it wasn't like Keon was really discreet, no matter how much Adria pretended she couldn't stand him. Relationship or not, they had been together for the past thirteen years, Mondays and Thursdays.

I caught Jahmad looking in my direction but I didn't bother acknowledging him. He wouldn't dare say anything to me out here in front of Keon, so for now I was covered.

"Y'all should come out with us tonight," Keon was saying. "We need to celebrate my boy's return."

Adria looked to me for confirmation but I shook my head. "I'm a little busy tonight."

"Doing what?" Keon inquired, raising a brow.

"Doing me," I said with a grin.

"All right. Well, if y'all change your minds, we rented a VIP section at XR, so y'all should come through."

Jahmad still hadn't said a word, and his silence was making me uncomfortable. I wanted to ask the question that was burning on my mind. Was CeeCee going to be there? But I wouldn't give him the satisfaction of knowing I was interested. So I too remained silent, and Keon and Adria carried on the conversation as if Jahmad and I weren't standing there like two heavyweight boxers.

Adria could obviously sense my discomfort, so she finally said, "We'll see," and grabbing my arm, guided me toward the house. "Girl, why don't you want to go?" she asked once we were alone inside.

"I told you I need to pack and I really don't want to be bothered with my brother or Jahmad tonight." And by *my brother and Jahmad* I meant *Jahmad.*

"Okay, well, we don't need to go with them. But how about we go out instead. It doesn't have to be a club. Something to cheer you up."

I frowned. "Cheer me up from what?"

"That bullshit at the job," Adria said like it was obvious.

I smirked. Leo had deposited $5,000 in my account, I noticed after we came from the bridal shop. I was cheered all the way up. But it would be nice to get out and splurge a little. Have some fun with my girl and not have to wonder who was buying me a drink because my broke ass couldn't afford it. Maybe even get a new outfit. The more the idea formed, the better it sounded. And why not have a little fun with Jahmad in the process?

———————

XR was once a three-story mansion on fourteen acres with nine bedrooms. Some rich guy had bought it, tricked it out with paint and strobe lights, and turned the place into one of the liveliest nightclubs in Atlanta. Saturday night was no exception.

Most of the grass on the property had been removed to make room for parking. A stream of luxury cars packed the lot, and attendants wearing reflective yellow vests and waving orange batons like plane runway agents attempted to manage the congestion. My car was still at the bank from earlier, where it was going to stay, more than likely, so I was sitting shotgun in Adria's car as she inched along behind the other vehicles.

I hadn't gone too crazy with the shopping. My bandage dress left little to the imagination in its deep burgundy hue. It wrapped around my body to hide the parts that could get me in trouble. I had paired the dress with silver jewelry, stilettos, and a burgundy wristlet that was just big enough to carry the essentials.

Adria had insisted she was going to wear something she already had, but when I insisted on paying, she had picked out a black-and-white romper with long sleeves and a low dip in the back. Between the two of us, it was a dead even tie for who was showing more skin.

I flipped down the visor once more to give my lips another coat of color. Of course, I had done the makeup for both of us, and our faces looked like they belonged on somebody's magazine cover. It felt good, being out with money to spend. I didn't know how the whole thing with Leo would work so I certainly didn't want to blow through every dollar. But I was eager to enjoy myself. And throw it all in Jahmad's face at the same time.

We were directed to a tight-squeeze space toward the back. I got out, already regretting the shoes I'd chosen for the long trek up to the building. But the music was blasting, the red-and-purple beam projector lights danced in the sky, and a crowd of people spilled out of the front entryways and onto the enlarged deck in the back. It had been raining earlier, so now a dense fog rose up from the slick pavement as we hiked up to the entrance.

Rather than wait in line, I led the way to the door, bypassing the groans and lip smacking from the waiting club-goers along the way. I didn't know what I was doing or if it would even work, but, hell, money talked, and I had enough to test the waters.

The bouncer, a bulky guy busting from a red XR logo shirt, stood at the door checking IDs. Behind him, two other men in the same shirt guarded the door and patted people down before they entered.

I stepped up to the first man and he eyed me warily. Immediately, I reached into my purse and pulled out five crisp hundred-dollar bills along with my ID. He looked from me to the money and behind me at Adria, who also flashing her own ID. Without a word, he silently took the cash and stepped aside for us to go through. I grinned. Shit felt like winning the lottery. They patted us down, and the door swung open, the rush of music and noise greeting us like a slap in the face.

XR was known for its theme nights. Tonight, it was apparently glow-in-the-dark. All of the lights were off, the room illuminated by glow sticks and glow-in-the-dark paint smeared on the cage dancers grinding on the elevated mini platforms. A fast-paced club mix blared through the speakers, bass thick enough to have the marble floors vibrating under my feet.

Off to the side, a set of floating stairs spiraled its way up to the second level, VIP, where multiple sections separated by sheer curtains and a stretch of circular leather couches were situated for perfect viewing of the activity below.

Asses clapped on the dance floor like an auditorium round of applause, and the men certainly stood back appreciating the view. When the DJ mixed up another beat, appreciative hoots and hollers rose up to roar in a deafening echo. We had come at the right time because the place was definitely in full swing.

Adria grabbed my arm and propelled me through the throng of people toward the standing glass bar that lined a mirrored wall off to one side.

A young ebony bartender with a neon bra-and-panty set and fishnets smiled as we approached. "What you drinking, ladies?" she said, slapping a monogrammed napkin in front of us.

"Hennessy and Coke," Adria recited, and I narrowed my eyes. Her order of her ratchet poison of choice meant she intended on getting all the way fucked up, verification that I would be driving home tonight, so I had to drink light. That's usually how it went when we went out. The responsible one was never really defined, but it was just understood when it came time to order drinks.

"Margarita," I said when the bartender turned her eyes on me. She quickly whisked away to make our drink orders, and I caught Adria scanning the crowd, probably looking for my brother and Jahmad. I had struggled not to look my damn self.

It was different, being back in the club scene. Of course that's all I had done when I was in college. That was my problem. It was no surprise to anyone to find me shit-faced drunk in my own throw-up and being woken up just to shower, change clothes, and hit the next party. Now, I didn't go as overboard, but the whole vibe was equally thrilling.

I felt a light touch on my arm. I turned, drink in hand, and stared in the face of an older gentleman. He was light-skinned, not usually my choice, but he did have a gorgeous smile. I could see the row of pearly whites even in the dim light. He stuck out sorely, because while every other man had on jeans or khakis, this guy wore a charcoal gray suit with a mustard yellow button-up undone at the neck. I guess it was his weak attempt to appear casual, though the rest of his attire completely contradicted that.

"You are beautiful," he said, leaning close to my ear so I could hear him over the loud music. "I know you are with your friend, but I was wondering if you wanted to dance." I kept my face neutral as I sipped on my drink, the watery taste of the alcohol doing nothing more than hydrating me. They really had to do better about these drinks.

"You don't even know me," I replied, and he smiled and held out his hand.

"Greg."

I paused before accepting it. "Kimmy."

"Now can we dance?"

Adria nudged my shoulder and laughed at my attempt at playing coy. "Girl, go dance with that man. I'll find your brother."

I nodded, took a sip of my drink, and sat it on the bar. I let myself be led out onto the floor, and he pulled me into his arms, more from the lack of space rather than the intent. I felt the music in my hips and began rolling against his body, allowing his arm to remain wrapped around my waist. Bodies bumped bodies, and the air was thick with a mix of perfume, sweat, and liquor, enough to cause the first beads of perspiration to dampen my forehead. I thank God I wore next to nothing because the heat had me wanting to take off the little bit of material I did have on to let my skin breathe.

He turned me around and I continued swaying to the music, feeling his eyes on my body as I turned this little sensual dance into my own personal show. Greg's hands were on my waist, then my thighs, rubbing up against my ass while his breath tickled the back of my neck.

Don't ask me how I made eye contact with Jahmad from this distance. But through the crowd, from the floor above, in the darkened room, there he was looking dead at me. He was on the VIP second level, leaning casually over the banister, the neck of a beer bottle between his fingers. Every so often, he took a casual sip from the drink but kept his eyes trained on me.

I suddenly felt shy and awkward. I had come wanting to see him see me, and now that I had his undivided attention, I was nervous as hell. And not to mention horny. Even from this distance I remembered that same look he used to give me right before he undressed me: narrowed eyes, a half smirk on his lips. And my body reacted on demand.

Even now, as I gyrated against Greg and my body seemed to hum to life, I imagined it was Jahmad pressed against me and I sank into that familiar memory. Damn, I missed him. I wanted him. And I felt his mutual feelings as clearly as if he had spoken them out loud.

The song ended and I turned, smiling appreciatively at Greg. "Thank you for that," I said.

"No, thank *you*, Kimmy." He pulled a business card from his breast pocket and passed it to me. I didn't bother glancing at it, just slipped it into my purse. "You going to use that or you taking it so as not to break my heart?"

I grinned, because it was more than likely the latter. With Leo on my mind and Jahmad on my heart, I had no room for another man. But Greg—he was cute and seemed sweet so I didn't see any harm in taking the card.

"We'll see," I responded with a flirtatious wink. No sooner had the words left my lips than I felt an iron grip wrap around my arm and snatch me around. I stumbled, the abrupt movement throwing me off balance, and my eyes ballooned when the man came into view.

Leo's face was about as dark as the room, so it took a moment for my eyes to adjust to his features. The menacing scowl, the forehead creased in the same rage that consumed his narrowed eyes, not to mention the damn vice grip I knew was going to leave a bruise on my arm.

"Leo, what—" I stopped when I saw his jaw clenching, and the look he gave me alone sent a piercing shudder through my spine. I swallowed the rest of the objection.

"What the hell are you doing here, Kimmy?" He didn't yell. Leo never yelled. But I read each word as it hissed through his tight lips and I wondered if I should answer.

The crowd had parted, no doubt wanting to witness the action on the dance floor. Greg stood behind me, and I winced when he placed a protective hand on my shoulder. *Don't do it, Greg. Don't be a hero.* Hell, now even I had no idea what Leo was capable of.

"You need to take your hands off of her," Greg said. He didn't seem intimidated but even the authoritative voice seemed minuscule compared to the aggressive stance and death daggers Leo was throwing in my direction. He didn't even take his eyes off of me.

"I'm her fucking husband, so I think you need to take your damn hands off of her," he said.

Either obedience or shock, I don't know which, but I sighed in relief when I felt Greg's hand leave my shoulder. Still clutching my arm, Leo led the way toward the entrance as I struggled to half run, half jog in the heels and not bust my ass.

I didn't realize how much I had been suffocating from the heat, or maybe it was embarrassment, until we left the building and the cool night air hit my face. It had started drizzling, tiny splatters dampening my hair and cheeks as we stepped to the limo waiting right there at the entrance. He opened the car door for me; once I got in, he didn't follow, instead slamming it shut and thumping on the roof to prompt the driver to pull off. I glanced behind me through the back window and watched him cross the parking lot and disappear between the row of cars.

I sat back on a sigh. What the hell now?

Chapter 6

My ass was scared.

As grown as I was and as corny as it sounded, I felt like I was on death row. That feeling of anxiety as you take one heavy step in front of the other while a line of inmates watches on in pity and remorse. The heart palpitations, the increasing adrenaline mixed with fear at what lay on the other side of the hall. The uncertainty of the certain. That was the best way to put it. You knew it was coming but the surrounding details were gray. What would happen? What would it feel like? And no matter how you try and turn your mind to something else, something positive, still the strength of your impending future hangs over your head and lies dominant in your subconscious.

That's what it felt like as the limo eased up to an iron gate. But instead of the electric chair, I was headed toward my husband. My body felt numb as I shifted to the edge of the seat, craning my neck to peer out of the window. But it was black with only the moon reflecting off what appeared to be a lake in front of us.

"Where are we going?" I questioned. Just my luck this driver was about to gut me out here in the middle of nowhere and dispose of my stupid ass.

"Mr. Owusu asked me to bring you back to his place to wait for him," he said, pressing a button on his sun visor. On cue, the gates swung open, exposing the paved driveway that wound into the distance before being swallowed by darkness. Of course, his house. I had never been, but instantly I saw the isolation fit Leo perfectly. He wasn't really flashy, that was my job. So, no, I didn't expect anything other than a residence set apart from the rest of civilization.

We crept along the paved driveway, bending around a glistening lake with the call of crickets like a melody against the night sky. A few ducks circled the water near the banks, a few crossing the path so we had to stop a moment to let them pass.

The mansion itself didn't seem to suit him. I eyed the massive house as the limo maneuvered up the circular driveway to brake under an awning. I didn't know what I'd been expecting, but to picture Leo living in something this large nestled amid lush acreage of perfectly manicured lawn seemed a bit far-fetched. Probably Tina's doing. Leo was way too low-key for this type of place.

Being so far from the road was obviously privacy enough, because they had foregone blinds altogether. Now, only a few lights shone brightly through the oversize second-floor windows, exposing every furnishing down to the paintings on the wall.

As soon as we stopped, I opened the door and stepped back out into the night air, tugging at the hem of my dress, which had risen to expose nearly all of my ass. A wonder that I was in love with this dress on the mannequin and I thought I was the shit in the club. Now I felt like nothing more than a cheap gutter rat.

"Where's Leo?" I asked, glancing around.

The driver had circled the car to close my door. "He'll be along. You can go on inside, Mrs. Owusu. The other wives are waiting."

I cringed. Would I ever get used to that? I turned and looked at the driver, an older black gentleman with wrinkles creasing his face. He looked like he could've been my grandfather. I wondered why Leo had him working for him. He should've been playing checkers in some park, already enjoying the benefits of having had to work all his damn life.

"Please just call me Kimmy," I said with a smile. "What's your name?"

"Eddie."

"Well, thank you, Mr. Eddie. Are you done for the night? Are you off anytime soon?"

Eddie blinked in apparent surprise. "Um, no, Mrs. Owusu. I'm on call for whenever you lovely ladies need me."

I shook my head. A shame. "Go home, Mr. Eddie. Get some rest. It's late. Don't you have a wife or someone waiting?"

He was shifting nervously as if he didn't know how to answer. "Uh, yes, ma'am, but she understands I have to work. We are taking care of my grandbabies and they're not cheap."

I suddenly felt sorry for Mr. Eddie. Well, if I was going to be Mrs. Owusu there were certainly some changes that needed to take place. "Well, take tomorrow off, then," I said. "With pay. You deserve it."

"But, ma'am—"

"Look, if Leo has a problem with it, he can talk to me." I grinned and added, "There's a new wife in the house."

"It's not Mr. Owusu, ma'am. It's the other Mrs. Owusu. She wouldn't allow it."

I rolled my eyes, my disgust for Tina increasing exponentially. She couldn't even give this man a damn break.

"No disrespect," Eddie added quickly. He tipped his hat and walked back toward the driver's seat. Then, as if he had been debating first whether to express it, he said, "Thank you, Mrs. Owusu. Not one of them has ever been as kind to me as you. Not one has even shown they care. That means a lot to an old man like me." He then lowered himself back into the car. Yeah, there were definitely going to be some changes. As soon as I could make them. But first, I needed to deal with Leo. The fear inched its way back into my spine as I remembered his harsh reaction to catching me in the club. The ink hadn't even dried on the papers and here I was already fucking up.

I turned back toward the house as the front door opened, surprised when it wasn't Leo, or even Tina, but Lena who poked her head through. She didn't look at me as I walked up, but a small smile grazed her lips as she opened the door wider for me to step through.

"So glad you're here," she said, and I had to think back for a moment. I believed those were the most words I had heard her speak. Hell, even her voice was low and raspy like it didn't get put to much use.

"Thank you," I said. "Where is Tina?"

"With Leo. They should be back soon." Lena lowered her head as we stood awkwardly in the doorway. For a moment, she seemed like she wanted to say something else. Or maybe she was waiting for me to say something. But then she turned and walked toward a staircase. "I'll show you to your room." Thank God. This chick was a little weird and it was making me uncomfortable.

The interior was as sweeping and majestic as the exterior with expanses of beautiful ceramic tile floors, elaborate archways, and heavily adorned chandeliers dripping from cathedral ceilings. A light jazz tune wafted from the built-in speakers as we headed up the grand staircase.

We stopped on the second landing, and Lena showed me into a bedroom at the far end of the hall, which she indicated was right next door to a guest room, separated only by an oversize bathroom that opened to both rooms.

The room was damn near the size of my parents' house, with a stone fireplace, a bay window overlooking an infinity pool, and a California king sleigh bed buried under a mass of decorative pillows in hues of purples and teals. Someone had already pulled down the duvet on the bed, tucking it neatly at the footboard to expose crisp white Egyptian cotton sheets.

"I hope you like these colors," Lena said, glancing around in hesitation. "I picked them out."

"Thank you," I said, nodding. The entire room had been done in purples and teals with accents of gray and white, from the paint color to the two chairs and ottoman positioned in the sitting room. It wasn't necessarily the colors I would've picked for myself but I liked it just the same. Something about the combination instantly calmed my nerves.

"Lena, you seem pretty nice," I said, stepping out of my heels. "Why are you so quiet?"

"I don't have much to say, I suppose."

I wanted to chuckle. Probably because Tina did enough talking for the both of them.

"Well, how do you like it?" I pressed, taking a seat on the bed. I patted the area beside me, but Lena stayed planted in the middle of the floor, rubbing her belly. She seemed to be deep in thought at what I assumed was a simple question.

Finally, she lifted a shoulder in a half shrug. "It's okay, I suppose. I just do what I'm told and stay out of everyone's way."

I frowned. What kind of relationship was that? And I certainly hoped Leo and Tina didn't expect me to just be that docile. "Well, what do you do for fun?"

Lena lapsed into another dazed look. Damn, had no one ever taken the time to actually talk to the girl? She acted as if I were quizzing her for the SATs. "I read," she answered finally. "Leo has a very nice library. And I write. Not as much as I'd like to, but I still try to do it when I feel inspired."

"But do you go anywhere? Like hang out with friends?"

"No, not really. I don't have many friends."

"Well, what about family?"

Lena's face seemed to fall the more and more I pried. She shook her head. "I don't have much family either."

I wondered if that was by choice. Lena seemed content, but

maybe that was just a facade. More than that, she seemed lonely. And slightly troubled.

"Well, since I'm here, maybe we can hang out some."

Lena's eyes seemed to brighten at that. "I'm not sure how much fun I am carrying around this little load."

"How far along are you?"

"Eight months."

"Girl or boy?"

"I don't know. Leo wanted it to be a surprise."

I stood and held my hand out toward her stomach. "May I?"

She nodded and took a step in my direction until my hand was now resting flat against the taut skin over her navel. It was firm and, as if the baby could sense the extra attention, a small nudge pressed back against my palm, startling a gasp from my lips.

"You felt that?"

Lena giggled at my reaction, and I grinned. Kids seemed like such a far-fetched thing for me. I mean, I wanted them. Eventually. But to imagine being pregnant now, the idea seemed too foreign. I couldn't even see myself as a mother.

"I'm glad you're here," Lena said, looking me in the eyes for the first time. Her face remained neutral but in her eyes, as large as they were, I detected something. Worry. And that was the second time she had expressed that.

I nodded and dropped my hand. Both of our heads whipped toward the hallway as a door opened and slammed shut with such force it seemed to echo throughout the house. Without a word, Lena turned and scurried from my room, leaving me alone to wait as two sets of feet busied around downstairs. Leo's heavy feet were damn near stomping in a quickened pace and Tina's heels clicked leisurely as if she were taking her time.

It seemed like his body was framing my doorway in less than five steps, and now he stood, looking me up and down in disapproval, as he made in his way inside my room. Damn, I wished I had changed. I still wore my club clothes; I might as well have been completely naked underneath Leo's menacing glare.

"I see you've found your room," he said, his voice surprisingly calm.

"Lena showed me," I murmured. I could barely hear my voice over the pounding of my own heart. The suspense was killing me. I wished he would go ahead and yell or fuss or whatever he was going to do so we could get it over with.

"What were you doing at that club, Kimmy?"

The better question was, how the hell had he known? But for some reason, that didn't seem like a good tactic. "I just went out with my friend Adria," I said. When he didn't speak, I rushed on. "It was innocent. I promise. We were just out having a good time. I didn't know I couldn't go out."

"Who was that guy?"

For a moment, I had almost forgotten about Greg. I cursed myself as my own hesitation only heightened the suspicion. "Nobody. I mean I wasn't with him." I felt the first few hitches of a quiver and tried to keep my voice as calm as possible. "He just wanted to dance."

I felt the slap before it even registered that Leo was close enough to do it. The impact was enough to have me stumbling backward. I clutched my face, shock knocking my ass completely speechless as my cheek stung.

"I'm sorry," he said, though he sounded anything but. His voice carried that same calmness, and the way he looked at me was obvious that he was not sorry for hitting me, but sorry that I "made" him. "Promise me that won't happen again."

That what won't happen again? That I won't go out? That I won't be hit? That I won't be seen with Adria? At that point, I was confused as hell but all I could do was nod. He reached for me and I ducked, prepared for the next round of hits. To my surprise, this touch was gentle as he caressed my burning face. He then put his lips to mine and all I could do was stand there, frozen. It was taking my mind a moment to register what the hell was happening until I felt his other hand slide up my thigh and under my dress. He shoved his hand between my legs, and I gasped at the sudden intrusion. I wasn't even wet. But then he softened his fingers and began moving them in a circular motion, and my kitten purred to life. Pain, then pleasure? Was that how pissed Leo operated?

My knees weakened, and I leaned into him as he used his other arm to circle my waist and support my weight. I moaned as he continued fingering me, his thumb gingerly massaging my swollen button and his index and middle fingers stroking my walls in a sensuous slow dance.

"Please," I uttered the words, not really sure what I was begging for. Leo kissed me, hard, his tongue forcing its way into my mouth, and I dissolved like putty in his arms. He quickened his pace and I grinded against his hand, coaxing the orgasm. "That's it," I urged as I felt my muscles begin to tighten. "Right there, baby." Then, as quickly as he started, he stopped, snatching his fingers away with enough force to have me crumpling to the floor.

I know my look was confusion mixed with irritation as my eyes met his. Was this some sort of punishment? He didn't bother looking back. Just wiped his fingers on his pants and walked from the room. "Clean yourself up and go to bed. I'll deal with you later." He shut the door behind him with a satisfied click that left me alone, frustrated, and still trembling from the impending orgasm. Could I really endure this for the next year?

Chapter 7

The knock on my door had me groaning and rolling over in the luscious sheets. The mattress felt like it was hugging each and every inch of my body and lulling me into a sleep so deep I didn't want to leave.

"Mrs. Owusu." The voice was muffled through the closed door and the persistent knock followed. "I'm so sorry to bother you, but it's time for your fitting."

My eyes felt heavy as I struggled to lift them. A quick look at the wall clock let me know it was a little before seven in the morning. I threw the covers over my head. I had only been here a week and had barely seen the maid, Ayana, but the Jamaican accent told me it was her asking to get her ass beat by waking me up so early.

A week. It felt like so much longer than seven days had gone by since I'd been snatched from the club, much to my embarrassment. I hadn't left the grounds since—mainly because I felt weird asking, and no one offered—so I took the opportunity to explore. And there was plenty to explore.

The home was absolutely majestic, and under any other circumstances, my ass would have been relishing the maid service, infinity pool, movie theater, gourmet kitchen, huge bedrooms with plush carpets, and even the stable with three Arabian horses Leo had named Larry, Moe, and Curly. I was scared shitless of the animals but I enjoyed watching them graze and roam, their skin seeming to glisten in the sun with the rippling of muscles.

Now I saw why Leo chose the property. It was peaceful out here. And with the amenities it was like a little resort. The place was so big I really didn't see Lena, Tina, Leo, or the help unless I went looking for them. But in just a few short days, the gorgeous walls had become my prison, the huge floor-to-ceiling windows a mere reminder of my captivity on the expensive estate.

"Mrs. Owusu." This time Ayana's voice was nearly pleading, and for that reason, I mustered up enough strength to pull off the covers and throw my legs over the side of the bed.

"Come in," I called, and she did, quickly scurrying into the room with an ivory garment bag held high so as not to let it drag on the floor.

"I'm so sorry," she said again, making her way to the closet door to hang up the bag. "But Mr. Owusu wants you to fit once more before the ceremony tomorrow."

I waited for the butterflies or, hell, even the nervousness at the reminder of my wedding tomorrow, but nope. Nothing. It felt like a business arrangement. Like it was just for show. I didn't even know who we were doing this for anyway. According to Tina, the "marriage" was official when I signed the papers. Neither my family nor friends were coming or even knew about it. And Leo had already done it twice before. So I didn't understand the big presentation. Between caterers, bands, and decorators that had paraded through all week, I calculated Leo was spending well over $50,000 on this wedding. Which was ridiculous as hell, in my opinion. He could've given me that money. I'm sure I could've found a lot more to do with it than spend it on a phony wedding ceremony and reception.

I spared Ayana an absent glance as she busied herself with opening the sheer curtains, allowing the sun to spill into my room. I hadn't meant to be rude. Ayana was actually a sweet woman, though she really didn't talk much. I was just so tired for some reason.

Tina had taken the lead in planning everything, but she had insisted I shadow the process so it appeared that my suggestions were taken into consideration. They hadn't been, but I suppose she could at least tell Leo that she had tried. So here I was agreeing with a double layer white chocolate cake, and I didn't even care for chocolate, along with a multitude of other details, just to feign interest in the whole affair.

Last night we had been up overseeing the setup, watching as they placed ivory folding chairs with royal blue sashes on the lawn angled toward the gazebo on the lake, also decorated in blue floral arrangements and sashes. The perfect location, since that's where he had married Tina and Lena, of course.

Ayana unzipped the garment bag and pulled the dress into view. "After you try this on, Mr. Owusu requests to see you." I nodded, struggling to keep from rolling my eyes. He would find the most inconvenient time to "request to see me." Damn, it couldn't wait until after breakfast?

I removed my red lace teddy and tossed it on the bed. One of my other wifely duties as assigned. I had to wear something sexy to bed in case Leo popped up on me at night. He hadn't bothered me since that first night just yet, and he was usually gone through the day. So I was curious what he wanted with me today.

I allowed Ayana to help me into the dress and zip it up in the back. It fit perfectly but was still unflattering. Maybe something a woman in her forties would wear.

"You are so beautiful," Ayana complimented as she tugged and pulled on the material, making sure it fit in all the right places. "Mr. Owusu won't be able to take his eyes off of you."

She removed my dress and passed me my robe to cover my naked body. "Would you like me to draw you a bath first, ma'am?"

I shook my head. I didn't think I would ever get used to someone waiting on me hand and foot.

She left the room, and I moseyed over to the bay window and sat on the seat, folding my legs underneath me.

Adria had called me I don't know how many times. She was worried. I hated that. I needed to tell her the truth. Tina and Leo had told me not to talk to her, and honestly, that didn't faze me. I hadn't returned her calls because frankly I didn't know what to say. I'm sure she had seen the fiasco at the club like everyone else. What was I supposed to say? *Girl, I know it looks crazy, but it's not what you think. He's really my husband and he just got a little jealous, even though he has two other wives.*

I shook my head. Reaching into my nightstand, my fingers flew across the papers and other scattered items to rummage for my phone. The first phone I came to was the one Leo had given me. My "business" phone, I called it. Only he called me on it and I needed to answer. My personal phone was on vibrate so I had missed the few additional calls and text messages that came through. In addition to Adria, my dad had called twice. And Jahmad had texted. I deleted the text without even reading it. I thought about it briefly before punching in the digits to call my parents. I was sure they were just as worried.

"Hey, Mama," I greeted once she picked up.

"Girl, where have you been?" she snapped. "You leave out of here to go to some club and don't return or call for nearly a week. All you had to do was say you were going to stay with Adria for a few days. What is wrong with you?"

I made a mental reminder to thank Adria for covering for me. "I'm sorry, Mama, it's just been really busy. I got fired last week so I've just been trying to find another job. Applications and interviews. You know how it goes." Lies, lies, and more lies. I swallowed the guilt and pursed my lips to keep from confessing just as quickly.

"Oh." Her voice had softened. "Fired you? For what? And why didn't you tell me?"

"Because it was for a stupid reason, Mama. And it was embarrassing so I was just trying to handle it."

"Sweetie, you know you could have talked to us. We would have helped. Do you need some money?"

I scanned the lavish room with all of its expensive furnishings and chuckled. "No, ma'am, I'm fine, I promise."

"Okay. Well, your dad stepped out to a meeting, but will you be at service tomorrow?"

No, I was too busy getting married to a married man. The realization had my heart hurting. Of course I didn't expect my father to walk me down the aisle and my mother to sit in the audience crying tears of joy, but it would have been nice to have them there. No one from my side of the family would be present, for that matter. Not sure why it hurt. This wasn't real. That's what I kept telling myself. But still . . .

"I don't think so, Mommy, but I'll try for next weekend."

She grunted, no doubt her expression of disbelief, but she didn't push.

We ended the conversation, and I typed in a quick message to Adria. I couldn't talk to her right at the moment. Talking with my mom just reminded me how I had placed myself in this lonely position, and the shit was depressing me.

I started typing that I would call her later, then reconsidered, erased it, and typed a new message.

Hey Girl. I'm so sorry for just now reaching out but it's been so busy. Let's meet for brunch and I'll explain everything. Thanks for covering with my folks. Love you.

I sat my phone on the window seat and crossed to the dresser to pull out something to wear. They, and by they I meant probably Tina, had gone shopping for me so when I arrived, I had dressers and a closet packed full of designer clothes. I tossed on a burgundy bodycon sweat-dress and went into the bathroom to brush my teeth.

Twenty minutes later, I walked downstairs to find Leo. His office was the first place I headed to. He wasn't home a lot, but when he was, he was usually in his office. I had messed around and asked him once what he did for a living and he told me his family had money and he did a lot of international business. Whatever that meant. I didn't know how that coincided with him being gone so much but I didn't care. The less I saw him, the quicker these weeks would fly by. Sure enough, Leo was in his office, and by the look of the scene through the French doors, he wasn't alone.

Leo was sitting in the executive office chair behind his desk. But he sure as hell wasn't working among the numerous papers strewn across the desktop. He was leaning back, his eyes closed, and his face reflecting a clear expression I easily recognized, since I had put that same expression on him on many an occasion. He was turned to the side, so all I saw on the floor was Tina's ass and heels peeking from the side of the desk as she sucked him off like an experienced head master.

I froze at the door, my eyes fixed on the sexual encounter I had stumbled on. For some reason, I felt angry. Angry that it was happening at all, that these two didn't give a damn about respect in this house to be doing it in the open for all to see, that Tina could sample Leo and here I had been left the other day to finish the job myself, and I had been waiting every night for him to come to me, but that visit never came.

Leo arched his back and began pumping her mouth, his face contorting as he was about to bust. He moaned; I heard it through the door as he shot his seeds on her tongue and leaned back in relief. Tina rose to her feet, wiping her lips with her fingers. She leaned over, and they shared a passionate kiss, she no doubt passing him all of his sperm-coated spit.

Not caring that the door was closed, I knocked twice on the glass pane and opened it. Leo's eyes opened in my direction, but neither of them broke the kiss.

This was definitely awkward. I knew I shouldn't feel disrespected, but this blatant display of affection was enough to make me sick. "You wanted to see me?" I said, crossing my arms over my chest. He nodded, finally giving Tina one last peck and beckoning me to come closer.

"Tina, leave us for a moment."

Tina didn't seem too happy but she nodded and, not looking at me, stalked out the room. It seemed like she had an attitude. I didn't know why. She was the one who just sucked down our husband. Hell, I hadn't even wanted or meant to break up their little early-morning sexcapade. I was comfortably sleeping in before I had been "summoned."

I walked to the desk as Leo gave me the biggest grin. I certainly hoped he wasn't expecting me to pick up where Tina left off. His slacks and underwear were still around his ankles and his now flaccid dick was glistening in saliva as it rested on his hairy thigh. I wanted to gag.

"You want to take care of that?" I nodded toward his exposed package.

He chuckled. "What? You don't want a taste?"

"I'll pass, but thanks." Though I honestly didn't think I would ever get the sordid vision out of my head.

Leo pulled up his pants, stuffing his dick back into place. He then patted his lap for me to sit down. I obeyed.

"You know we never really had a chance to talk about the club thing," he said, kissing the back of my shoulder.

"If I recall, you talked with your hand," I mumbled, the memory still fresh. To my surprise, he found that funny.

"I hate when women make me do that," he murmured, his lips still against my arm. "I just need you to never disrespect me like that again. You understand, right, my love?"

I pursed my lips shut and nodded. Of course I understood. He hit women and played the victim. And his money bandaged that fact. No, it wasn't like he beat me, but he could. And by the mindset he had just revealed to me, he wouldn't hesitate to "put me in my place" if he felt he needed to.

"I want you to see something." And just like that, the subject was over. I wasn't even sure what we had accomplished but apparently, it didn't even matter. Leo had spoken and his words were gospel.

He rose to his feet, lifting me with him. "Come outside." Taking my hand, Leo led me through the office and down the hall to the front door.

As usual, the limo sat parked right outside the door but we bypassed it and headed in the direction of the six-car garage. I waited while he punched a code on the keypad and the gears ground to life as one of the doors lifted. My eyes widened in shock.

The back of a brand-new pearl white Porsche slowly came into view, the tag reading *Kimmy1*. I squealed in delight and damn near leapt into Leo's arms. Lord knows I needed a new car, but the luxury Porsche was certainly not what I had expected.

"Thank you, babe!" I said, planting a kiss on his lips. Remembering the dick sucking fiasco, I stopped short before he could slip me his tongue and instead squeezed him in a tighter hug.

"Just think of it like a wedding present." He fished in his pocket and passed me the keys. I was grinning from ear to ear. Now I wouldn't be confined to the house like some hostage. Now I could make moves like I wanted, including going to see Adria in a few hours. This car was like a breath of fresh air.

"I'm going to take it out for a spin after breakfast," I said casually.

Leo lifted an eyebrow. "Really? Where are you going?"

"Just out, sweetie. Maybe to the mall or something. I can't let you get me a car and not drive it. What good is that?" I feigned a pout. I could tell he was still skeptical but he nodded anyway.

"Just for a few hours," he said, patting me on the ass. "I'm serious. I don't want you gone all day. And make sure you take your phone and answer it immediately when I call."

I bit my tongue to keep the smart remark from falling from my lips. I would have to find a way around his possessive ass. But at least for now I could go and see Adria without everybody on my back. I was glad too, because I had so much to talk to her about. But I'm not going to lie, I feared how she would react to the whole ordeal.

I pulled up to Sweet Auburn Seafood and wheeled my baby into the underground parking garage. This thing drove like butter, with an engine so quiet I had to keep checking to make sure the car was still on whenever I stopped at a light. It had a burgundy leather interior, and Leo had gone all out with the bells and whistles. Better still, the neon lights on the dash had displayed a mere three miles when I first slid behind the wheel. I was in heaven.

The valet gave me a ticket and I walked around to the restaurant, removing my Gucci sunglasses as soon as I entered the dimly lit lobby area. It was prime brunch hour so the place was packed, which I had figured it would be. Thank God I had made reservations.

"Kimera, party of two," I told the hostess, who quickly scanned the list.

"Yes, ma'am, right this way. The other member of your party has already arrived."

She didn't even have to tell me, because I had just caught Adria's eye across the room, sitting patiently in a corner booth. I smiled in her direction. She didn't. Even after the hostess showed me to the table and I slid into the seat opposite her, Adria still made no move to speak and kept her face neutral.

"Don't give me that look," I said with a sigh. "I know you're pissed. Damn, that's why I said we should meet up so I could explain."

Adria released a breath I didn't know she had been holding and shook her head. "You don't get it," she said quietly. "I'm not pissed. Well . . . maybe a little, but I'm more hurt than anything. You got something going on, something major obviously, and you can't even respect this friendship enough to confide in me. I mean, damn. We only have eighteen years of history behind us."

I nodded as my heart cracked. She was right, and I deserved that. I lowered my eyes to the mimosas she had already ordered, one for each of us. I wanted to take a sip so badly, but I figured I didn't need to stall. Just get it out before I lost my nerve. The guilt was already eating heavily at me.

"No, it's not that," I confessed. "Honestly, yes. I do have something going on, but more than anything, I wasn't sure what you would say or how you would think of me after. So I kind of kept it to myself."

Anger flashed in Adria's eyes. "I would never judge you, Kimera," she snapped. "Who the hell do you think I am?"

"I know. I'm sorry. I guess it's a little embarrassing."

Adria sat back, shaking her head. She stared at me long and hard before she spoke again; her words seeped through lips tight with restrained anger. "You get snatched out of the club last week in front of me, your brother, Jahmad, and everyone else. You don't resurface until today. Ignoring calls and text messages. None of us knew what the hell had happened. Your folks were worried sick when your brother told them what went down at the club and here I go, trying to smooth things over. Now you pop in here today looking like you just stepped off a runway and in a fancy new whip, I see." She paused to nod toward the Porsche key I had sitting on the table. "And to my relief everything is going gravy for you. But you are too 'embarrassed' to give me, of all people, an explanation? Looks like you're living the good life to me. What is it? You found some kind of sugar daddy who you can suck and fuck for a few dollars?" She bit off the words like it stung her throat to say.

I opened my mouth to speak but she rushed on, her voice clogged with tears. "I don't even care anymore. Forgive me for actually giving a fuck about you." She began gathering her things and shifted toward the edge of the seat to slide out of the booth.

"I'm sorry." I was nearly frantic. I couldn't lose my best friend. Not over this. "Please, Adria. Stay. Let me explain."

She paused, clearly pondering if she should oblige. Finally, she leaned back against the seat and crossed her arms over her breasts. She hadn't even bothered to remove her purse from her shoulder. But at least she was still here to listen. I took a deep breath. Here goes. "I took Leo up on his offer."

First, her face crinkled in confusion as she obviously had to think about what I was even saying. Then, recognition as my words brought back our conversation. She sat up, her mouth open as I saw the montage of thoughts play across her face.

"Wait. Wait. Are you saying you married that dude who already has a wife?"

My nod was slow. "It's complicated. Something like that, though."

"'Something like that'?" she echoed, and I lowered my eyes.

"It's not a legal marriage. We are going to have a little ceremony and be in a relationship. Like we've been doing."

"While he still has a wife."

I nodded again.

Clear and utter shock had her staring at me as she struggled to find the words.

"Why—how . . ." She shook her head again. "Why are you

doing this?" And there. I could see it. Regardless of what she had just said, there was the judgment. She was looking down on me.

"Because I want to," I said simply. "I listened to what they had to say. It is a great deal. And it's not even official-official because polygamy is not legal. Basically I'm doing exactly what I was doing before when I was seeing Leo knowing he had a wife. But now I'm being compensated."

"So wow, I was right on both accounts. You did find a sugar daddy and you are prostituting." She scoffed. "Unbelievable."

"That's not how it is," I said. "But this is one reason why I didn't want to say anything. It's my decision. It's done. I'm not asking no one's approval."

She grunted. "Yeah, I got it. Did you even tell your folks?"

"It's really no one's business."

"Then what's there to be embarrassed about, since you stand so firm behind your decision?"

I opened my mouth to speak and shut it again when no words came out. It wasn't something I wanted to go shouting from the rooftops. But if I was happy with the financial benefits, what difference did it make?

"I'm getting a shit ton of money," I reasoned. "Enough so we can start our business. That's a great thing, Adria."

"I don't give a damn about that store if it means you sacrificing your morals and selling yourself short," Adria snapped. She blew a breath through her nose and said, "Kimmy, you deserve so much more than that."

"I'm happy with it."

Adria's eyes narrowed in doubt. "Are you really happy?" she asked.

My thoughts flipped to Leo hitting me, the "punishment," the office encounter this morning, and even the ceremony tomorrow. Then I glanced down at my expensive clothes, thought about the mansion and about my checking account, which hadn't seen those types of figures in this lifetime. Not to mention my car. And I didn't think I had even begun to touch all the "perks and benefits" as outlined in my contract. I was satisfied. Wasn't that the same as happy?

"Yes," I answered finally, though now I really wasn't sure.

"Then that's enough," Adria said and forced a smile. I smiled too. That was enough. For now.

Chapter 8

I had never had an out-of-body experience. They say it usually happens when you're in the hospital or maybe when your life flashes before your eyes right after a traumatic experience. I think it's much like straddling between conscious and subconscious, that peripheral medium of purgatory where you aren't really in the driver's seat anymore but more of a passenger in your own life. At least that's what I assumed it felt like. That was surely what seemed to be taking place as I walked down the aisle.

It was overcast with a few sporadic sprinkles of rain that I felt on my arm and that rippled the water of the lake. Not at all a pretty day for a wedding, but it did match my mood nonetheless. But I will say the yard had been beautifully decorated and now, more than a hundred people were seated in the carefully arranged folding chairs. A mass of people I didn't know. Leo's friends and colleagues, a few snatches of his family here or there. But no one from my side. Not even Adria.

She had asked yesterday if she could come support. No, she wasn't condoning it, but her love for me outweighed her disapproval of my decision. I lied and told her it was going to be a simple courthouse thing for formality's sake. My heart couldn't bring me to tell her she wasn't invited. That Leo wouldn't approve. And Lord knows I wanted her there.

I continued my slow trudge down the silver silk runner, gripping my bouquet like it was a lifeline. My vision was slightly obstructed by the birdcage veil, but I could clearly see Tina and Lena, both standing against the bank of the lake with ivory dresses of their own. Theirs looked nearly identical to my dress except theirs were the shorter version. Their wedding rings caught a sliver of sunlight that peeked through the clouds, and my eyes dropped to my own engagement ring. *Wife number three. Wife number three.* That thought was resonating in my head with each step, closer and closer to Leo waiting in the gazebo.

All eyes were on me; a few clicks of the camera as the photographer froze this moment in time. The moment I made the biggest decision in my life. Decision or mistake? It was too soon to tell. I wondered how my face looked on the film. Did I look as nervous as I felt? Did the makeup hide it enough? Could he tell I hated my dress and the lace neckline was itching the hell out of my skin?

The music, Kenny G's "The Wedding Song," blared through the speakers, the sultry jazz instrumentals creating a beautiful sound track that would have been memorable had all this been real.

The runner stopped and gave way to the wooden walkway that led out onto the water. I started across, my kitten heels clicking across the wood planks. I risked glancing down at the water and caught my saddened expression reflecting back before it rippled away amid a school of fish. It felt like the longest trek of my life, getting across that walkway.

Leo met me in the middle of the water, holding out his hand with the biggest grin on his face. He certainly did look handsome with his fresh twisted locs pulled back into a neat braid that went down his back. He had chosen an ivory suit that seemed to glow against his dark complexion.

I wiped a sweaty hand on the thigh of my dress before placing it in his. "You look so beautiful, my love." He raised the back of my hand to his lips and then kissed my palm.

I forced a smile. "Thank you."

It all would've been so perfect. Everything was nice and right where it was supposed to be. The music, the whole ceremony, it would've been so nice. But something was missing. And that was why my heart wasn't in it. That was why I just feigned smiles, nodded along, and recited my lines like a mindless zombie. It felt like a movie and I was just acting the part. Bad acting, probably, but acting nonetheless. Hence the out-of-body experience. Hell, I don't even remember what I vowed, considering Tina had written them for me. I don't remember the kiss or the broom being placed in front of our feet and us holding hands and leaping over the stick to thunderous applause.

But here I was, now after a multitude of pictures and praises. I had been instructed to change into a white cocktail dress that brushed my knees and cinched at the waist. At least I was comfortable and the dress was cute, though I had no idea who picked it out.

The reception was inside and with good reason, because no sooner had we journeyed back up the aisle as love partners, husband and wife number three, than the sky opened up. An all-out downpour had guests running for cover from the storm. I told myself it was a sign. Even God himself couldn't bless this.

"Congratulations again, Kimera." It was Leo's father, Obi, a much older yet just as handsome version of his son. Leo had flown him in from the Ivory Coast just for the day. Leo's mother I hadn't met; I was told she was too sick to make the trip.

Obi pulled me in for a hug, the smell of his Cuban cigars immediately consuming my nostrils. He kissed my cheek and held me back by my shoulders to look me up and down.

"My son is a very lucky man," he said with a wink. "Much more beautiful than his other wives, but I'll deny it if you ever tell them I said that."

I wasn't sure how to take that, but I thanked him anyway. "How is your wife?" I asked.

"Which one?"

His question was genuine, but I still had to keep from rolling my eyes. Damn, I knew he had multiple wives too. It was my first assumption after thinking about where Leo could've gotten it from. It was a generational thing.

"Leo's mother," I clarified. "Leo says she's not feeling well."

Obi pulled out a cigar and fired it up, letting a stream of smoke trail lazily from his lips. "Yeah, that's why I'm leaving right after this. The chemo is making her sick all the time, and they just found another spot on her brain. It's pretty aggressive cancer."

He spoke with such compassion that for a brief moment I thought he seriously loved her. But then I counted the five other wives he had in the room and reconsidered. But, damn, I hadn't known it was cancer. Leo just kept saying sick. I wonder if he knew how serious it was, or if he was in denial, or just watering it down for me so as not to dwell on the circumstances too long. If he was hurting, which I would think he was, he hid it very well. And apparently so did his father.

Obi left me to my thoughts and went to mingle with the other guests, kissing another wife and laughing at a joke someone made while they clicked champagne glasses in a toast. I watched him wrap an arm around the shoulders of two women and both leaned in, almost obediently, to kiss his cheek. How could he be so sociable while his wife lay thousands of miles away dying? Is that how it would always be? If I got sick, would my husband actually be there to take care of me or would he continue on with life, since he had alternatives?

Speaking of which, Tina walked up and handed me a glass of champagne. She self-toasted by clinking her glass against mine before taking a healthy swallow. "So?" She smiled. "How does it feel?"

What kind of question was that? How was it supposed to feel?

I felt . . . incomplete, if I had to be honest with myself. Like I settled. And though I had been welcomed into a relationship with not one but three other involved parties, I had never felt lonelier. But I kept thinking about the end game and merely nodded. Eye on the prize.

"Fine."

"He'll sleep with you tonight," she informed me like we were going over the offensive plays in a championship game. "Be ready with your lingerie. He'll cuddle with you afterwards too, and he'll spend the night in your room. Just a heads-up."

I glanced at Tina and watched her eyes narrow. I followed her gaze and saw she was looking at Lena waddle toward the punch bowl. "I'm sick of looking at that bitch," she mumbled so low I had to question if I had even heard it. "Wish she would hurry up and drop that baby." She strolled off and disappeared into the crowd, and I frowned after her. What the hell was all that about?

I stood at the full-length mirror, white see-through mid-thigh teddy clinging to my curves like a second layer of skin. I turned, admiring the way the material accentuated my body. With the matching white fishnet tights, I looked good enough to eat, if I did say so myself.

I had been pretending all day with the fake ceremony, but I sure as hell couldn't pretend I wasn't excited about the wedding night. More than the fact that it was Leo was the fact I was getting some, period. I'm not sure if it was intentional or purely coincidental, but he had been walking around here feeling up and tonguing down Tina and Lena every chance he got. Meanwhile, he had my thirsty ass on a drought and my poor kitty hadn't had any attention, other than my own hand, in weeks. Situation aside, I had always been physically attracted to Leo, and now with him in such close range day in and day out, the lack of attention had me about to bust.

The knock on my door had the ache intensifying. I gave myself a final once-over before heading to the door.

My grin turned into a deep frown when I saw it wasn't Leo on the other side of the frame, but Ayana. "What is it?" I snapped. I didn't bother trying to keep the attitude out of my voice. Dammit, I was ready for some action.

"Mr. Owusu was called for an emergency and he requested you be up and ready at nine-thirty sharp tomorrow morning."

My face fell. I felt the disappointing tears sting the corners of my eyes. I just nodded my gratitude for the information.

"Would you like me to get you something?" Ayana asked at my silence.

Unless she could get me some dick, I didn't need her pressing and pampering me. So I shook my head and closed the door. He had the nerve to leave me alone on our wedding night and then called himself making demands? Be up and ready? Ready for what? Ready for when he had time for me? He could kiss my ass.

Suddenly feeling suffocated, and the ache between my legs not helping, I quickly threw on a t-shirt and some jeans, stuffed my feet into my Coach shoes, and headed downstairs.

Lena was on the couch in the great room, her face buried in the pages of some book she seemed to be toting around with her these days. She looked up when I descended the stairs and pushed a pair of glasses farther up on her nose. She watched me without watching me as I crossed into the kitchen. It was obvious she wanted to speak, probably ask me where I was going at eight o'clock at night, but she didn't. Instead she murmured, "Tina will be looking for you. She'll tell Leo."

I ignored her. At that point, I really didn't give a damn. I would deal with the consequences later. Right now, I needed out of this prison.

I hadn't even realized I was headed to my parents until I wheeled my car up the driveway and parked behind my brother's truck. The lights were on, which meant they were up. I sat parked outside for a moment, trying to decide what my purpose for being there was. The diamond engagement ring and band suddenly felt heavy on my finger, and I slid them off, dropping the set into my purse. Then I climbed from the car and headed onto the porch.

"Did you lose your key?" Mama asked when she opened the door. "I know you haven't been gone that long." I smiled as she kissed my cheek. The little things. No matter where I went, this place always felt like home.

"No, ma'am. I was just being lazy and didn't feel like digging for it."

"You hungry? We just finished eating and I was about to clean up, but I can make you a plate."

I hadn't thought much about food, but my stomach growled in appreciation. All I had eaten were little finger foods at the wedding. Shit with no taste, but I had nibbled anyway to keep my mouth busy.

"Oh, that's why I see Keon's car here," I said, side-eyeing my brother, who was thrown on the couch in the living room. He flipped up his middle finger, and I reciprocated the gesture.

Home-cooked meal smells still lingered in the air as I joined my mother in the kitchen. Pots and pans of cabbage, macaroni and cheese, cornbread, and barbecue chicken rested on the stove and cluttered the tiny countertop. The family sure had dug in because there wasn't much left, but I was grateful just the same. Mama passed me a serving spoon and a plate, and I began piling the food on.

"They not feeding you at Adria's?" she asked with a laugh when she saw my huge portions.

"No, that's not it." I winked. "No one can compete with your cooking. You know that."

"You're right." She looked me up and down as if she were searching for something. I kept my eyes averted. My mom could see right through me. She always could.

"Where's Dad?" I asked, lifting the lid on another pot.

"He ran out with Jahmad to get something for the car."

I nodded, though my heart quickened at the mention of Jahmad's name. I didn't know why I was surprised he was here. Hell, before he left for Texas he was *always* here. It just never bothered me before.

"What have you been up to today?" she asked, running water to begin washing dishes. I thought again about the day's events and could only shake my head. Married. I was married now.

"Nothing too much."

"Are you sure you're okay, sweetie?" Mama stepped closer, trying her best to read my face. "You seem a little distracted."

Distracted was the least of it. Try disappointed, horny, somewhat regretful, nervous. A few more choice words played around on my tongue, none of which I dared express. I just shook my head and feigned a smile. I had been doing it all day so it seemed like it was becoming more and more authentic.

"I'm a little tired, Mama" was all I said, and she didn't comment any further.

I had plowed through half my plate in the dining room when I heard the key turn from the garage door. My dad entered first, a confused frown on his face. He glanced at Keon before turning his eyes on me. "That your Porsche out there?" he said, pointing a thumb in the direction of the car.

I froze. Shit. I hadn't really thought this whole thing through. I could tell him it was a friend's car, but then why the hell would a borrowed car have the plate KIMMY1 on it? Damn, maybe it had been a mistake coming over here.

Suddenly, my throat felt dry, as everyone's, and I do mean everyone's, eyes turned to me. I took a deep swallow of lemonade before giving what I thought was a nonchalant nod. Like it was every day broke young women like me managed to ride in, let alone own, a brand-new luxury vehicle.

Mama came in from the kitchen, drying her hands on a towel. "Where did you get that?" she asked.

"It was a gift," I admitted and stopped at that. No way would I divulge the rest.

"Who would give you an expensive gift like that?" Mama placed her hands on her hips. She didn't mind pressuring and she damn sure didn't mind asking questions no one else was going to.

I kept my eyes downcast, pushing the last of the macaroni around with my fork. "Just a guy I'm talking to."

I caught the silent exchange between my parents; behind my father, Jahmad stood against the wall, watching me just as intently. I wasn't able to gauge his reaction but part of me felt triumphant he had been here to witness this little bit of information. That's right. He had his little hood rat CeeCee and I had some mystery boss boyfriend giving me cars and shit. Checkmate.

"A guy you're talking to?" my mom echoed, prompting me to tell more.

I just nodded.

"My Lord, girl, I don't know what you're into but it doesn't sound like nothing but the devil."

I don't know why I was surprised. I knew that was coming sooner rather than later. Suddenly, I didn't have much of an appetite. Not even for the key lime and red velvet layer cake I could smell baking in the oven. I rose and headed for the stairs.

"Can we just drop it, please? It's not that serious. I promise." But that was a lie. It was that serious.

I collapsed on my bed and stared up at the ceiling fan blowing a gentle breeze in my room. It was interesting. Being in that huge house was nice, don't get me wrong, but I was still waiting on that familiar feeling. Like I was where I belonged. The feeling like I got now, in a bedroom three fourths the size of my closet at Leo's house. Not sure if it was the stark décor or the personalities of my other housemates, but it felt like more of a museum over there. And me, well, I felt like a visitor just passing through and not allowed to touch anything or roam too freely.

I felt him before I even realized he was there. Something about

Jahmad's presence was overpowering, but in a somewhat welcoming way. I leaned up on my elbows and met his eyes at the door. He hadn't even stepped in my room but I could feel him in every inch of it. "Did they send you up here to interrogate me?" I asked when he made no move to speak.

Jahmad leaned on the doorjamb, shoving his hands in his pockets. "Not really. I came to do that on my own."

"Oh, is that so? Why do you even care?"

He lifted a shoulder in a half shrug. "Why do you?"

"I don't." I rolled my eyes, trying my best to play up annoyance I didn't feel. I had been craving his attention, and now it was exciting me. My kitty was almost purring out loud.

"Why you keep playing with me, Kimmy?" He took one step into the room, shutting the door behind him, and my heart skipped a beat as the lock clicked into place. But he didn't come farther. It was like he was waiting on a sign. Some sort of permission either in my eyes or my body. I kept my face neutral.

"I'm not playing with you."

"Then why you avoiding me? Giving me all this attitude?" Another step.

"I'm just not trying to be bothered with you. CeeCee made it very apparent that there were boundaries and she's right. We both need to abide by them." My breath quickened as he took two more steps, this time positioning himself right in front of me. I angled my head to keep my eyes on his. His package was inches from me, and I could almost smell the desire permeating from his pores. Or maybe mine. I couldn't be sure. But, damn, I wanted him. That much was certain.

He got down on his knees in front of me and I waited, willing him in my head to continue. I crossed my arms over my chest to keep my body from trembling. His hands were now on my knees and I'm sure he could feel my body responding, as much as I tried to hide it.

He lowered his head between my legs and kissed my kitten

through my jeans. That was all it took. It felt like she was cream-
ing from that alone, and I leaned back and arched up my hips,
urging him to take the jeans off and devour me. "Ready?" he whispered.

We both knew the simple question had been a dare, and I
would be damned if he would continue to taunt me. It was just a
test. I had to reassure myself. Just sex, and I had absolutely no
feelings for this man whatsoever. I would like nothing better than
to prove him wrong. He leaned up to me and stopped a breath
away, as if waiting for me. I gripped the back of his neck and
dragged his face to mine.

Peppermint. I relished the flavor on his tongue, used my own
to caress the roof of his mouth and swallow his moan in response.
His grip tightened on my arm, seemingly urging me for more, or
demanding it, I couldn't even be sure. But Jahmad seemed to be
not only reigniting that passion I had long since buried, but coaxing it, propelling it, until it was erupting into new sensations that
made me feel like a stranger in my own body.

He sucked on my bottom lip, and I quivered. His body hummed
against mine. I felt the power I had over him as much as I was
weakened by the power he had over me.

He fumbled with my shirt before snatching it over my head
and cursing under his breath in response. I glanced down to
where his eyes were focused, and suddenly remembered I still
had on my wedding night teddy. "Why you so damn sexy, girl?"
he whispered before assaulting my mouth again. I moaned into
the kiss, my body becoming enflamed with desire. I tongued him
back just as fiercely, relishing his familiarity.

Jahmad took his time undressing me, and I trembled underneath his delicate touch. He had always been such a patient and
passionate lover, giving every inch of my body special attention
that it was enough for my mind to hit orgasmic bliss before he
had even journeyed to the other parts of my body. He used his
tongue to massage each tender nipple, moaning as if I tasted like

the most delicious thing known to man. I was murmuring words that didn't even make sense and struggling to keep from screaming too loud myself. Part of me had forgotten I was even in my parents' house. A small part. The other part didn't give a damn.

He buried his mouth between my legs, the soft facial hairs caressing my skin as he licked and sucked me like a pacifier. I bucked against his mouth assault as his tongue darted out to lick the flavor of my juicy fruit. I threw my head back and squeezed my eyes shut against the eruption of ecstasy. "Oh, Jay." His name fell in a stuttered whisper from my lips as I gripped his head with my thighs and gyrated on his face.

I hadn't even come down from my euphoria before his body lay on top of mine. He nudged my legs apart with his knees and inserted himself, my walls expanding to take in the dick that I had long ago claimed as mine. It had been so long. Damn, my body was on another level, but the last thing I wanted to do was some bipolar-ass shit like shed tears at the glorious feeling. So I just hugged his frame to mine and enjoyed the sensation as he slow stroked. I felt my juices polishing his dick as he worked himself to loosen me up. Our bodies were slick with sweat as we made love to our own little rhythm. At that moment, nothing else and no one mattered. And as he quickened his thrusts with the impending orgasm, the confession staggered from my lips, coated with authenticity and blissful content. "I love you, Jahmad." We clutched each other and came together.

Chapter 9

It was a mistake.

Before I had even opened my eyes, my body became aware of the cool chill left exposed from what was a warm body. The sheets felt cool and empty underneath my hand, the hand that had rested on Jahmad's chest before I dozed off. My lids slid up, further confirming what I already knew. It was a mistake because I had let him open me up once more, body and heart, only to leave me holding the pieces of both in the end.

I sat up, allowing the sheets to pool around my waist. I reached for my phone, not surprised when I didn't see a call or even a text from Jahmad. Figured. He'd gotten what he wanted.

Part of me tried to convince myself that he had to sneak away. That we were at my parents' house and the morning couldn't find him in my bed or my dad would be ready to kill him and me both. Not to mention my brother. That was enough to sooth my head but definitely not my heart. No, my heart knew better.

I love you. My own words from last night came back to haunt me; I could've kicked myself for my vulnerability. His silence afterward had spoken loud enough.

A low ringing had my eyes dropping eagerly to my phone. Nothing. I glanced to my purse hanging on the door. Of course. Not my personal phone. My "business" phone. My Leo-only-I-better-always-answer phone. On a groan, I tossed my legs over the side of the bed and padded to my purse to retrieve it.

"Where are you?" he snapped before I even had time to speak. I pulled the phone away from my ear and glanced at the clock. It was 8:34 in the morning. Damn, what time did Ayana tell me to be ready?

"I'm on my way," I lied, already snatching my jeans from the floor. A brief flash of Jahmad easing them down my hips had me smirking at the memory. That man had my ass sprung. And I hated and loved him for it.

"Answer me!"

Leo's harsh tone brought me back to the conversation. "How are you at your parents' house when I told you to be ready this morning? And why are you staying out all night?"

"Sweetie, I'm sorry. I . . ." His words replayed in my head, and I paused. "Wait a minute. How did you know I was at my parents'?"

"Just get your ass home now." *Click.* I frowned, pulling the phone away from my face. Notifications cluttered the screen. Six missed calls and eleven text messages from Leo just this morning. Not to mention a few more from the previous night. Can't say I was surprised about that either. Lena had said Tina's tattletale ass would go blabbing. But what the hell did she do? Follow me? How did Leo know I was at my parents'? And what else did he know? Jahmad?

I dressed, straightened up my room, and even sprayed a few squirts of perfume I had on my dresser just for good measure. I figured my parents were up, well, my mom for sure, but I snuck out anyway. I didn't want to have to rehash last night's conversation. I still didn't have any answers. Well, none except the truth, and I sure as hell couldn't give them that.

On the drive to Leo's, I debated calling Jahmad. What would I say? What now? Deciding I could disguise the call as an attempt to see if he made it home safely, I punched in the same ten digits he'd had since forever and cradled the phone to my shoulder.

"Hello?" The voice had me nearly swerving off the side of the road. It was a woman. Groggy with sleep, but it was clearly a woman. I pulled the phone from my ear and eyed the digits I had dialed. Maybe he had finally changed his phone number after all.

"I apologize, I must have the wrong number. I was looking for Jahmad."

She chuckled. "No, this is his number. He's in the shower. Who is this?"

I hung up. The hurt sunk back in, deep and familiar. So he left me to run back to his woman? What the hell did I expect? And wasn't that what I was doing?

Leo was waiting for me outside, and no sooner had I pulled up than he sprinted to my door and grabbed my arm. "What the hell where you doing out all night?" he said, snatching me from the car. I stumbled against him, struggling to pull my arm free.

"I went to visit my folks," I said. "I didn't know I couldn't do that."

"Well, why didn't you answer my calls? I told you to always answer my calls."

"Leo, I was sl—" I couldn't even finish. The knuckles on the back of his hand slammed into my jaw with such force I bit my tongue and swallowed the rest of the words. Pain pierced the side of my face, and I turned to run before he could pull me back and hit me again. Two steps, and his hands had grabbed my neck, turning me around and slamming my back against the side of the car. I coughed and sputtered as his grip tightened.

"Don't you ever let this shit happen again, Kimera," he hissed, his eyes glazed with anger. "Do you understand me?" I clutched his wrist, attempting to pull his fingers from my throat before he cut off my air supply. A meager nod was all I could get out before he finally let me go. I sucked in a greedy breath and coughed as the air stung the inside of my throat. Leo just stood over me. I waited, afraid of his next move.

"I'm running out of patience. I'm tired of having to tell you how to be my wife." He leaned down and grabbed the back of my neck, forcing my face to angle to his. "Get your shit together, Kimera, or it's only going to get worse." With that, he let me go.

All I could think as he walked away was thank God he didn't notice I wasn't wearing my rings.

Slow footsteps had me looking toward the front door. Not Leo this time but Lena. She made her way to me and, leaning down, took my arm to help me stand. "You okay?" she asked.

I nodded and spit on the ground. A small spot of bright red blood splattered on the pavement at my feet. I wasn't in too much pain, but more than anything, I was fearful. The rage I had just witnessed was enough to put the fear of God in me. And it made me wonder what else this man was capable of.

Never in all the time we dated had Leo been anything other than sweet to me. I don't think I ever recalled him so much as raising his voice. And not that eight months was enough time to get to know a person, but it was sure as hell long enough to see any abusive tendencies. Which is why it was all taking me by surprise.

"Has he ever put his hands on you, Lena?" Not that it was any of my business, but I had to know.

She shook her head.

"Not even before the pregnancy?" I pressed.

"Well, Leo and I weren't together that long before I got pregnant," she said. "Only a couple months. And we spent the whole time trying to have a baby. I wasn't really doing much else so. . . ." She trailed off with a shrug, and a look of pity crossed her face.

I nodded my understanding. She wasn't out in the streets trying to rekindle old flames and turning up at clubs with her best

friend. That was why Leo was digging into my ass. I wasn't be-
having.

Tina stood in the doorway, her arms crossed over her breasts.
She looked me up and down and merely shook her head before
stepping to the side to allow us to pass through.

"You're really making it harder on yourself," she said with a
smirk. "Leo is a very easy man. All you have to do is follow the
rules."

"What rules?" I snapped, rolling my eyes.

"The rules in the contract."

I racked my brain trying to remember the fine print. "All I did
was visit my parents," I said. Then as an afterthought, I added,
"But of course, you already know that because you followed me
last night, didn't you?"

Tina chuckled and shook her head. "Why would I do that?"

"I don't know. Ammo. You just love having something over
me. Something to go run back and tell Leo."

Tina stepped closer, her eyes piercing mine. "There would be
nothing to tell if your ass would just do what you're supposed to
do. Make things easy on all of us. Your lip is bleeding, by the
way." She turned and sashayed into the hallway, and it took all of
my power not to tackle her ass and beat her into the hardwood
floor.

Lena steered me to the living room, but I shrugged out of her
grasp, turning instead toward the stairs. "I'm just going to go lie
down," I told her. "Thank you."

"Okay. Do you need anything? Want me to have Ayana bring
you an ice pack or something to eat?"

I ran my tongue over my lip. It certainly felt swollen and I
could taste the metal of drying blood on my skin. As hungry as I
was, food was the last thing on my mind.

"No thanks." I turned again before Lena's words stopped me
in my tracks.

"She's right, you know."

I looked over my shoulder, staring down at her from a few steps up.

"Tina," Lena answered the silent question. "She's right. She and Leo both are a lot easier to get along with if you don't buck the system. Just go with the flow."

I didn't bother responding. Just resumed my ascent up the stairs. It made sense, sure. But I still didn't have to like the shit. No matter how logical it seemed.

No sooner had I gotten to my room and lay across my bed, clothes and all, than the door opened and shut. Only one person in this house would barge in without knocking, so already knowing the visitor, I didn't bother looking up.

The bed sank under his weight, and Leo lay beside me, draping his heavy arm across my waist. "I'm sorry," he whispered. His voice was so soft, it was a wonder I heard him at all, but still, the surprise had me turning my head to look at him.

He was staring at me intently, but sorrow had long since replaced anger and his eyes held the sincerity in his apology. A single tear fell from the corner of his eye and trailed down his cheek. "I'm so sorry," he repeated. "You have to understand, my love, I'm really not like this. I don't put my hands on women."

I know. Just me. But I kept silent and watched him struggle for the right words.

"You asked me before," he went on quietly. "If I loved you. When we were at Atlantic Station. I do have love for you, Kimmy. I don't even know where it came from. It's confusing the hell out of me right now. And it just scared me when you weren't here last night when I came home. I didn't sleep. I needed you. I thought . . . I thought you had left me." Leo's thumb trembled as he rubbed my swollen lip. I watched a little blood smear onto his thumb before he pulled me in to a passionate kiss. His lips were gentle on mine, and at first the pain was like a pinch, then a sting as he used his tongue to massage it. But his tenderness did have me melting and for a moment, a brief moment, I forgot he was the one who had caused it. It was as if he wanted me to feel every piece of genuine regret for his actions.

His words echoed in my head as he deepened the kiss. Love, huh? Ironic how just a few hours ago I was murmuring those same words to Jahmad, my heart longing to hear them in return. But they had dropped from Leo's mouth, whether he was actually serious or not. And me, well, there was a part of me that had love for Leo, when he wasn't acting crazy. But my heart, I knew, belonged to Jahmad and that had been so for years now. No matter how I tried to take it back. And that hurt. Knowing he didn't feel the same way, knowing that I was indeed settling with Leo. But if you can't be with the one you love, love the one you're with, as the saying goes. And, no, it wasn't all good, but it was good enough for now. And it would be for the next year.

Leo undressed me, not bothering to linger on the foreplay. I had come to expect this. Leo wasn't that big on the pregame. He was ready for the main attraction. So a few kisses and licks here and there, and he was already whipping out his dick and bouncing it on my thigh to make sure it was hard enough. I sighed. She wasn't even wet. Plus coming behind that wonderful lovemaking with Jahmad, Leo wouldn't even be able to deliver. Like I mentioned before, I was physically attracted to the man, but the sex wasn't the best. But it had never been a problem because at the end of the day, he would spend hella dollars to keep me satisfied.

He inserted the tip, and I grimaced as the raw meat rubbed against my tender folds. Jahmad had certainly put some serious work on her because just the mere thought of having sex right now did nothing for me. But Leo didn't seem to mind dry pussy one single bit. He inserted it the rest of the way, and I wiggled against his package, struggling to get my own juices flowing.

"Oh, Kimmy," Leo was mumbling as his thrusts became quicker. "Oh, my love. You do this to me."

My mind wandered to Jahmad, and I smiled, struggling to tune him out. I pictured Jahmad's head nestled snugly between my legs like he had wanted to make a home there. Live in it. Plus, he actually cared about me and what was going on in my life. That shit was a major turn-on. And Jahmad would never in his life hit me. Emotional pain, sure. His womanizing ways caused plenty of that. But physically, hell no. Never. I wasn't sure which was worse. And at what price?

Leo worked his hips a little longer before I felt his meat throbbing with a nut. No way was I about to catch mine, so I just moved in tune with him, urging him to bust so he could climb out and go ahead about his business.

He howled. I mean a full-fledged wolf cry as he spewed his cum all up and down my walls. His weakened body collapsed on top of mine, his breath hot and heavy on my neck. I remained motionless. Hopefully, this was enough to keep him good long enough. And if not, he certainly had Tina and Lena to take over where I left off.

When he shifted, I thought for sure he was about to leave, but instead, he pulled me against his body as we snuggled under the covers. Pretty soon, I was listening to silence and I assumed Leo had dozed off. But I was wide awake, my mind reeling from the previous night's events.

"I have something for you," Leo said suddenly and nearly startled me as his voice cracked the quiet. He kissed my forehead.

I sat up as he climbed from the bed, strolling over to his jeans, which lay in a pile on the floor with our other clothes. A thin white envelope was in his hand as he crossed back to the bed and passed it to me.

"What is this for?" I asked, even as I began tearing it open.

"Because you're mine," he answered and leaned over to kiss me again. I shuddered at the possessive statement. "You ever been to Negril, Jamaica?" he was asking as I pulled out the plane tickets. My grin spread so hard it split my lip even wider, but I wasn't even worried about that. My eyes beamed in excitement. It felt like winning lottery tickets in my hands. All other thoughts faded as I pictured myself lying on the white sand beaches, my skin heating and growing red in the island sun. I may not have remembered everything in my contract like Tina kept throwing in my face, but I damn sure remembered the perks and benefits.

I thumbed through the boarding passes, my smile fading as I realized there were more than two tickets. My eyes scanned the names and my face fell. Damn, it looked like it wasn't going to be a couple's trip after all.

Chapter 10

I would've been better off staying at home.

Don't get me wrong, Negril was absolutely beautiful. The weather was perfect and the entire Sandals resort was surreal with its gorgeous expanse of beach and catered amenities. No, all of that was perfect and completely worth the trip. It was Leo's wives who overstepped their boundaries. And by wives, I mean Tina.

I asked Leo why he didn't leave them at home. Lena was eight months pregnant and too far along to be traveling anyway. And Tina, well, her intrusive ass was just in the way, and I hadn't planned on being stressed out on my vacation. I told him it was our honeymoon, and why couldn't we just go out and enjoy each other? Leo reminded me that I wasn't the one who got all of his attention, and just like that, the conversation was over.

So all four of us boarded the plane to fly out to Jamaica that evening, with nothing more than the beach clothes on our backs. Leo said we would shop when we arrived.

We landed in Montego Bay and from there, we hopped in a cab that took us an hour away to Negril, just in time for a candlelit evening dinner and drinks beachside at the open-air restaurant.

It was warm out, and all I wore was a sheer sundress that dipped low in the front and back with a high split on both sides to show off my legs. I sat beside Lena, sipping on my third rum punch and side-eyeing Tina, who had pulled Leo out on the floor to dance. Every so often he would turn and blow a kiss in my direction, and I smiled casually. I didn't like the half-assed attention.

I glanced at Lena as she shifted in her seat for the umpteenth time that evening. Her face was furrowed in a frown clearly expressing her discomfort. "You okay?" I asked, concerned.

"I'm good." But she didn't sound good. "Just a little tired."

I nodded, feeling bad for her. Neither of them should be here anyway and I had tried my best to get Leo to comply with that request. Tina, I didn't want to come for my own selfish reasons, but Lena for the baby. She looked about ready to pop any second.

"Do you ever get jealous?" I asked, almost to myself. Leo and Tina had started slow dancing, embracing each other and swaying their hips to the sensual trumpets of Hugh Masekela's "No Woman, No Cry." They looked sweet. They looked right. Brown skin against brown skin and holding each other like long-lost lovers do. I immediately regretted the question as soon as it left my lips. I don't think I was jealous of them so much as I was jealous of the attention. My mind flashed back to Jahmad and just as quickly, I shook him from my thoughts. Lena followed my longing gaze.

"No, I don't get too jealous," she admitted. "Tina has always been number one in his life until you. And I'm okay with that. Leo has helped me when my family turned their backs on me. I'll always be indebted to him for that."

My eyebrows lifted. Damn, she had said a mouthful there. "What do you mean?"

Lena sighed. "I got mixed up with the wrong group of people. People I thought were my friends. Got me strung out on drugs, into some stuff you would be surprised about. My family has never been very active in my life so I kind of raised myself. Then, I was homeless, couldn't find a job, all kind of things. I was at my lowest low, and then I met Leo." She nodded in his direction and her lips turned up in a small smile. "I didn't know about Tina at first, but I appreciated Leo and everything he did for me. Got me clean and back on my feet. Asked me to marry him, and well . . . I accepted because how could I say no? It was after the ceremony he told me about Tina. Then he asked for my help in return." She rubbed her belly. "Said to think of it like a surrogacy. Tina can't have kids, you see, and he wanted kids. A lot of them." She shrugged. "And I thought it was a fair deal."

Wow. I would never have known. Lena was so quiet; who knew she was the shell of such a broken interior? My heart went out to the woman and her sordid past. And the choices she didn't think she had. But still. Something else she said clawed at my confusion.

"What do you mean, 'She was number one until me?' " I asked.

"Leo talked about you all the time. To everyone who would listen. It was clear he had serious feelings for you before he even realized it. Everyone knew. Even Tina. Maybe he had love for her at one point but now, it's like he just tolerates her. They argue all the time."

I was still confused, turning my attention to them once more. My face was still sore from his hand and a bruise had begun to color my cheekbone, now easily covered with the makeup I had applied before the flight. He sure as hell didn't act like he had feelings for me. And argue with Tina all the time? When? I hadn't heard him turn his anger to anyone but me. The only time I'd caught them together they sure as hell weren't arguing. Unless they were arguing before her mouth was full of his dick.

"I don't get their relationship," I murmured, more to myself.

"I think he grew to love her at one point," Lena said, taking a sip of her water. "But I heard it was an arranged marriage, so I guess they had to find a way to make it work."

Now that was certainly news to me. The two continued dancing like a couple in love, hardly like the estranged pair Lena was making them out to be. At that point, I didn't know what to believe. But I knew there was even more to the situation than anyone was letting on.

They sat down, clearly winded from the dancing, and giggling at whatever inside joke they shared. Leo slid right next to me and immediately draped his arm across my shoulders, nuzzling my neck. He reeked of Tina's perfume.

"You having fun, my love?" he asked, and I nodded, though it was far from the truth. I just hoped this vacation was salvageable. Maybe I could do my own thing tomorrow and leave them to themselves.

The waitress came over with fresh drinks I didn't remember ordering but was grateful for anyway. "You two make a beautiful couple," she complimented in her thick Jamaican accent as Leo snuggled closer to me. "How long have y'all been together?"

"Almost a year," he said, beaming. "But we just made it official."

"Aw, how sweet! Honeymoon in Negril. We get a lot of that." She eyed Tina and Lena. "Let me guess. Friends?"

"His other women," Tina snapped. "He's with all of us."

The waitress was obviously taken aback, but she just chuckled, hoping to ease the tension. "Oh, it's a joke?" she said.

Tina rose and, leaning to Leo, grabbed him by the collar and brought his face to hers. She tongued him down as if she had a point to prove. Embarrassment had me lowering my head as the waitress looked on in shock.

"Now." Tina plopped into Leo's lap and circled her arm around his neck. "Don't *we* make a beautiful couple too?"

━━◆━━

I hadn't heard from Jahmad since the night of our little affair. I hadn't even given too much more thought to little Miss CeeCee, who had picked up his phone when I called. I figured it was better to keep busy and not think about it. Massages, shopping, parasailing, swimming with the dolphins. Out of sight, out of mind.

So I surely didn't expect to see his name come up on my phone while I lay out on the beach during our second to last day on the island.

Lena was sitting on a beach towel in the sand, writing in a little purple pocket-size journal she liked to carry around. Leo was out in the water and Tina was laid out sunbathing on a lounge chair in her itty-bitty bikini. Huge-framed sunglasses dominated her face and her hat was pulled to shadow her face from the sun. I couldn't tell whether she was awake or asleep, but she hadn't moved in a good forty minutes, her face angled out as if she were looking toward the sea.

I pulled my phone from my beach bag and rose to wander out closer to the water while I spoke.

"Hey," I greeted, struggling to keep the excitement out of my voice. I had to remind myself this man had up and left in the middle of the night and hadn't bothered to dial my number since. Not to mention CeeCee answering his phone while he was washing my juices off in the shower.

"I'm glad you picked up," he said. "I figured you would be mad." Damn right I was. Pissed was a more accurate term. But I wouldn't give him the satisfaction.

"No, of course not," I said, feigning ignorance. "About what?"

"It doesn't matter. I'm glad you answered because I really wanted to talk to you. Do you think we could meet later?"

I stepped to the water's edge, allowing the gentle waves to push the current up to my ankles. Overhead a seagull made a loud call as it soared across the sand.

"Sure. I'll hit you up when I get back," I lied. I had no intention of calling him when I returned to Atlanta.

"Oh, you out of town?"

"Jamaica."

"Wow, really?" His voice heightened in surprise. "By yourself?"

"Who said I was by myself?" I said and could only chuckle at the silence.

"We need to talk about the other night."

"No, we don't."

"So what, Kimmy? It's better to act like it didn't happen?" Yes. So much better. As much as I didn't want to, feeding into this, what was It? Thing? We were playing a dangerous game. I thought again about Leo's reaction. Very dangerous.

"It was a mistake," I said, already regretting the words as they left my lips. "A terrible mistake. You're engaged, I'm seeing someone. What are we doing?"

Jahmad's sigh was heavy. "That's the thing. You got me second-guessing . . ." He trailed off, and my heart lifted in anticipation.

"What do you mean?" I prompted. I tried to make the question sound casual, but the hope was easily detected.

"Listen. I'm sure about a lot of shit. But being with you, us together. That I'm not certain about. And it's that gray area that fucks up my head. The unknown. I thought I knew what I wanted. I thought I had found it in CeeCee."

Didn't know how that last part was possible but okay. "And now?"

"Now. I don't know. That's why I want us to talk. Sort this shit out. See where we go from here. The last thing I want to do is hurt you, Kimmy. I care about you too much."

I felt my love for him deepening. Jahmad had never opened up to me like that. No, he didn't say "love," but for once I didn't feel like my feelings were being stepped over or pushed to the side. We both knew what I wanted to hear. But of course I couldn't very well make him say it. I didn't know what to think or feel anymore.

I'm not sure if the little conversation had made me feel better. Who was I fooling? Bottom line, I still loved that man. Maybe it was better this way. If he admitted to loving me back, then what?

I promised to talk to him soon and hung up. Still deep in thought, I hadn't heard Leo sneak up behind me. He grabbed me around the waist and lifted me in the air, startling a panicked gasp from my throat.

He was wet from the ocean, his beautiful locs cascading like a waterfall down his back. I relaxed when I saw him smiling, realizing he was close to hearing my conversation but thanking God he hadn't. "Who you talking to, my love?" he said, planting a kiss on my cheek.

"My dad," I said. Funny how easy the lies came now. Like second nature.

"When do I get to meet them?" All seriousness had replaced amusement, and I scrambled to find an excuse. He sure as hell couldn't meet my parents. All hell would break loose.

"Soon," I said finally. Though it would be a cold day in hell first. He had mentioned inviting them to the wedding, but I quickly made up some excuse about them being out of town. I just prayed he didn't bring that up again. I didn't know how long I could stall before that request became a demand.

"Where do you think you're going?"

Tina's question had me halting in my tracks. We hadn't been home from the airport but thirty minutes before Leo got a text and left abruptly. I had waited an additional five minutes before snatching my purse, keys, and shoes and was damn near running to the door myself.

I turned, eyeing her as she closed the distance between us, her arms crossed over the cleavage spilling out of the top of her maxi dress. I didn't bother hiding my irritated sigh. "Out," I snapped, readjusting the strap of my purse on my shoulder. "I didn't think I needed permission."

"Not permission." Tina's lips seemed to turn up in a knowing smirk. "Just a simple question. I would hate for Leo to get back and wonder where you are. We both know how he gets about you."

The gloating was more than obvious, which made my stomach turn in disgust. She appeared to be relishing in the simple fact that Leo didn't use his hands on anyone but me. Maybe it would be better if I played nice.

"Look, I'm just going to my parents' house," I said, content with telling half the truth. "I won't be long."

Tina made sure to keep the smirk in place but she didn't bother responding. Before she could come up with something else to delay me further, I turned on my heel and took long, brisk strides to the door. Let her feel empowered. I had somewhere to be.

Jahmad was waiting in the driveway as I pulled up to my parents' house. He was on the phone, leaning against the back of his black Expedition. It was obvious he was fussing with whoever was on the other side of that conversation and by the look of his furrowed brow, the person was pissing him off.

I pulled up behind his truck and he locked eyes with me through the windshield. I smiled, hoping to ease his tension, as well as my own nervousness. Just like he suggested while I was in Jamaica, it was time for us to have "the talk" and I remained hopeful as I stepped from my car.

"Yeah whatever," Jahmad mumbled into the phone and instantly hung up as I neared him. He shoved the phone in his pocket.

"Everything okay?" I asked.

"Much better now," he said and a smile touched his lips, though I could still read the uncertainty in his eyes.

I leaned a hip on his truck, close enough to have our shoulders brushing.

"How do you feel about me?" he started, catching me off guard. I kept my eyes focused in front of me, watching a car pass by. He already knew the answer to that question. Of that, I was certain.

I sighed. There was no need to beat around the bush. "Jahmad, let's be honest. I've had feelings for you since I was young."

"Why didn't you tell me before I left for Texas? Back when we were . . ." he trailed off and I nodded my understanding. Back when we were sex buddies.

I got up enough nerve to look sideways at him, my gaze meeting his. "Would it have mattered?"

He broke our eye contact, now staring off into the distance. Yeah, I didn't think so.

"I was young," he admitted, his frown returning as if he were disappointed in his admission. "Young, dumb, reckless. I probably knew while we were together it was more serious for you than it was for me. But honestly, I didn't care. And that is what's eating at me. I led you on. I got your heart involved. And I was too selfish to admit I was wrong. Or to stop messing with you." He met my eyes again. "I am so sorry Kimera. For real. That was some foul shit and you didn't deserve it."

His apology was sincere and my heart melted with his compassion. I blinked back tears and placed my hand on his. "It's cool, Jay," I said. And it was. I hadn't expected any of this. Jahmad had certainly grown from the boy I puppy loved to the man who had my heart and soul.

"I broke it off," he murmured, almost to himself. "With CeeCee. I couldn't do her the same way I did you. It wasn't fair to her nor me. And there was no way I could marry someone else when I was still so uncertain."

I swallowed, thinking about my wedding rings I had stuffed in the inside pocket of my purse as soon as Leo's house faded in my rearview mirror. If only I had that same mindset.

Jahmad's phone rang, interrupting the silence between us. He shoved his hand in his pocket to stop the notification, immediately engulfing us in the quiet once more. I would bet my bank account that was CeeCee. In another life, another situation, I would have felt bad. But not today, not now, and surely not with Jahmad. This one was mine.

"So. Now what?" I asked, my heart fluttering with expectancy.

Jahmad's hand lifted to my face and he brushed his finger down my cheek. I closed my eyes and released a quivering sigh. "I'm saying," he said. "That I want to see where this goes. I'm saying that I can't keep denying I have feelings for you too. I'm saying, I know your ass is hungry so why don't we get something to eat."

I laughed and leaned in to kiss him. His words were music to my ears. The kiss deepened, Jahmad's tongue dancing with mine before he pulled back, a sudden intensity in his eyes as he stared at me.

"No games Kimera," he added, simply. "I'm not into that shit anymore. If we are going to have something, let's keep it real with each other."

I hesitated briefly before nodding my understanding and kissing him again. I couldn't bring myself to actually speak at the moment. My lies were better left unsaid.

Chapter 11

I certainly hadn't planned on this little shopping spree. Especially not with my husband's wives. Hell, after the little Jamaican family-moon (as I was calling it), I had been trying to find ways to spend as little time as possible together. But when Tina announced at breakfast that she was in the mood for shopping, I would've been lying if I had said I wasn't low-key excited. Not that I needed anything else, but still. Clothes, shoes, and spending someone else's money certainly had my interest piqued.

Lena requested to stay behind, but Tina gave Leo some kind of look and he told her she had to go. I felt bad for her because the poor thing looked like she needed a massage and a wheelchair. I made a mental note to suggest the former to Lena soon. Who knows. We might end up being friends in this whole situation.

We all piled into the limo, and Eddie drove us to Phipps Plaza in Buckhead. I'm sure we were bound to draw a few stares, and I couldn't blame any of them. Not only were we four black people in an expensive outlet mall but four black people who didn't seem to fit in any way, shape, or form with one another. We clashed. Hell, even I would have to question our connection if I were on the outside looking in. You had a black man with a pregnant woman in a floral, long-sleeved dress that looked like she needed to be rounding up prairie dogs outside of a farmhouse. Then

Tina's flashy ass was trying to draw the most attention in some kind of shimmery gold ensemble that was excessively elaborate for a shopping excursion. I, the most sensible one, it seemed like, had dressed down in a Burberry sweat suit. Sure, it was designer, because that was all that was in my closet now. But still, I needed to be able to quickly try on clothes. And with Leo spending money and it not coming out of my account or off my credit card, I planned to take full advantage of this little outing. Mall traffic was light, but that was to be expected. Who just up and goes on a shopping spree in the middle of a Tuesday afternoon? Only the Owusus.

A couple of hours and $13,000 later, at least from my receipts alone, Leo suggested we grab some lunch from the mall restaurants. Tina, Lena, and I followed the waitress to a corner booth while Leo excused himself to the restroom.

Once we sat down, Tina tossed a look over her shoulder before turning to us and lowering her voice. "After we are done, I want to get Leo something from the Armani store."

"For what?" I asked.

She frowned. "Damn, we can't do a 'just because we love you' type of thing? Does it have to be for an occasion?"

She and Lena both gave me a questioning look as if I should have known better, and I suddenly felt foolish for being so insensitive. I kept my mouth shut.

"I was thinking a nice new suit," Tina went on. "You know our husband can wear the hell out of a suit. I think it would be great for the Mayor's Ball, don't you think?"

Lena just nodded along while my ears perked at the last question. "Mayor's Ball?" I echoed. "What Mayor's Ball?"

Tina shook her head as if she were trying to explain calculus to a five-year-old. "I know you're new to all of this, Kimmy," she said with a smirk. "But please try to keep up, sweetie."

It took every ounce of my strength not to haul off and slap this chick in her smug-ass mouth. By the grace of God himself, Leo walked up to our table and slid into the booth beside her. Clearly, the tension was thick, because he immediately paused and looked between us.

"Everything okay, ladies?"

"This bitch wants to get slapped," I murmured.

If he heard me, he certainly didn't let on. He turned to Tina with a frown.

"What happened?" he asked.

"Nothing." Tina grinned and tossed me a condescending wink. "I was just telling our wife here about the Mayor's Ball. It's a big thing, and of course, we wouldn't want to miss it."

Leo nodded and slid into the chair beside me. "She's right. We look forward to this. What? You don't want to go, my love?"

I sure as hell didn't. A Mayor's Ball sounded fancy. Not to mention crowded with a ton of spectators watching as we paraded around in this little foursome. Though it would be nice to get all sexified and rub elbows with the elite, I would be too busy being ashamed to have any real fun.

My mind struggled to come up with some excuse as to why I wouldn't be in attendance. "When is it?" I stalled.

"Next weekend. My love, you know you have to go, right?" Leo leaned over and planted a kiss on my cheek. I knew better. It wasn't a question, and it certainly wasn't up for discussion.

"It'll be fun," Tina chimed in. "I'm sure you've never met the mayor before, right? Or any of the political officials in this city. And Leo is very well respected among these people. Even Lena wants to go." She nudged Lena's shoulder and obediently the woman gave a slight nod, though it was clear that was the furthest thing from the truth. "We just have to find her something to wear. A lot of the formal dresses don't look too good on fat people."

"Or on your whack-ass body shape," I snapped, immediately coming to Lena's defense.

Tina narrowed her eyes. She looked as if she wanted to say something else but the silent, narrowed eyes Leo was throwing at her obviously said a mouthful, because instead of responding, she just pursed her lips shut. I just shook my head. I knew it was only a matter of time before our interactions surpassed words. I was ready for this uppity bitch to catch these hands.

The waitress came, took our orders, and left us alone once more. We remained quiet before Leo spoke up. "I would love for you all to dress alike this year," he said casually. All three sets of our eyes whipped around to stare at him in horror.

Tina spoke up first. "Leo, baby. That's a bit much, don't you think?"

"For once I have to agree," I said with a frown. Already picturing all three of us dressed in matching outfits like some Great Value Diana Ross and the Supremes was enough to make me back out altogether. Fuck that, I would just catch one of Leo's ass whoopings before I waltzed in there dressed alike. He was definitely tripping.

Apparently there was a certain power in the three of us on some united front, because Leo held up his hands as if in surrender and chuckled. "Okay, okay. I want my girls to be comfortable and happy. Let's do different dresses, but they'll have to be the same color. Y'all decide."

Tina relented with a shrug. "Fine," she said. "I can pull off any and every color. It's these two we'll have to worry about."

I smacked my lips and rose from the table. I knew I needed to get to a safe zone because Tina was making it a point to grate all up and down my nerves. Besides, I no longer had an appetite anyway. "I'm going to run in a store really quick," I stated before anyone could question my departure. Then, just to piss Tina off, I added, "I want to get my husband a nice little surprise."

I couldn't see her reaction because I immediately put my arm around Leo and proceeded to press my lips against his. I could feel her eyes tearing daggers into the side of my skull so for that alone, I was satisfied. Even Lena had to chuckle at my move, and I couldn't help the cheeky grin that broke my face. Checkmate, bitch.

I wandered back into the mall and headed toward the Gucci store just because it so happened to be the closest one. I wasn't looking for anything in particular, just wasting time, really. And trying to get out of the same breathing space as wife number one. I stopped at the entrance as something else caught my eye. A "For Rent" sign sat on a stand in front of the adjacent storefront. My grin spread, and I stepped closer to peer through the window. Sure, Phipps had a Sephora, MAC, and an Ulta. But they didn't have a Melanin Mystique. I pulled out my phone to save the contact information for the vendor space. I would have to talk to Adria about it. Even if we didn't settle on this location, seeing this was just a reminder that I needed to be making this task my priority. I couldn't let a year pass me by and I didn't have that store up and running for us. Then this whole thing would have been a waste.

Satisfied, I crossed into the Gucci store, letting my eyes roam over the store's clothes with their signature brand logo, appreciating the smell of luxury that hung in the air. It was so interesting how just a year ago, I couldn't dream of entering, much less owning anything out of this mall. And now, it had become so normal it was almost unimpressive.

A case containing watches and jewelry caught my eye. I leaned over the glass to take a closer look. One particular watch stood out. The face contained two rows with glistening black diamonds surrounding it. The signature green-and-red stripes with engraved G's decorated the entire black band. It was definitely an eye-catching piece.

"Lovely, isn't it?" The sales associate, a young brunette with freckles peppering her nose and cheeks, flounced over to assist me. Without asking, she opened the case and removed the watch from its neat perch on the stand. "Three-karat diamonds," she went on, laying on the pitch. "Completely authentic and exclusive. Also customizable. Absolutely perfect for that special man in your life."

I had to agree. Nodding, I smiled in approval. Yes, I could see the watch on his arm nicely. "I want it," I said and immediately dipped into my purse for my credit card. I didn't bother asking the price, nor did she volunteer it.

I followed her to the register and handed her my card. When I signed the receipt, I saw the watch was $1,695. Before tax. I didn't bat an eye as I scribbled my name with a familiar flourish. Kimera Davis would have never in the history of nevers been able to remotely afford to drop $1,700 on an accessory. Lucky for me, I wasn't Kimera Davis. I was Kimera Owusu.

The associate boxed and bagged my watch and handed it to me across the register. "Excellent choice," she said. "He's going to love it. I'm sure your husband appreciates having a thoughtful and caring wife such as yourself."

It took a moment for my mind to register her words as I noticed her eyes zeroing in on the huge engagement ring and wedding band set seemingly twinkling in the fluorescent light. I merely nodded, though I had no intention of giving this to my husband. But she was right. I was a caring and thoughtful wife. Just not to my husband.

I left the store, not really looking forward to joining Tina and the gang right now. Maybe I could find a restroom to escape to so I could have a few more minutes of alone time. I had suggested we split up as soon as we had come to the mall, but no, doting husband Leo wanted us all together like the dysfunctional family we were. I groaned as I turned, making my way back to the restaurant. Might as well get it over with.

"KayKay."

I froze at the familiar voice and squeezed my eyes shut, hoping and praying the source was not who I thought it was. Apparently God was on a break, because sure enough, Keon strolled up to me, his arm around the shoulders of some white chick I had never seen before. And probably would never see again.

I swallowed, trying to make this interaction as normal and as short as possible. "Hey, Keon. What are you doing here?" And more important, I sure as hell hoped Jahmad wasn't with him.

He nodded his head toward the woman, who gave me a friendly wave. "Amber, my sister, Kimera; Kimera, this is Amber. Just shopping. What about you, big time?. Since when do you buy shit not off the clearance rack?"

He was right, but no less amusing. "Whatever. But look, I have to go," I rushed. I just needed to leave. Fast. Before—

"There you are," Tina's voice was right behind me, and my breath caught in my throat. "Leo told us to come looking for you."

Keon was clearly sizing the two ladies up, and without a second thought, he held out his hand in Tina's direction. "Hey, I'm Kimmy's brother. Have we met?"

I saw the light bulb go off in Tina's head, so I knew the words were coming before they even left her lips. Her look was slow and meticulous as her eyes shifted from me to my brother. She had me. And she knew it. "I'm Tina," she said, the gloating karma in her voice as thick as maple syrup. "This is Lena. We are Kimmy's sister wives."

Chapter 12

"It's really not what it looked like." I shifted the phone to my other ear as I listened to the silence coming through the line. I was supposed to be getting ready. I should have been completely dressed by now because I knew any minute Leo was going to announce it was time to go. Instead, I sat in my Victoria's Secret black lace bra-and-panty set trying to defuse the mess that had happened at the mall earlier that week.

Keon had never been the stubborn one of the two of us. Usually it was me who wouldn't budge or fold. But, oh no, not this week. He was showing his ass this week and his little attitude was making me anxious. I knew he wouldn't tell our parents, but Lord help me if he messed around and let it slip to Jahmad.

The silence drew on so long I thought Keon had hung up on me. To be honest, I was surprised he had even answered the phone this time. I had wanted to talk about the "sister wives" comment Tina had not so accidentally let slip out when she met him. I had quickly dismissed us right after and promised I would explain later, but apparently Keon wasn't trying to hear it, because he had been ducking and dodging my calls since. Until now.

"Oh, it's not what it looked like?" Keon echoed, clearly agitated. "Well, explain to me what the hell is going on, Kimera? If it's not what it looked like. That other chick wants to tell me something about sister wives, and wouldn't you know it, you do have a big-ass rock on your ring finger to prove it. So what? None of that is true?"

I sighed. There was no lying my way out of this one. "It's not even real," I said. "I just signed a contract to act like I am married to this guy. But technically he already has a wife. A legal one, I mean."

"Wait, so this dude has more than one wife? And you're cool with that?" His shock carried through the receiver so strongly that I was ashamed to admit that, yeah, I actually was.

"He treats me good," I responded gently to keep from answering the question. "He takes care of me and he's really sweet. It's really not as bad as it sounds."

"Wow." He blew out a shallow breath. "Just . . . wow."

"Are you mad?"

"Not mad. But disappointed. I can't believe you would stoop that low for some nigga. Like you desperate and can't get nobody else."

I winced. His tone was harsh but more than that, the words were beginning to cut, whether he intended it or not. "It's not going to be forever or anything. It's really just right now." I stopped short of telling him my motivation was the money. That confession, I'm sure, would make it sound even worse.

He was quiet again and I let out a sigh. "I know you don't understand or agree," I said. "I know it's not the best circumstances. But can we just go with it? For right now?"

"I mean, I don't have a choice. But I'm not about to be chumming it up with this dude on some brother-in-law shit."

He was serious, I knew, but the fact that the statement carried bits of his snarky humor was enough to appease me for the moment. My lips curled in relief. "I don't expect that," I said.

"Look, I just love you, Kimmy. I know I'm the last person you should look up to for relationship advice and how a man should treat a woman. I know I ain't the best man because I don't care about none of them chicks. I do care about you, though. And I know what you deserve."

My smile widened. "I know it's all out of love," I said. "Thank you. And can we please just keep this between us? I don't want any of this getting out."

"Hey, you already know that's not my style. Your ass gone mess around and give Mom and Pops a heart attack, though." He laughed, and I had no choice but to join in because he sure as hell was right. "I tell you what," he added. "Just gone head and pawn me your ticket to Heaven because we know you won't be traipsing up the golden stairway."

I rolled my eyes. "Oh, like you haven't done worse?"

"Please, girl. Next to this, your boy is looking like an archangel."

I laughed as I hung up on him. I was glad this hadn't damaged my relationship with my brother. I knew the situation wasn't the best. He and Adria both had expressed that. Thing was, what, if anything, could I do about it?

I stood up and walked over to the Versace gown that was still hanging inside of the garment bag. We had decided on gold to wear since Leo insisted we color-coordinate for the Mayor's Ball. I wanted to make sure my dress made a statement, and it certainly did with the faceted stones and sequins adorning the corset bodice before giving way to a flowing satin-silk skirt. The back out would complement my fresh haircut and the long side slit in the front would give just enough leg to keep it sexy, yet classy. I was dreading going to this function, but I was definitely ready to be seen in all my elegant splendor.

Not even ten minutes after I slipped on the dress, the knock came at my door. "Mrs. Owusu." Ayana's words were muffled through the door. "The others are ready. Mr. Owusu says you all should be leaving in the next five minutes."

"Ayana, come in, please," I called.

Obediently, she opened the door and the woman scurried into

the room and shut it behind her. Her eyes landed on me and ballooned. I even thought I heard a little gasp from her parted lips. I
smiled. Good. Just the reaction I was going for.

"Mrs. Owusu, you look absolutely stunning," she said with a
nod to confirm her statement.

"Thank you. I just wanted a second opinion."

"Well, you certainly will get a number of them tonight, and
they all will be raving about you in that dress." Her smile was genuine, and it definitely soothed my nerves.

"What will you be doing tonight?" I asked.

"Oh, uh, probably just cleaning. Is there something you would
like me to do, ma'am?"

"Yes. Please take the night off. Don't you have family or something?"

Ayana seemed at a loss for words. She clasped her hands in
front of her and shuffled her feet, her eyes falling to stare at something on the carpet. "Well, yes, but—"

"You should go be with them. When was your last off day?"

Ayana's shoulders lifted in a hesitant shrug. "I-I don't remember, ma'am."

"You and Eddie take the night off. I will tell my husband."

She seemed frozen in shock at the direction, and I could only
shake my head. I didn't know what Leo or Tina were thinking to
not give these nice people a break. I knew Eddie was older and
had his wife and grandchildren. Ayana, well, I didn't know much
about her family, but she was a young, attractive woman who
looked to be in her mid-thirties. Surely there was something or
someone she could get into for a few hours while we were away.

"But Mr. Eddie will be driving you all to the Mayor's Ball,"
Ayana pointed out, and I shook my head.

"We'll rent a driver. Eddie needs a break too." Either fear or
disbelief had her feet still rooted to the carpet, so I walked over
and placed my hands on her arms. The gesture was meant to be
reassuring, but I was surprised when Ayana flinched at the touch.

Damn, what had this family done to her? "Just go," I reiterated, my tone as comforting as possible. "You won't get in trouble. I will talk to Leo myself. I promise it'll be okay with him." Of course I didn't know that for sure, but I was banking on Leo being enthusiastic that I was taking initiative like I was part of this family. After all, that was what he wanted, right?

Ayana looked like a slew of thoughts jumbled in her mind and threatened to spill out but she merely nodded and left me alone. I sighed. Well, at least she could be free for the night. I, on the other hand, was not so lucky.

My phone rang and I quickly snatched it up from the dresser. It would have to be a short call with whoever it was. When Leo meant five minutes, he meant five minutes to the second.

My face lit when I saw the number and I swiped the screen to answer the call. "Hey, you," I greeted.

Jahmad's laugh was pleasant and refreshing. "Well, this was certainly a surprise."

"What are you talking about?" I feigned innocence, though I knew exactly what he was referring to. I was just glad he liked it.

"You know what I'm talking about."

"But did you like it, though?"

"Of course. I really appreciate it. This means a lot that you were thinking of me."

I couldn't have stopped smiling at that moment if someone had paid me. I'm sure to come home from work and see I had been there was a surprise in and of itself, but the Gucci watch I had left in his mailbox was completely unexpected.

I'll admit, the gift was bold. But since I had been back from Jamaica, Jahmad and I had been talking more and more. It was easy enough with Leo being away from the house so much. Hell, I had even started to think maybe he was working on wife number four. But with Jahmad keeping me distracted, I was just fine with Leo's absence. I just hated I hadn't been able to break away to actually see him again yet. It had been damn near a David Copperfield magic trick to get the watch to his house after I convinced him to give me the address.

"Thing is, though, how could you afford something like this?"

I figured he would ask something like that, so I was already on my game. "Oh, it wasn't that expensive," I lied. "Picked it up in Jamaica. You know they have brand items for much cheaper over there." I rushed on before he had time to ask a follow-up question. "I just hate I couldn't be there when you came home to catch your reaction." If it wasn't for the fact I had to get ready for this damn gala, I surely would have been. The pout was evident in my voice, I'm sure.

"And next time I see you, I'll be sure to show you how much I love it."

His flirt had my delicate flower throbbing to life, which doubly increased my disappointment about my night's commitment. "You be sure and do that."

My door opened abruptly and Leo entered, not even bothering to knock. I guess I should have expected that. Leo had already made it clear on several occasions he wouldn't ask for permission to enter anything he had paid for. Damn privacy.

I froze, the phone still to my ear, Jahmad's words not really registering as Leo lifted a questioning brow. To play it off, I casually held up a finger to him. "Hey, I got to go," I spoke cordially into the phone. "I'll talk to you later."

"Okay, have a good night, beautiful."

"You too." I hung up and tossed a smile at Leo, still waiting patiently by the door. "Sorry about that, handsome. My dad."

He nodded, and if he didn't believe me, he surely didn't voice it. Instead, his eyes roamed my body hungrily; I was thankful the dress was enough of a distraction. "My love, you look simply amazing."

"I'm glad you like it." I saw he had chosen an ivory tux with a gold handkerchief peeking from his breast pocket. "You look pretty good yourself, Leo."

He nodded. "I came up here to check on you and see if you had seen Eddie. He's not answering his phone, and it's time to go."

"Call another driver, sweetie," I said, grabbing my clutch and breezing toward the door. "I told him and Ayana they could have the night off."

Leo's hand caught my arm before I could walk by. "What?"

"Baby, they deserve it. I didn't think you would mind," I said. I didn't see the slap coming, so I had no time to block his hand before it connected with my face. The force of the blow had me stumbling, and I quickly grabbed the banister to keep from tumbling off my six-inch heels.

"Next time, ask me first. You don't make those kind of decisions."

I held my breath, almost expecting another hit, but Leo strolled past me and descended the stairs. "Clean yourself up," he said. "It's time to go."

I felt the first sting of tears threaten to seep from my lids. Not from the hit, though that hurt enough. My sore cheek could vouch for that. No, I wanted to cry in shame. The abuse was becoming so habitual now, I shouldn't even have been surprised. And I felt like a complete idiot because if anyone else, Adria or anybody, had voiced to me they were going through something like this, I would have been the first one to help them pack their shit so they could get away. But, of course, it was different when it was yourself. And dumb or not, I knew I wasn't going anywhere. Not until I got everything I was entitled to.

Tina appeared at the base of the stairs, her arms crossed over her chest. The smug look on her face had me quickly turning away and storming back into my room.

When I checked the mirror, I saw my makeup was slightly smudged and my cheek carried a reddish tint from the slap. A little concealer, a little more eyeliner and mascara, and I looked good as new. My mind was all over the place, but physically, I was poised, polished, and ready to get back into character. I prayed the rest of the evening would go as smoothly and as quickly as possible, though I didn't get my hopes up too much. I honestly never knew what to expect with this family.

———◆◆◆———

As usual, downtown Atlanta was lit up like the Vegas strip. The congestion was illuminated by bright neon lights on the marquees of restaurants, theaters, and hotels. Taxicabs and a variety of vehicles stuffed the roads, and the sound of car horns rang out in a harmonizing chorus. Every kind of pedestrian, from Atlanta-crazed tourists to half-naked club-goers, cluttered the sidewalk so that it looked as if the concrete had been replaced with boots, sneakers, and heels. No matter if it was three in the afternoon or the early brushes of dawn, my city was always awake.

Our limo driver finally pulled up to the sidewalk of the Marriot Marquis, and hotel valets hurriedly ran over to assist. I had been briefed on the way over. Work the room, but if it wasn't about politics, try not to talk too much. That wasn't going to be an issue, because I didn't know a thing about the current officials in charge so I couldn't add much value to the conversations anyway. And since I would rather have been left alone, I was just fine with staying to myself.

We emerged from the vehicle, and immediately I was blinded by the flashes of the press's cameras. Apparently, this was as big a deal as Tina had made it seem.

I still hated the idea of us color-coordinating like we were. Lena had on a swooping light gold chiffon dress with lots of lace, folds, and sashes. She looked almost angelic, and the dress accentuated her belly just right, just enough to be noticeable without dominating her figure.

Tina had chosen more of a rose-gold, form-fitting gown with plenty of beads and sparkle. It was long-sleeved with a high neckline, but the hemline was short in the front while cascading like a long waterfall in the back. She had pulled her weave into a neat bun at the base of her neckline. Frankly, it was a little tacky and way too extra, but hell, so was she, so I guess it worked.

Tina walked to Leo's left, gripping his waist with a huge smile for the spectators. Lena walked on his right, and I opted to walk on the other side of Lena, as far away from Tina as possible. I felt like my dress up against hers would clash as badly as our personalities.

The city had rented out one of the ballrooms in the hotel and even went so far as to reserve rooms in case people got a little carried away with the open bar. The futuristic-themed room was predominantly white with banquet-style tables. White leather circular couches were sprinkled throughout the room to allow for leisure, resting from the jazz music that wafted through the speakers. I noticed an entire accent wall had been decorated to look like a starry night sky, and massive screens displayed the mayor's name and picture.

I guess we were a little late because the party was already in full swing when we entered the room on the red carpet. Leo propelled us through the throng of formal gowns and alcohol-induced laughter. I was bored already.

Tent cards displayed *Owusu* on one of the tables, and I immediately slid into one of the chairs beside Lena.

"Come on, Leo, let's dance." Tina hadn't even bothered to sit down before grabbing Leo's hand and pulling him to the floor. On a roll of my eye, I turned to Lena, who was also watching, her hand making absent circles on her protruding belly. She and I both took a labored breath, though not necessarily for the same reasons.

"I don't know how you deal with it," I murmured.

Lena smiled, knowing full well what I meant. "You get used to it," she said. "Tina thinks everything is a competition, but she really doesn't compete with anyone but herself."

I had to laugh at the truth in that statement.

At one point, Lena had excused herself to go to the bathroom, and Leo and Tina were still out on the floor. I wanted so badly to find someplace to retreat myself, because time sure as hell felt like it was moving backward.

"Excuse me, pretty lady."

I glanced up as a young black man, probably in his mid-twenties with a low fade and a black three-piece suit, walked up to stand near my chair. I couldn't help but remember Leo's reaction with the club situation, so my eyes slid to see if he was still engaged on the dance floor. He was.

"May I help you?" I asked.

"You mind if I sit down for a bit?" He gestured to the empty seats at my table, and I shrugged. The table was reserved, but I really didn't see the harm.

"Thank you. I'm Clayton, by the way."

"Nice to meet you, Clayton. Kimera."

"Well, Ms. Kimera. Are you here alone? Why you sitting over here by yourself?"

"This is not really my thing," I admitted. "I just came with . . ." I paused in thought. "Some friends."

"Well, are you at least having fun?" Clayton said with a sympathetic laugh.

"Bunches. Can't you tell?"

Clayton smirked. "Just bubbling over, I see," he teased. "To be honest, this is not really my thing either. I'm just here with a friend for moral support."

"Good friend."

"I try to be." Clayton nodded his head in the direction of the dance floor. "Those your people?"

I glanced at Tina just in time to see her pull Leo closer against her and sneak a little lick to his earlobe. "Something like that."

"Isn't that Leo Owusu?"

I nodded. "It is."

"And is that his wife?"

"Yep."

Clayton looked at me, his eyes seeming to dance underneath his bushy eyebrows. "And where do you fit into all of that, Kimera?"

Damn, I wish I had asked how I was supposed to address that question. Did everyone know about Leo's multiple partnership? Was it public knowledge? Supposed to be discreet? I thought a moment longer before going with the latter.

"I'm just a friend of Tina's."

"Oh."

I couldn't tell, but Clayton almost seemed a little disappointed. He started to say something else, but the movement behind me stopped him. I looked back to see Dr. Lin approaching, and I gave him a little smile.

"Good to see you, Dr. Lin," I greeted. "Come on and have a seat. Clayton here was just keeping me company."

I turned as Clayton got to his feet, a shaky smile in place. "I better get going, but it was nice to meet you, Kimera." And with that, he disappeared into the crowd.

"What was that all about?" Dr. Lin said as he slid into one of the available seats.

"No idea."

"Well, it's good to see you all out together." He glanced to the doorway, where Lena had stopped one of the waiters with a tray of appetizers. Apparently she had found something to nibble on.

"It's weird," I told him. "Being out all together. I mean, I do it for Leo, but it makes me uncomfortable."

Dr. Lin waved away the confession with a hand and a comforting smile. "Don't stress yourself about it. It's understood about you all, even though it's never been completely expressed. But everyone who's anyone that knows Leo knows about his relationships."

For some reason, Dr. Lin's comment did not feel like a good thing. And I know he meant it to ease my discomfort, but I could already feel it rising. The more people who knew, the more questions. And the more likely the lid was going to fly off this thing, and it would be shown in the worst way. And if that day came, I just hoped the damage to my life was reparable.

Chapter 13

"Well, look at you, Mrs. Celebrity." Tina entered the kitchen and tossed a folded newspaper on the dining table. "Looks like you officially made it to the big leagues with the rest of us."

I glanced up from my omelet with a frown. Tina didn't elaborate any further but simply grinned like she knew the punch line to some ridiculous joke.

Rolling my eyes, I put down my fork and unfolded the paper. And damn near choked on my food.

Right on the front page was a huge picture of Leo, Tina, Lena, and me at the Mayor's Ball. Someone had apparently caught us as soon as we had stepped from the limo. Newspaper ink had the picture quality not looking the sharpest, but it was clear enough for me to be discerned among the other two women. And even more clear was the caption: *LEO OWUSU ATTENDS MAYOR'S BALL WITH GORGEOUS WIFE AND LOVE PARTNERS.*

"Shit." I dropped the paper as if I had been burned. "Why the hell didn't you tell me this would happen?"

Tina shrugged. "It was bound to happen. I told you Leo was very prominent with these people."

"But an article in the paper?" I was horrified. What if my parents saw? Members of the congregation? Jahmad? Panicked, I quickly scanned the article to see if my name was mentioned.

Thank God it wasn't, so maybe, just maybe I could deny it was me. I frowned when I caught a small photo next to the author's name. My mind flashed back to the man who had sat with me at the table before Dr. Lin had shown up. Clayton. Sure enough, Clayton Arnold was the author of this mess. Of course. A damn journalist. And here my dumb ass thought he was just trying to be sociable.

I stood, leaving Tina's gloating ass sitting right there at the table, and carried the paper with me to my room. Without a second thought, I punched in Adria's number and waited impatiently for her to answer.

"Girl, I just tried to call you." She was nearly yelling once she picked up. "Have you seen the paper?"

I groaned and collapsed on my bed. "Yes. That's what I was afraid of. Adria, what am I going to do?"

"Calm down. You can't really tell it's you."

"You're lying. Otherwise you wouldn't have thought to call me." Her silence elevated my fear. If she could recognize me, chances were someone else could too.

As if on cue, my phone beeped in my ear signaling an incoming call. I pulled the phone away from my face and, sure enough, my mom's number flashed across my screen. Oh, hell no, I definitely couldn't talk to her now. I swiped to reject and squeezed my eyes shut. Now what was I supposed to do?

<hr/>

I didn't immediately go inside.

My parents had seen the newspaper. What else was the reason for the twelve missed calls and four voicemails? I hadn't even bothered listening or returning the calls. Just got dressed and came on over. This conversation was better had in person anyway.

A few more minutes ticked past, twenty to be exact, before I got up enough nerve to step from the car. They knew I was out here. The living room window was right beside the driveway, so as silent as my luxury engine was, they still knew when someone pulled up. But like me, I'm sure they were also dreading this conversation. I took a breath. Better to get it over with.

I used my key to enter and, as I expected, they both were seated on the couch. Waiting. They hadn't been long home from church because both were still in their Sunday best.

My mama used the remote to click off the TV and crossed her arms over her chest. The tension was so thick you could cut it with a knife. Where I had been comfortable just moments prior, now the air was too stuffy, my clothes feeling way too tight.

I sat down in the armchair opposite the couch, wishing she had left the TV on. The silence was deafening.

"You come in and can't speak?" Mama broke the quiet, her tone clipped with restrained anger.

"I'm sorry."

"For not speaking? Or this?" The newspaper was thrown on the coffee table, hitting the glass with a sickening slap that made me flinch. The crumbled picture stared at me, almost taunting.

"It's not as bad as it looks." The lie left a bitter taste in my mouth. Of course it was as bad as it looked. Maybe worse.

"How could you do this?" My mother had gotten up and was now pacing the floor so hard it was a wonder she didn't walk a hole in the carpet. "Everything we've done for you, Kimera? And you pull this? What are we supposed to think of you? And I'm sure some of the church members have seen it."

I slid my eyes to my dad. He didn't utter a word, but the way his veins were bulging in his arms, I could tell it was taking everything in him not to. He looked like he was about to bust.

"Why, Kimera?" my mom asked, turning pleading eyes back to me. "Why would you do this? On what earth and in what Heaven did you think this would be a good idea?"

"I'm sorry," I said again.

"What the hell is a 'love partner,' anyway?"

I opened my mouth and shut it again. "We're all just . . . together," I mumbled.

"Like married or something?" Mama was nearly hysterical, tossing her arms wildly. "What? Swingers? What the hell does this mean? How did y'all even pull this off?"

"It's not official, Mama."

"Then you need to end it." My dad's voice didn't lift an octave but still carried enough power and command to rock me to my core.

"Your father is right," Mama jumped in. "All he has worked for. All we have—"

"Sandra." My dad's hand lifted to stop my mother's rant, but his eyes never left mine.

Whatever silent communication they had took place, because as if she understood, my mother turned on her heel and stormed from the room.

I averted my eyes, instead focusing on the fingers that had begun to twist the bottom of my shirt. I suddenly felt nine again.

"I'm disappointed in you," he stated evenly, his words hurting more than any physical abuse from Leo. "But I'm disappointed in myself."

Confused, I looked at him and saw that he had indeed lowered his head in shame. "Daddy, what do you mean?"

"Colossians 3:18," he replied. " 'For if someone does not know how to manage his own household, how will he care for God's church?' "

Slowly, his words settled on me like an itchy blanket. "No, Daddy."

"How could I have not known what was going on with my own daughter?" His face went slack, and I chanced crossing to him.

"I'm sorry, Daddy," I said again, touching his hand. "I never meant for any of this to get this bad. And certainly not for it to reflect negatively on you. Or the church." And now, I was riddled with guilt. Not only were my own indiscretions put on display for the world to see, but I felt stupid for not realizing how personally my dad would take it.

"More than that," he said, "I don't want it to reflect negatively on you, Kimera. You deserve the utmost respect, but you have to respect yourself first. You deserve the best."

Like father, like son. Keon had said something to that same effect. Not that I didn't believe it, but the way my world was set up right now, this was what was best for me. For the time being.

"I imagined my daughter getting married to a nice, respectable man," my dad went on. "Have me some spoiled grandbabies. To be honest, I assumed you and Jahmad would get together."

I remained quiet. With luck. I was working on that.

"But I definitely didn't expect no foolishness like this. Why, Kimmy? What's the purpose?"

I didn't want to tell my dad it was for money and risk making myself look even worse. I couldn't add gold-digger to the list of names that might have run across his mind about me when he first saw that article.

"Leo is a good man," I lied. I thought he was at first, but living with him had definitely changed my perception.

My dad's sigh was heavy. "Look, I'm not going to agree with all of your decisions and I don't expect you to tell me every little thing that goes on in your life. But I hope you would always strive to do right by God, your mom, and I. And yourself. So whatever this mess is you're tied up in, it's dangerous. You need to get out of it. Then repent, baby girl. Get yourself right before all of this gets out of hand."

Chapter 14

It looked different.

I hadn't stepped foot in Word of Truth Christian Center in, and I felt guilty admitting this, years. My dad's church had certainly grown in both building size and location since then. I almost didn't recognize it.

As I pulled up to the cream stucco building on the hill, set atop a large expanse of beautifully landscaped lawn with a huge gold cross adorning the front, I just remembered when my dad had first pursued what he was called to do.

He had started ministering to folks on the street and opening our home to homeless people in the community to give them access to a warm bed and a hot meal. The first building he could afford was in a plaza next to a check cashing place and beauty supply store, and it only seated twenty-three people comfortably, three of whom were faithfully me, my mom, and my brother. I chuckled as I remembered having to sit on that hard pew in my Easter dress with its abundant frills and lace. I was uncomfortable, but I knew not say anything or my mama would hand my ass to me when I got home.

My dad had moved twice since then, each building growing with his followers. Now this church, between its cushioned pews and even more spilling onto an oversize balcony that overlooked the pulpit, easily accommodated five thousand people.

I maneuvered my car into an available space and started the long hike to the double doors.

It was really impressive what my dad had done with the place. He'd given the entire building a makeover inside and out, and he was constantly updating to high-end finishings and extra accommodations. Like the brand-new playground I spotted on the side, complete with slides, jungle gyms, and a swing set. He was one of the only pastors I actually saw make use of the building fund he was constantly soliciting money for.

No one recognized me at first, and for me that was a good thing. Especially with the newspaper fiasco circulating. No, today's visit wasn't me finally taking my folks up on their invitation so much so as it was a social call. This was the only place I could meet Jahmad, and it wouldn't raise suspicion. After speaking with my parents, I had decided to finally tell him the truth. He still hadn't come across the article yet, but I wanted him to know what was going on before he saw it sensationalized in the paper. I couldn't have him assuming the worst about me. Not when we had been making such progress. Since I knew I would be followed and it would somehow get back to Leo, I thought my folks' church was as good a place as I was going to get. Leo couldn't really argue with my spiritual growth.

I followed the crowd and found a seat toward the large stained-glass windows. Service had already started, and the choir had everyone on their feet singing along. I just sat and watched them, nodding along with the words I didn't know.

My phone vibrated and I pulled it out, eyeing the screen. My lips curled into a smile.

I'M HERE, the text read. I quickly sent a reply. **ME TOO. NEXT TO THE WINDOW TO THE LEFT SIDE.** I turned to look at the door, craning my neck to see the incoming traffic. Ushers continued to direct the last few stragglers, but no Jahmad yet.

The choir finished two more songs, and Deacon Michael—at least I thought it was Deacon Michael, but it had been so long I couldn't even remember if that was him—led us in a prayer. Then I saw Jahmad shifting through the people in the pew, headed in my direction, and I scooted over to make room.

We didn't speak as he sat down and took my hand. His fingers stroked my knuckles and my heart soared. He used his other arm closest to me to wrap around my shoulders, and I snuggled into him because it felt so right. This was how it was supposed to be. He had to feel this chemistry between us. Not just sexual; it was hitting on all levels.

My dad was never one to dress in a traditional robe. Just like he didn't request that of members of his church board or choir. Everyone complemented each other in service color schemes but that was the extent of it. Today's colors were blue, black, gray, and teal by the look of it.

It amazed me how my dad took on such a dominant and passionate aura when he stepped behind that pulpit. He spoke with such reverence, each word dripping with anointing. He didn't do all of that yelling and jumping around, just spoke from his Spirit. And his message seemed to always be right on time.

Today's message was walking in the love of God in relationships. I'm not sure if he purposely chose that knowing what was going on with me, but for some reason, I still felt convicted. My marriage wouldn't really get anyone's stamp of approval. Not to mention I spent nearly the whole service thinking of Jahmad and how I couldn't wait to feel him inside me. I had to remember where I was and pray for my thoughts, because they were surely lustful.

One more prayer, altar call, and the service was over. Jahmad stood with my hand still in his, and I followed him out of the pew.

"I didn't realize how much this place has changed since I've been gone," he said as we walked down to the front. "Feels good to be back."

I nodded. It did feel good.

My dad was in front of the stage, shaking hands and giving kind words to the crowd that had gathered.

My mama spotted me first and she walked over. "Hey, Kimera," she said with a tight-lipped smile. She was clearly still pissed from our previous conversation, because the greeting wasn't warm, just polite and cordial. She didn't give me a hug or touch me in any way. I wondered if Jahmad noticed the attitude. When her eyes glanced down at my hands still linked with his, she lifted an eyebrow. *Shit.*

I pulled my hand away and cleared my throat. The gesture couldn't have been more obvious, but still, my mother just looked at both of us, not speaking.

Jahmad shoved his hands into his pockets. "That was a powerful sermon today," he said, breaking the silence.

My mama nodded, narrowing her eyes. "It sure was, Jahmad. It sure was." I wish I could read her, but she kept her face as blank as possible.

"Baby girl." My dad's voice was thunderous as he walked up to hug me. He, at least, was more welcoming than my mother, despite the hurt I had caused. "So glad you could make it out this Sunday. You too, Jahmad." He nodded in his direction before turning questioning eyes back to me. "You two came together?"

"No." I quickly spoke before Jahmad had a chance to. "We just saw each other when we came in. Not together," I added. My dad gave a slow nod and slid a look to my mother.

"So you two coming back to the house for dinner?" Mama asked after another moment of silence. "I'm going to fry some pork chops."

I felt Jahmad's eyes on me. "We'll see," I answered, because I really didn't know. It seemed like I had to promise an arm, leg, and kidney just to get out of the damn house for church. As pathetic as it was, I felt like a prisoner in Leo's house, and every time I managed to leave, I wondered if an ass whooping was waiting for me at home.

We moved out of the way to let others come and shake my dad's hand. I couldn't help but feel they had carried on an entire secret conversation behind our backs, right there in front of us.

It was probably very questionable. First they find out I'm in a poly relationship and now, here I am, arm-in-arm with Jahmad at church like we're a couple. I was actually more concerned about my brother finding out about Jahmad, considering they were best friends and since he also knew about my marriage. And Leo was still adamant about me introducing him to my family, but I already knew that was completely out of the question given the circumstances.

"What do you think your parents have to say about us?" Jahmad asked as soon as we had made our way to the Fellowship Hall. My hand had once again found its way into his as we walked close enough for our arms to brush.

"I don't know," I admitted. "I don't even know what to say about us, honestly."

"Well, instead of your parents' house, do you maybe want to go somewhere and talk about it?"

I started to nod but my eyes slid behind him, the person coming into view having me blinking to make sure my vision was clear.

The crowd had dispersed for the most part, but I would know that damn red dress anywhere.

It had to be one of her favorites, because I saw her in it too often. It was way too tight and too low-cut to be appropriate for church, with her titties all but spilling out of the top. She was looking right at me, her face in an amused smirk.

I quickly pulled my hand from Jahmad's. "One sec," I said, already headed in her direction. "I see someone I know."

Tina crossed her arms over her bust as I stopped in front of her. "Old friend?" she asked casually, her eyes sliding in Jahmad's direction.

"No, the better question is, what are you doing here?" I hissed. "Did you follow me? Damn—" I covered my mouth, remembering where I was. "Dag, Tina, what is wrong with y'all? I can't even go to church without y'all hunting me down?"

"It's not even like that. Leo wanted to surprise you."

At the mention of his name, my neck snapped around, my eyes darting in all directions. Why the hell was he here? How did he find me? Had he seen me with Jahmad?

"He's in the car," Tina clarified. "I thought you would be happy that your husband wanted to accompany you to church. This is your family church, right? Are your parents here?"

Damn, it's not like she was yelling, but she made no point to talk in a lower tone, so anyone within earshot was all in our conversation.

Jahmad was looking in my direction with a questioning expression, and I held up a finger for another minute. If Leo was on the phone, maybe. But I didn't see how I could weasel out of this one with him sitting right in the parking lot.

Tina saw the exchange, I'm sure, but she didn't speak on it.

I walked to the door and stepped outside, immediately spotting the limo at the curb. It wasn't like it was exactly inconspicuous, and every member, it seemed, was looking, pointing, and trying to peek at the vehicle that was so out of place. Leo got out as soon as he saw me descend the church stairs with Tina fast on my heels. He opened his arms for a hug. "Hey, my love—" but I was already cutting him off.

"Leo, what are you doing here?" I said curtly. "How did you know I was here?"

Leo's smile faded. "My love, what's wrong?"

I shook my head. I was so damn frustrated, I could feel the beginnings of a headache throbbing at my temples. "I just want to come out the house for a few hours without having to worry about you and Tina on my back," I admitted.

"I'm sorry, my love. That's not why I'm here."

"Then why are you here?"

"It's Lena," he said.

Chapter 15

When we arrived at the hospital, Lena had already been wheeled back for the emergency C-section. Leo had brought me up to speed on the way over, that she had woken up that morning to a pool of blood staining her sheets.

As soon as we burst into the hospital, he informed the nurses who he was, and they immediately gave him scrubs and rushed him down the hall to surgery. Tina and I waited in the lobby, passing the time between walks to the vending machine down the hall.

The more time that passed, the more and more I felt my anxiety rising. Lena and I hadn't spoken too much since we got back from Jamaica. She spent more and more time in her room sleeping, stating she was exhausted and the pregnancy was draining her. Her drowsy spells were more frequent and for longer periods of time, but, hell, I had never been pregnant so I figured that was normal.

The waiting room was nearly empty as visitors came and left. My body was growing numb from the stiff chairs, and I was constantly having to shift and reshift to ease the aches in my back. Had it not been such an emergency, I would have loved to be able to stop by the house to switch out of the dress, stockings, and heels I had worn to church. Because between the clothes and the smell of antiseptics in the air, I was becoming uncomfortable.

I glanced down the hall once more where Tina had disappeared for what seemed like the twentieth time. She must have been just as restless as I was, because she certainly couldn't remain seated too long.

My phone vibrated in my purse, and I pulled it out, glancing at the notification. I checked to make sure Tina was still gone before sending a quick reply to Jahmad. I figured he would wonder what the hell was going on. Here we were, seemingly making a little progress, and I just up and ran out on him. He asked who the mystery woman was and what was with the limo. I came up with the best lie that I could. Tina was a friend of mine, it was her limo, and she had come to tell me about an emergency with her sister. She needed me there for moral support.

DAMN, I'M SORRY TO HEAR THAT, his text read. **IS THERE SOMETHING I CAN DO?**

AW I APPRECIATE IT BUT WE'LL BE OK. I SHOULDN'T BE TOO MUCH LONGER.

OK. YOU WANT TO MAYBE GET TOGETHER THIS EVENING?

I did. Lord knows I did. But the chances of me being able to get away were pretty slim to none given the new baby. Hell, I didn't even know if I would be making it out of the hospital tonight.

CAN I CALL YOU LATER AND LET YOU KNOW?
OK.

"He's still back there?" Tina's voice had me nearly dropping my phone. I quickly scrolled off of the messages and dropped the device back into my purse. She sat down, a chair away, popping open a bag of cookies.

"I guess so," I answered. "Haven't heard anything yet."

"Hm." Her grunt was nonchalant as she crossed her legs. "Well, they sure need to hurry the hell up. I'm not trying to be here all night."

Funny. I had been thinking the same thing, but it sounded so heartless hearing it out loud. Or maybe just because it was her.

"I just hope the baby is all right."

Tina popped another cookie on her mouth. "He'll be all right." To my surprise, her face softened as a smile touched her lips. For a moment, she actually looked . . . normal. Not the bitch I'd grown accustomed to. "I can't wait to hold him."

"Him? It's a boy?" I frowned, remembering what Lena had mentioned. "I thought Leo wanted it to be a surprise."

"He did. He doesn't know. But I just couldn't wait. I suspected it was a boy but I just had to make sure. So little Leo Jr. It makes so much sense to have his dad's name."

Interesting. Tina seemed to be getting more and more excited the more she talked about it. I guess she had a weak spot for babies. The more I thought about it, though, the more I realized that I hadn't seen much in the way of preparing for a baby. The nursery, the toys and baby essentials, the car seat. I guess I had missed all of that or maybe I just was not paying attention. Or hadn't cared enough to look for it.

We sat in silence a little longer, Tina now fiddling with her cell phone and me just absently staring at the soundless images playing on the wall-mounted TV.

Finally Leo pushed from the back doors, a huge grin plastered on his handsome face. He looked funny in his green hospital scrubs and his locs stuffed under the mesh bonnet but the joy that radiated from him was strong enough that anyone could tell from miles away.

"A boy," he announced before planting a sloppy kiss on my lips. He turned and lifted Tina in the air and kissed her too. I tried to ignore the attention, but I know his public display of affection had drawn the curious stares of several visitors sitting in the lobby.

"Aw I'm so happy for us, baby," Tina said with a grin. And she seemed like she really meant it. Me, on the other hand, I really didn't know how to feel. My mind was on too many things as it was, namely when I would be able to see Jahmad again. But it was good to know the baby had arrived safely.

"Eight pounds, six ounces, twenty-one and a half inches long," Leo informed us. "Little Leo is going to be tall."

"How is Lena doing?" I asked.

"She's good. Recovering. Sore, she says, but they're taking care of her."

Jahmad crossed my mind again. Maybe . . .

"Listen, babe, can Eddie take me home? I really need to get out of these church clothes."

Tina smirked, looping her arm with Leo's. "No, stay," she insisted. Her concern actually might have sounded genuine if I didn't know any better. "We need to be here for Lena. We are all one big happy family here, right?" I caught the little squeeze she gave to Leo's arm before he nodded.

"Right, my love," he said. "Lena needs you. She needs all of us."

I had no further objection, so I kept my mouth shut. Guess I was stuck.

We went down to the nursery and peered through the glass. I scanned the row of bassinets, babies swaddled in the customary white hospital blanket and blue or pink hat, some crying, some sleeping, until my eyes stopped on the one that read "Leo Owusu Jr." The nurse picked him up and held him up, and my heart melted. He looked just like Leo, his round eyes staring curiously, his chestnut complexion smooth over his plump cheeks. Tina squealed, and I couldn't help but smile stupidly as I stepped closer. He looked like a little baby doll.

"Let's go check on Lena," Leo suggested. "They can bring him up to the room."

We rode the elevator upstairs and found Lena's room halfway down the hall. We entered a large pastel-blue hospital room, the substantial size I was sure an added bonus of being wife number two. The scent of latex and disinfectants stung my nose and the buzzing from a monitor near the bed quietly echoed in a steady rhythm that harmonized with Lena's shallow breaths. I grimaced, eyeing the woman in the bed. Lena sure as hell looked horrible. She was tucked underneath starched sheets with an IV hooked up to her arm. She appeared to be weak, eyelids barely lifted. But what did I honestly expect after a woman had just given birth?

Lena managed a weak smile as we all crowded around her bed. Leo leaned over to kiss her forehead. "I'm proud of my girl," he was saying, gingerly brushing loose strands of hair from her face.

"Thank you," she murmured, her voice weary.

"Leo Jr. is doing good," Tina said. "Looks just as handsome as his father."

"You need anything, my girl?" Leo asked.

I smiled. It did warm my heart to see him tending to Lena. One thing I could say, he certainly cared about each of us in his own special way. When he wanted to show that side of himself.

Lena shook her head and let her lids lower. She looked peaceful. I was glad she was finally getting some rest.

"Maybe we should go," I whispered, nodding in her direction. It looked like she was trying to go to sleep.

"The doctor wants to run a few tests," Leo said. I had to really listen, but I thought I could detect a hint of concern in his voice. "Something about her blood being low. I'm not sure."

"She'll be fine, Leo." Tina held out her hand for Leo to take it. He did and the two headed toward the door.

I turned to follow before I heard the faint whisper. I had to pause to even be sure I had heard anything at all.

There it was again. I turned back to the bed and saw Lena's lips moving. She had opened her eyes once more and was lifting an arm in what looked to be a struggling "come here" gesture. "I'm coming in a bit," I told Leo before making my way closer to the side of Lena's bed.

She looked paler than usual, which was hard enough for a black woman, but her skin looked as if it was absent of all color. And warmth. I brushed her cheek with the back of my hand and, sure enough, it was cool to the touch. I shuddered as an eerie feeling came over me. If having a baby did this, then I sure as hell wasn't planning on any. Ever. I hoped that part wasn't in the contract.

"You okay?" I asked.

"I'm scared." Her voice was barely a whisper.

I frowned. "Of what?"

"I think something is going to happen."

"To who? To you? To the baby?"

Lena's eyes slid to the closed door before shifting back to me. Sure enough, fear had replaced the weariness.

"I don't know," she admitted. "I just . . . have a bad feeling." Her head lolled to one side, and I glanced over at the IV drip, making its way down the tube through some needle to spread through her veins. Before I could ask another question, a gentle snore showed she had fallen asleep just that fast.

I readjusted her covers and took the opportunity to mimic Leo's move by kissing her on her forehead. I don't even know why I did it, but I felt compelled. "Get some rest," I whispered in her ear, though I knew she couldn't hear me.

I left the room and shook off the sudden heaviness that seemed to weigh my body down. I tried to push Lena's words out of my mind, chalking it up to the drugs. When she came home from the hospital in a few days, she probably wouldn't remember what the hell I was talking about if I even brought it up.

I caught up to Tina and Leo back in the lobby downstairs. Tina had her arms around his waist, snuggled against his chest. She just insisted on hogging the man. I mean, damn, his other wife did just have his child. He should've been in there by her side, making sure she regained her strength. But once again, Tina had to make it about her.

"Oh, good, Kimmy." Tina turned to me as I entered the waiting area but she didn't bother moving from her comfortable position on our husband. "I was just trying to see what we were doing tonight. You going back to the house, right?"

I felt like it was some kind of setup. Again I thought about Jahmad and how, disappointedly, I would have to accept being held hostage tonight. "Of course," I said with an overly chipper smile. "Where else would I go?"

I started to walk past them when somewhere in the distance an alarm sounded, and we dodged a few nurses as they ran down the hall. We started in the direction of the elevators just as Dr. Lin stepped off, looking slightly frazzled. Without speaking, he grabbed Leo's arm and steered him down the hall, out of earshot.

I don't know what he said but whatever it was, it had Leo pushing past him and running into the stairwell with Dr. Lin fast on his heels. I frowned.

"What was that about?" I mumbled, almost to myself.

Tina shrugged. "Not sure."

"Do we need to go with them?"

"No, we don't even know where they went. They could've gone to the nursery or they could have gone back to Lena's. Let's just wait here."

An hour later, it wasn't Leo who met us in the lobby but Dr. Lin. I stood, surprised at his solemn expression. Where was Leo? And what the hell had happened?

Chapter 16

The first time I had experienced death, I remember I couldn't have been more than six. My dumbass brother had brought home a frog he had found near the lake at our elementary school. Of course I didn't like frogs and I thought the thing was absolutely hideous. But after a few weeks, Kermit started to grow on me.

Keon had made him a makeshift home out of a shoebox with holes poked in the top and patches of grass we had pulled up from outside and sprinkled in the bottom of the cardboard. I had even colored a lily pad and some trees on the interior, and we were really happy about our little pet. Until he escaped and Mama found him in the kitchen, and she splattered his ass all over the linoleum.

He had just been a frog, and I was young, but when I came home and saw him in the trash, I damn near had a heart attack. I mean the full-out ugly cry with a runny nose, wheezing, and puffy face under a faucet of sloppy tears.

Since then, a few cousins and a great grandfather I never knew had passed away but no one close to me. So I hadn't had to deal with death before.

But Lena's death put me back in mind of Kermit. I hadn't

known her long but in the short amount of time I did, we'd gotten close enough that her passing hit me in the gut.

Postpartum bleeding, they said. I had heard of complications during pregnancy but they seemed more uncommon than common. Apparently, in recovery, Lena started hemorrhaging and lost a lot of blood. Her body went into shock and slowly shut down.

I was surprised I hadn't cried. I'd wanted to. Felt I needed to. But the tears didn't come, though I felt my heart hurting. Tina, on the other hand, seemed too preoccupied with the baby. She damn near moved into the nursery and rarely left that baby's side. Even while he slept, she would just stare at him lovingly, her hand through the bars of his crib for his little hand to grip her finger.

Honestly, I'm sure Leo was grateful someone was taking care of his son. He was dealing with Lena's death the hardest, and he just stayed cooped up in his room for the most part. He didn't really have anything to say to any of us. When he finally did emerge just to lock himself in his downstairs office, it was evident he was so far gone in grief he hadn't given two fucks about his appearance. His locs were disheveled and he hadn't bothered to shave so the beginnings of a beard had a hideous stubble coating his chin.

I felt bad but, honestly, I didn't know what to do. So we all just trudged around the house like zombies, disconnected from each other and everyone else. The only reprieve I had was that I had been left alone to talk to Jahmad. Plus with everyone worrying about themselves, I was even able to sneak away and back before anyone realized I was gone. It was my way of escaping.

I was surprised that Lena's funeral was empty, except for us. And by us, I mean me, Leo, Tina, and Leo Jr. in the first pew and Ayana and Eddie directly behind us. That's it. Not a mother, father, or cousin in the church.

I remembered Lena telling me she didn't have any family. Well, I guess any that was still active in her life. But still. I would've expected more than just us, especially remembering the number of people that were at our wedding. But then that was for show. A staged performance where an audience was needed. This. This was real life. And a funeral is where you see people's true feelings. Or lack thereof.

Leo had been so out of it that Tina had taken the reins in preparing this service. Probably another reason for the lack of people in attendance. She had picked out an antique white casket with rose-gold embellishments. Lena looked beautiful as she lay on the pink crepe cushions. As if she were just sleeping. The makeup had revived her, and minus the pregnancy weight, she looked like the woman she probably was before this whole ordeal.

Sorrow engulfed me as I thought again about the last time I saw her in that hospital bed. She was frail but alive. She had murmured something about being afraid. Maybe she knew this was coming. I've heard some people know when they're about to die. A feeling. A vision. Maybe Lena was trying to prepare me. Never did it cross my mind that was going to be our last conversation.

Leo had buried his face in his hands, but the trembling, slumped shoulders made it more than obvious he was crying. To his left, Tina sat quietly staring ahead. Expressionless. She looked more like she was sitting in a class listening to a lecture than at a funeral.

Beside her feet, Leo Jr. slept soundlessly in his carrier. He was plump for a newborn and had a full head of curly black hair. He was the perfect blend of his parents, with Leo's nose and mouth and Lena's innocent, wide-set eyes. As he slept, the gently parted lips, the long eyelashes tickling his cheek, his face looked nearly identical to his mother's as she lay in the coffin. The comparison made me shudder.

There was no eulogy, no pastor, just some soft music playing in the background as we sat. I was almost pissed at Tina for not doing more to make this homegoing an actual service, but then I was just as pissed at myself for not doing the same. We should have done more by her. Lena deserved better. Guilt racked at my nerves until I was forced to tear my eyes from the casket to keep from sobbing out loud.

It had started raining by the time we trudged back into the house after the ceremony and burial. Leo didn't say a word to any of us. He just disappeared into his office. Part of me wished there was something, anything, I could say, but I was at a loss for words. I felt as if I needed comforting myself.

"Kimmy, come with me for a minute," Tina demanded, and she turned, carrying the baby with her to the stairs. She didn't even bother waiting to see if I was behind her. I could have raised a fuss about the bossy attitude, but frankly, I was too weary. And now was just not the time. So I quietly followed.

The nursery was huge. Much bigger than I would expect for a child, let alone a baby. Someone had decorated the entire room in Dr. Seuss. Blue walls had Thing 1 and Thing 2 and of course the Cat in the Hat drawn on them, and sheer red curtains covered the huge bay window. Dr. Seuss book covers had been cut out to spell "Oh the places you'll go, Leo Jr." along the wall behind the convertible crib.

Tina sat down in an oversize red recliner, the baby lying on her chest and sucking on his pacifier. She began lightly bouncing him, prompting his tender giggle in amusement. Even with his lips peeled back, he kept the nipple of the pacifier firmly planted between his gums.

"Thank you." I hadn't realized I was going to say it until the words left my lips. "For handling him. I'm not a mother in any way, shape, or form, so I would be lost."

"I know." Her tone softened when she nuzzled Leo's neck. "I've always wanted kids but . . ." She trailed off on a shrug. I remembered that Lena had told me Tina couldn't have kids.

"Ayana cleared out Lena's room," Tina said, changing the subject. "There's a couple boxes of her stuff downstairs that we need to go through." She stared pointedly at me, and I took the hint. *We* meaning me. I didn't know how I felt going through Lena's things. I wasn't even sure what to do with any of it, but I'm guessing Tina thought there was something of value or something Leo would want.

Ayana had marked the boxes and placed them against a wall in the hallway outside of Lena's bedroom. The door was open, and I peered inside. I didn't know what I was expecting. Her smell, her books, those little ugly floral dresses she always wore tossed on her bed. But everything had been stripped and cleaned, just like Tina said, the lingering smell of Pine-Sol hanging in the air. All of Lena the woman had been scaled down to these two moving boxes that sat at my feet.

I stooped down and opened a box. Not too much. A few pictures of Lena when she was younger. In the first picture, she couldn't have been any more than two years old and dressed in a pumpkin Halloween costume. She had a kiddie pout on her face, as if she wanted to be anywhere but where she was. I chuckled and sifted through the rest of the box's contents.

An antique jewelry box looked like it carried more sentiment than value. Some notebooks. I peeled back the spiral cover on one and scanned the words. Poetry. I forgot Lena told me she liked to write. Without thinking, I pulled out the two notebooks, and a peek of purple caught my eye. Lena was always writing in that damn journal. Probably more poems. I set that on top of the others and carried them back with me to my room. I'm not sure what compelled me to take them. Not sure if I should. But it felt right. I felt like she would want these to live on and not just be tossed in the garbage.

Standing at the dresser, I flipped open the journal, my fingers running down the worn pages of Lena's elaborate handwriting. Her letters were art in and of themselves. Something like calligraphy. Coupled with the beautiful words of her poetry, it made her poems all the more powerful. The first few pages were nothing but poems. Dark, sad poems about suicide, sorrow, and loneliness.

I murmured the words to myself, feeling her passion resonate in my soul. A cry for help. It was enough to make anyone's heart ache.

About a third of the way through was when she must have started the diary. The date registered a year ago. And from the look of it, she had just met Leo. I grinned, listening as her voice was captured through the description of the man she and I both had feelings for. Obviously she had been drawn to his looks just as strongly as I was. It was weird, reading her thoughts and even more seeing Leo through her eyes. But somehow, I felt closer to the woman I wished I had gotten to know more.

Movement caught the corner of my eye, and I gasped as Leo's silhouette came into view. The journal fell from my fingers.

"Damn, Leo, you scared me. Why are you in my room?"

Leo lowered himself to my bed. "I come in here all the time," he admitted. "Your room always calms my nerves." His eyes dropped to the journal at my feet. "What are you doing with that?"

I stooped to retrieve it and sat it down on the dresser. "I just— Tina told me to go through some of her things. I didn't think it was right to just throw it out."

Leo nodded. "That was sweet, my love," he said, his voice gentle. He patted the empty space on the bed next to him.

I took the hint and sat down, allowing him to pull me into his arms. There was a slight odor hanging from his pores and his now fully grown beard scratched my skin as he nuzzled my neck. He held on with such need and desperation that I turned and wrapped my arms around him as well.

"My love," he murmured, his words muffled against my neck. I rubbed his back, not really sure how to respond.

Finally, I said, "Hey. What is it? What can I do, Leo?"

His sigh was heavy as he pulled back and searched my eyes. For what I didn't know. Love maybe?

"It's like my world is crashing down on me," he admitted. "I just don't know what to do."

I lifted my hand to gently stroke his face. "Hey. You'll get through this, Leo. I promise. It'll get better. You have a beautiful son to take care of. Don't forget what's important."

"Listen." His red-rimmed eyes seemed to bore into mine. "If something happens to me, just know I've chosen you. Okay? I know it was hard to come around with this whole thing, but you did and I appreciate you for it."

Stunned, my lips parted, but no sound came out. "W-why are you saying this, Leo? What do you mean if something ever happens to you? Are you sick? Is there something I should know about?"

He shook his head. "First Lena and now . . ." I saw the first few tears trickle down his cheeks. "My mother. She's getting worse. They've called in hospice." Damn. And here I was so wrapped up in myself I had neglected to realize how much Leo was going through. With everything going on at once, it was a wonder this man hadn't had a nervous breakdown. I pulled him back into my arms, hugging his neck tight.

"Oh, Leo, I'm so sorry." And I truly was. I felt like shit for being so selfish. "When did you find out?"

"My dad called me this morning. I have to ask you something." He placed his hands in my lap and took another labored breath.

"I'm going to fly out to be with her. I want you to come with me. I need you to come with me."

"Me? Don't you mean us?"

His smile was hollow. "No, not her. Just you. She can stay here with the baby. I'm sure she would love that."

I opened my mouth and shut it again. Go to Africa? Hell, I was still reeling from Lena's death, and now his mother? "For how long?" I stalled, and Leo shrugged his shoulders.

"Until." He left it at that, and I knew what he was thinking. *Until she died.* I swallowed the lump in my throat and averted my eyes. I couldn't do this. He looked so vulnerable, so pitiful and helpless. And his heart was crying for me. And I couldn't do a damn thing with it.

"Leo. I can't," I whispered. "My parents, my family . . ." *Jahmad.* I couldn't be away from that man any more than I already was. And fly to Africa for an undetermined amount of time? Could be three days. Could be three months. I just couldn't. No matter how much Leo needed me.

I kept my face down as I shook my head slowly. I couldn't bear to look him in the eye while I disappointed him further.

"My love, please." His words were heavy with ache. "I need you so much."

"No, you need to be with your mom," I said. "And your family. I'll be here when you get back."

Leo looked doubtful. "Can you at least consider coming out there for a little bit? Maybe in a few days, and you can stay for like a week?"

"Okay." I knew it was a lie even as the words left my lips. But that seemed to appease him for now. He kissed my lips, this time longer and more passionately. I could taste the desperation on his tongue. His hands lifted to caress my breasts and though I wanted to stop him, though it felt like I was cheating on Jahmad, I let him remove my shirt and bra. He wanted to be needed and, hell, I couldn't even remember the last time we'd had sex.

Afterward, I lay in the sheets, letting him cuddle me and listening to his light snore. But my mind kept wandering to Lena.

As if on cue, Leo Jr.'s cries lifted above the silence but didn't last long as Tina's hushed whisper soothed him back to silence.

I'm sure Lena would be rolling over in her grave knowing Tina was so possessive of her baby, and here I was, so hands-off. The baby seemed like the only form of life in this house. The rest of us, well. The rest of us were just existing.

Chapter 17

"I want to give you something."

I don't know why, but my heart felt like it was going to burst out of my chest at the simple sentence. I lifted off of Jahmad's chest and stared down at him. He looked content, still coming down from the wild-ass sex we had just had. His arm was thrown casually behind his head, exposing every bend and angle in his lean body. The sheets rested at my waist, exposing my skin to the chilly air. He always kept it freezing at his townhouse, and my nipples let him know it every time. And the sales associate and I had been right. He loved that Gucci watch and rarely if ever took it off.

It had been nearly three months since Leo left. My time at the house had become less and less until finally, I hadn't bothered sleeping there at all.

Leo and I did talk on the phone often. Nothing intimate, though. He was mostly filling me in on his mom's deteriorating condition and how nice it was being back around his family in his native land. He usually ended the call with begging me to fly over and me making up some half-assed excuse why I couldn't before I climbed back into Jahmad's arms.

"Give me something?" I echoed. At his wink, my grin spread,

and I reached down to grab the bulge between his legs. He laughed.

"You already got that, girl," he said, but he let me stroke it anyway. "It's something else."

He leaned up and planted a kiss on my lips. I moaned, his tongue playing with mine and sending my body into a frenzy. I don't know how he had my body so receptive to him. He made it come alive without my permission. But it was hella sexy.

I started to deepen the kiss, but Jahmad pulled away with a sly grin. I could've slapped him and married him right then and there. "Why you trying to get shit started again?"

I laughed. "Because you like it."

"True." He pulled out of my arms and swung his legs over the side of the bed. I licked my lips as the muscles in his thighs seemed to almost bust when he stood and made his way over to the pants he had thrown on the floor. "It's not much," he murmured, rummaging through his pockets. "But I thought it was time for you to have it."

He brought it back in his fist, slid back in the bed, and reached his hand out to me.

A key. I just stared at the silver metal winking up at me from the palm of my hand. How could something so simple mean so much? I had a $208,000 wedding ring hidden in my purse, Well, $208,369.12. they said when I had it appraised, but yet this $2.00 key to Jahmad's place meant more to me than that ring.

I wasn't going to cry. Well, shit, I lied just that quick, I realized as I felt the first few tears sting my eyelids. Jahmad's lips touched my forehead as I closed my fingers around the key.

"So," I said on a shaky breath, "does this mean what I think it means?"

"What do you think it means?"

A stampede of thoughts swamped my brain, so I really didn't know which one to address first. He wanted me around on a more permanent basis? Were we an item? Did he love me?

"Yes," Jahmad said as if reading the thoughts that seemed to cross my face. "It means what you think."

I nodded. I was not sure which one he answered but satisfied just the same. But just as quickly, the fear began to settle in. The more serious we got, the more dangerous. I was still Mrs. Owusu. One of two now. How the hell would Jahmad feel about me if he found out? And what would Leo do to me if word ever got back to him?

———•◦•———

"Fuck." Fear had the word stuttering from my lips as I leaned over the marble sink. Just when I thought my life couldn't get more complicated, here comes a damn curve ball.

My grip tightened on the counter, my eyes narrowing at my reflection in the mirror. I hadn't picked up much weight, thank God. Not enough where it would be noticeable, at least. The three positive pregnancy tests sat on the lip of the bathtub, bringing on another wave of nausea. *Positive, positive, positive.* What a damn lie. Sure, I was positive I was pregnant, that much was certain, but as far as knowing which man, either the man I was married to or the man I was in love with, was the father? Negative. Absolutely negative.

I lifted my tank top, eyeing my stomach in the mirror. I turned to the front, then the side. Sure, my tummy had rounded a little. It had a little more pudge than normal but I had chalked it up to all the good food and sex and I was getting from Jahmad. For the life of me, I couldn't imagine being pregnant. An image of Lena suddenly flashed in my mind and the chilling reality had me snatching my shirt back down to cover my belly. She had died from childbirth. How likely was that to happen to me?

Quickly, I grabbed the three tests from the tub and carried them back in my room, then stuffed them in my purse. I couldn't throw them away and risk Ayana, or even worse, Tina finding them. Especially when I was rapidly coming to the conclusion I had to get rid of it.

The well of nausea was beginning to subside. I took another sip from the ginger ale I had had Ayana bring me earlier. My phone's shrill ring filled the air, and I glanced at the clock on my nightstand. Weird. He usually called in the morning here to take into account the six hour time difference. The digits on my clock read eight p.m., which meant it was the middle of the night in Ivory Coast.

"Hello?" I felt it before he even responded. Something about his silence said it all that not even five thousand miles' difference could hide. I sighed under the weight of his grief. "Leo, I'm so sorry," I murmured.

"I wish you had met her," was his solemn reply. "I wanted so bad for you to meet her."

His statement probably wasn't meant to instill guilt but it came nonetheless. If I had to be honest with myself, death scared the hell out of me. And someone dying, let alone watching them die was enough to shake anyone's sanity. How could I be there for Leo if I couldn't even handle it myself? Plus, even with the purest of intentions on my part, me going to that length for Leo would have everyone perceiving my feelings to be stronger than what they were. Especially him. And Lord knows I didn't want that.

"When will you be back?" I asked instead.

"The funeral is Friday. So I'll be back probably Sunday or Monday."

One more week. One more week to get rid of a baby, spend more time with Jahmad, my family, Adria. Do everything I wanted to do before I was held hostage again. Considering how it was before Leo left, I was sure things would return to how they used to be. Maybe even worse, because grief had Leo being extra clingy.

"How's my son?" Leo asked.

Hell if I knew. Tina kept the baby. She even referred to herself as his mother. And I certainly didn't mind. It made things easier. But of course I couldn't tell Leo I had no clue how his baby was. "He's good," I lied. "Getting big."

"Good. I'll call Tina later and speak to her. When I get back I want to talk to you about some things."

Shit. "Things like what?"

"Just some changes." His answer was evasive yet final, so I didn't bother questioning him further. "Do me a favor and go check on Leo Jr."

I frowned. "Why?"

"I need you to spend more time with him. Get to know him. Shouldn't always just be on Tina."

We hung up, but his words still echoed in the air. Why was he suddenly so concerned about my relationship with his son? It was ironic he would mention this right when I found out about my pregnancy. And what changes were about to take place?

Chapter 18

"Girl, are you sure you want to do this?"

I sighed at Adria's question. She was my girl and I appreciated her support with this, but, damn, I wished she would stop asking that question. Of course I wasn't sure. It wasn't about that. It was about what I *had* to do. I didn't have a damn choice.

"It's better this way," I answered with a nod of affirmation. "My life is too complicated right now to worry about a baby."

Adria sat right beside me in the clinic lobby, and though she didn't say anything else, I felt her eyes on my profile. Probably looking for some sign I wouldn't be able to go through with this procedure. But I kept my face stoic, my eyes trained on the receptionist ahead. I silently willed her to call my name, not because I was anxious to get this underway but more so because I wouldn't have to be subjected to Adria's scrutiny.

But one thing I did appreciate: my friend might not have agreed with me on a lot of shit these days, but she was right by my side whenever I called.

"I take it you didn't tell Jahmad," she said, still studying me. "Or Leo, for that matter."

It didn't surprise me she knew about Jahmad, though I had never told her myself. "Of course not. This is not their decision to make."

"But at least you could've—"

"Adria, please." I massaged my temples as the first twinges of a headache began to pulsate. "I recall a certain fifteen-year-old sitting exactly where I am, feeling exactly the same way I felt. And I remember her best friend doing nothing but holding her hand and comforting her."

Adria pursed her lips and averted her eyes because she knew I was telling the truth. I had sat with her when she had the abortion as a teenager, not saying shit other than "Girl, it's going to be okay." I hadn't asked her anything about the baby's father, though I suspected it was my brother Keon, but she didn't divulge and I didn't ask. She seemed embarrassed enough that it had happened, placing her into that teenage pregnancy statistic we had heard so much about in school. But we sat, waited, had it done, had another friend's older sister drive us home, and we hadn't uttered a word about it since. Like it never happened.

I hated to have to even bring it up now, but, dammit, my nerves were already rattled enough as it was. Leo was coming home that evening. He had something important to discuss with me. He must have reiterated it several times until I was about to burst with curiosity. Even more strange was that he hadn't talked to Tina. The details of his flight and his arrival I told her because he hadn't bothered to. She seemed just as bothered to be kept out of the loop, but she dared not say it. But it was more than obvious that somewhere along the way, the roles had changed. And though I had married him last, somehow I had become first in his life. And I sure as hell didn't know how to take it. Nor did I want to play that position.

Plus my feelings for Jahmad hadn't made this any easier. I wished I could see him. But knowing me, I wouldn't want to leave him. I had gotten so used to not having to rush during Leo's absence. And because Leo had made it very clear my ass needed to be at home to greet him, I had decided maybe not seeing Jahmad tonight was for the better. And after today, well, who knew. We would have to cross that bridge when we got to it.

A nurse called my name and led me to the back of the clinic. First things first: some vitals, I was told. Then it would be taken care of. *It. It.* The staff kept referring to the baby as such, perhaps to establish the disconnection to make this process easier to handle. I didn't know what it would take, but I wouldn't ever be able to associate "easy" with this decision. It left a bad taste in my mouth and I felt like I was going to throw up all evidence of my meals from the past week. But still, I sat silent as she pricked my finger for a blood sample, checked my height and weight, and laid me on the exam table for the ultrasound.

It was quiet for a moment, the only sound that could be heard at first were the nurse's movements as she busied herself with prepping me, smearing the warm gel on my stomach and moving the probe around my uterus, her eyes on the monitor. Then, a whooshing sound broke the silence and a quick heartbeat filled the air. I wanted to cry as I heard the first few sounds of my child's life. I could see movement on the screen, and I had to shut my eyes to keep from looking. I tried to concentrate on something, anything else. Not if the baby was Jahmad's, would he have that same adorable smile? Or if it was a girl, would she have my dimples and button nose? Then, the nurse removed the device from my stomach and I again was engulfed in quiet.

The rest of the process went by in a blur. A disclaimer, some papers needed to be signed, and I knocked back what they told me was mifepristone, a pill that would stop the pregnancy. I was sent home with some antibiotics and another pill, misoprostol, to take in twelve hours that would empty my uterus; I was assured I needed to get pads because I would bleed heavily like a miscarriage. I nodded along like some crazed zombie, took my meds, and followed Adria back out to her car.

We were quiet on the ride back to my parents' house where I had parked my car. I felt weak, either from the medicine or the decision, I wasn't sure, but I didn't really feel up to driving. But I couldn't let Adria take me back to Leo's house. Tina would certainly have something to say then. Adria must have been thinking the same thing, because she said, "I'm not sure if you're supposed to be driving."

I glanced at the clock on her radio: 2:37. Leo wouldn't be home until nine o'clock that night. Eddie was supposed to be picking him up from the airport. "I'll take a little nap at my parents'," I said. "Then get up and go home."

Adria seemed satisfied by that decision, and she nodded as we pulled up in the driveway. She cut the engine off, then turned and offered a sympathetic smile. "I'm sorry," she said. "For earlier. You know I love you like crazy. I don't want you to think I'm not behind you with whatever you need."

Interesting how you could have all of the love and support and still feel alone. I wondered whether this was a side effect of the medicine or the whole abortion altogether, because I sure as hell felt empty. Like the shell of what I used to be. I kept telling myself that this was all necessary. That my hands were tied. But it sure wasn't easing this feeling.

"I want to tell you something," Adria went on. "You know I looked into a little more about why you got fired. Something about some records of you stealing money or something?"

I nodded along, urging her to continue.

"I didn't find anything. The person I know who does the time-keeping and verifications said there was no record at all of your drawers being short money."

"I know that," I said. "I told Aunt Pam it was a lie. That's why I didn't see why I was being fired. Or where the hell she had gotten her evidence from."

"Want me to ask her?"

I weighed the request and decided it wasn't worth it. Not like I needed the job, or, hell, even wanted the job anymore anyway. Shit was just puzzling, but it was water under the bridge, I guess.

"Thanks, girl, but don't worry about it," I said with a reassuring smile. "Could've been something got mixed up somewhere down the line. I'm pissed it happened but it's really not that big of a deal now."

Adria's eyes shifted toward my Porsche, sitting clean and pretty with its glare from the freshly detailed paint job. "I guess you're right," she murmured, but her expression was still troubled by her own news.

I hadn't been lying down too long before my mother knocked on the door and entered my room. I wanted to groan but I wouldn't dare be so bold or disrespectful. So I turned over as her weight sank my bed.

"What's going on with you, Kimmy?" She didn't bother beating around the bush. Her eyes narrowed, secretly telling me how I better think long and hard before I answered her.

"Mama, I'm really tired," I said, which was true. As soon as my body hit the mattress I felt like I could've slept for two weeks straight. My eyes were struggling to stay open as we spoke.

Mama shook her head. "That could be the case now. But something's been going on with you for a while now. And it hurts that you feel you can't come to me." She paused, waiting for me to respond, but I didn't. She patted my ankle. "Have you fixed this whole marriage mess?" she asked.

"I'm working on it."

She frowned, disappointed by the answer. "Is it Jahmad then?"

His name brought a small smile to my lips. "No," I said.

"So is it true? Are you two an item?"

Oh, how I wish it were true. I would hardly call us an item, considering I was a whole wife, or rather contract-bound love partner, to Leo.

"I've always liked Jahmad," she went on. "I'm not going to lie. Hanging out with that knucklehead son of mine, I never really knew his intentions. Is he some kind of playboy?"

I had to chuckle at my mom's description. "He was. He grew up."

Her face seemed doubtful, but she shrugged. "Does your brother know?"

"I don't think so. At least I didn't tell him. Why? Would it be a problem?"

"Well." Mama shrugged again. "I don't know. You tell me. It's a reason why you didn't tell Keon, though, isn't it?"

It was a reason I wasn't telling a lot of people. I had started to rub my stomach unconsciously, and I didn't realize I had been doing it until my mother's eyes narrowed at the gesture.

"It's not what you think," I said, lifting my hands in surrender. Not now, at least.

"I'll be glad when you do settle down, Kimmy. For real. Have some babies. Stop all this hoe-hopping and craziness you got going on. You and your brother."

I had to laugh at the abrasive term. "Did the First Lady really just call her daughter a hoe?"

"No. I said hoe-hopping. There's a difference." She nodded toward the door. "By the way, I've been meaning to ask. Was it the fancy man from the paper that bought you the car?"

Even more secrets, even more lies. How many tangled webs before I was able to break free, I wondered as I lowered my head. "Why do you ask?"

Mama stood but kept her eyes level with mine. "I get not telling everyone your business, Kimmy," she said. "But remember everything you do in the dark comes to light. If you're with Jahmad, be with him without all of the lies."

The truth in her words still tugged at my heart, and I merely nodded again, not exactly sure what to say to that.

I hadn't realized I had dozed off again until I opened my eyes and caught a glimpse of the blackened sky peeking through my blinds. I sat up and quickly snatched up my phone to check the time. *Shit.* It was 11:32. I was supposed to be back at home to meet Leo at nine. Quickly I grabbed my purse and keys and ran to the door. I was still weak, but fear can give you adrenaline you didn't know you had.

The rest of the house was asleep but I managed to make it outside without too much of a racket. All I could think was how Leo was going to kick my ass and why I hadn't heard the phone ring, because I knew he probably had called 1,002 times. I didn't even bother checking my Leo phone because I didn't want to see the notifications of missed calls and text messages. Better to just go right into the situation ignorant. Whatever it was, I knew it was going to be bad.

The blue lights caught my eye first as I pulled up the winding drive toward the mansion. The second thing that caught my eye was that every light seemed to be on, illuminating the entire house like some sort of holiday party was taking place. I know I was speeding, but I slowed down as I pulled up behind the two police cars in front. Since they were blocking the entrance and I wasn't able to get around them to the driveway, I just turned the car off and made my way to the door.

The front door swung open just as I reached for the knob, as if someone had been waiting for me and knew the very moment I pulled up. Tina had the baby in her arms, and despite her nightgown and disheveled hair, her face was surprisingly calm. "I've been calling you," she said. Her voice was low but I could detect a bit of hoarseness.

"Why? What's wrong?" I peered past her and caught the three

police officers who stood up from the sofa, their expressions solemn as they stared at me.

Tina began rocking the baby, more for her needing something to do with herself because Leo Jr. was clearly asleep, nuzzled against her breasts. "I'm sorry," she said. "There's been an accident."

Chapter 19

I always wondered how people could hold it together when dealing with tragedy after tragedy. When life was already at its all-time complicatedness of complications, it was like one of those infomercials that would literally stop the world and say, "But wait, there's more!"

Despite my upbringing, I have never considered myself a very spiritual woman. Sure, I believe in God, but I don't exactly live my life by the Christian values my parents have tried to instill in me. So when it came to prayer, I was severely lacking in that department.

But when the police described how Leo's limo had been involved in a car accident, I felt compelled to murmur a prayer that everyone involved was okay, that there would be some bumps and bruises, but there would be another day to live.

Eddie, the driver, died on impact. I thought of his wife, his grandchild he was raising, and how I had insisted time and time again that he go home and spend some time with his family. And now he wouldn't get that opportunity again. I imagined his wife being woken up in the middle of the night to the news that her husband left for work that day and would not be returning. That some recklessness had made her a widow. I hadn't been very close to the man. I hadn't shared much with him but a few kind words and too many rides to count, but I was saddened just the same.

I nodded to confirm I had heard the officer and made myself ask the question that had been burning on my mind since I drove up and saw the cop cars. "What about Leo?"

The officers exchanged glances before one of them spoke up. "He's been life-flighted to the hospital. We don't have any more news at this time, but his condition was critical."

I was already heading toward the door. "Which hospital?" I didn't even worry about whether Tina was coming along. Of course I wasn't shit for loving Jahmad, but cheating wife or not, I needed to be there. I just hoped I wasn't too late.

<hr />

Déjà vu.

I was back in the same hospital, back in that stale-ass lobby staring at the same mounted TV. Hell, it looked like the same news was flashing across the screen, though I couldn't exactly be sure of that, since I really wasn't paying attention the first time. But while that first time we were celebrating Leo Jr.'s birth, now we waited while Leo Sr. fought for his life.

I still tried to wrap my mind around our last conversation. I had tried to be patient, compassionate, and understanding just to appease him. I couldn't wait for him to get home. A lie. Missed him so much. Another lie. But honestly, I was desperate to take his mind off of his grief. He had seemed to lapse into a bit of a depression, and honestly, who could blame him? But who knew that last conversation would be our last—

No. I shook my head to clear the negative thoughts. I could not and would not think that way. But one thing was for sure: Leo and I certainly did need to have a conversation. I couldn't continue to live like this. It wasn't fair to either of us.

I racked my brain trying to remember some of the words from

that stupid contract. I needed to find my copy. At least I thought they gave me a copy. I didn't remember the details, but I vaguely remembered that if I left I would walk away with nothing. But at this point I didn't care. At least I would walk away. After months of this poly shit, I would finally walk away. I could only hope he would let me go easily.

Tina had come. I was not sure if it was an actual desire or obligation but nonetheless, she was there perched in one of the chairs with her arms resting on her knees. She had left the baby with Ayana. Now I was surprised as hell about that one. Leo Jr. had been damn near glued to her hip since we first brought him home from the hospital.

Another thirty minutes passed before a doctor pushed through the doors and glanced around the empty room before his eyes settled on us.

I remember the small things about that doctor. I remember how his glasses rested on his nose and he kept pushing them up on his face. I remember he had a warm smile and eyes the color of ocean blue. And how his watch was around $1,700. I knew that because it was the exact same Gucci watch I had bought for Jahmad that day in Phipps Plaza Mall. Go figure that. I focused on every detail of that damn doctor other than what he was telling me. That Leo was dead.

If someone had told me before that day that Tina was more emotional than I was, I sure as hell wouldn't have believed them. Not perfect, pristine, had-it-all-together Tina. But there she was groveling on the floor in fat, sloppy tears while I tried my best to hold it together.

"Mrs. Owusu," the doctor said, his eyes on Tina, "I'm going to need you to identify the body."

Tina nodded and staggered to her feet. "Can she go with me?" She gestured vaguely in my direction. Not *Mrs. Owusu*. Not *the other wife*. But *she*. The doctor nodded and escorted us down a hallway.

He stood next to us as we peered through a windowpane into an exam room. A body under a thin, white sheet was on a table in the center, and at the gentle knock on the glass, the nurse inside used both hands to pull back the sheet and expose the person underneath.

He could've just as easily been sleeping. I had seen him exactly like that on numerous occasions. But an eerie feeling sent a slight chill running up my spine, and I looked away. I had just talked to him. That was all that I could think about now. I had just talked to him. *My love, please, be home by nine at the latest. I know, Leo, I'll be there. You promise? I promise. Nine o'clock? Nine o'clock. Can't wait to see you . . .*

Now I was seeing him. And I wished like hell I would've waited. The nurse hadn't pulled the sheet down far, just slightly below his neck, but I saw the scratches and bruises peppering his face. I looked at his chest, waiting to see it rise as evidence that he was breathing, clearly not dead, but he remained still. Lifeless.

Tina sobbed and I stared. And she must have nodded in affirmation because the nurse draped the sheet back over his face.

The doctor showed us back to the lobby, and I was weak as I sank to the first chair I came to.

"Mrs. Owusu." We both looked up at the voice.

The man who greeted us gave a sympathetic smile as he held out his hand to me first. "Detective Vincent Wright." I accepted his extended hand. "First off, let me say that I'm so sorry for your loss," he went on, now speaking to both of us. "But I assure you we are going to get the people responsible for the accident."

"I thought it was just a car accident," I said with a frown. "What people responsible?"

"Further investigation revealed it may possibly have been a hit-and-run."

I don't know who gasped, Tina or I, but we were both stunned silent while we digested the new information.

Detective Wright handed me his card. "If you're up to it in a few hours, I would like you ladies to come down to the station to pick up his things we recovered from the accident. And please call me in the meantime if you need anything."

Tina's voice came out so hoarse it was almost unrecognizable. "Can I give you some information, Detective? Leo called me that night. I was on the phone with him right before."

Damn, I hadn't known that. That shit was eerie.

Vincent seemed surprised at her request, probably because it was so soon. "Are you sure you're up to that right now?"

"Yes. I don't want to forget any details. It may be minor but anything helps."

Vincent nodded his eagerness. "Absolutely. Anything helps."

The cop cars were gone when I arrived back to Leo's. Most of the lights had been turned off in the home with the exception of a few. Probably Ayana leaving them on for us.

Ayana only now. Just her. No Eddie. No Leo. Damn, it hadn't really occurred to me to check on her. The woman had been working for Leo for a long time, and she had known Eddie even longer. I wondered how she was holding up. But I didn't go in there to see for myself. Make sure she had just a few snatches of sanity. Lord knows I felt like I was slowly losing my mind. I couldn't bring myself to go into that house either. The house of a dead man. The house where we shared our memories. As unpleasant as they were, they were memories nonetheless. And the last ones I would have of Leo when he was alive.

I sighed and rested my head on the steering wheel. I had left the car running and now the engine caused a slight vibration on my forehead. A few lonely tears fell and dampened my lap. I would be planning another funeral. Two, if Eddie's wife needed us to. And the thought that kept lingering in my mind, and I didn't know if it was really selfish to think but that still didn't stop it: would I have been dead too had I gone with Leo?

Like I said, I wasn't the most spiritual woman, but I sure believed in God and his intervention. Was it a sign? Was this my wake-up call? What did all of this mean?

I suddenly felt scared, being out here against the pitch-black wee hours of the morning. I had rather go back to my parents' house, but it was nearly four in the morning now, and I didn't want to wake them. Plus I knew I looked like a train wreck, and I really wasn't up to answering their questions.

And I had a key, but I certainly wasn't going to Jahmad's place.

I waited a moment before I suddenly cranked up my car once more and headed in the direction of Adria's house.

Chapter 20

"*Do you love me?*" *Leo nuzzled my neck, his skin warm against mine. We were lying naked in bed, basking in the post-orgasmic bliss of some pretty rough sex. Uncharacteristically rough. Leo had ravaged my body much like, and I hated to compare, but like Jahmad did.*

Leo sensed my discomfort at his question and pulled me tighter against him. I sighed. "Leo, don't ask me that. You know it's complicated."

"It's a yes or no question, my love."

I shut my eyes because I knew he wouldn't quit unless I answered him. "Leo, I love you as a man. I love how you are. But I'm not in love with you." At his silence, I rushed on. "But it's not you, Leo. It's me. I'm just so torn right now and I hate it because it's not fair to you. You deserve so much better than what I'm giving you."

When he was still quiet, I turned my head to look at him and screamed. His corpse stared back at me, open mouth with scratches and bruises on his neck and face. His face was pale, his skin shriveled, and in place of his eyes were pitch-black irises that seemed to pierce into my soul. His body reeked of death. I snatched myself back, struggling to pull his heavy arm from my waist, my skin crawling with the maggots that had begun to feast on his flesh.

I gasped and snatched my eyes open, my labored breathing

echoing in the empty room. Not real. I blinked, struggling to adjust to the darkness. The smell of death that had seemed so prominent had been replaced with the faint scent of the cinnamon apple Glade candle Adria kept in the room. Though the ceiling fan spun on low overhead, my body felt sticky with sweat.

I sat up and swung my legs over the side of the futon. The lumpy mattress was uncomfortable, but that was all she could fit in the tiny makeshift office. But it was sure as hell worlds better than being in Leo's house. The vision of me wrapped in the embrace of his dead body had me shaking my head to free my mind of the image.

I couldn't remember the last time I'd had a nightmare. But I wasn't accustomed to being around dead bodies either. The image of Leo, lying on that exam table, would probably never go away.

The beginnings of a sunrise peeked through Adria's drawn curtains and, grateful, I climbed from the bed. It wasn't like I would be able to get back to sleep anyway.

Adria was already in the galley-style kitchen, hunched over the counter and muffling a yawn. "Morning," she greeted with a sleepy nod.

"Hey. I didn't wake you, did I?"

Adria gestured toward the Keurig beginning to hum to life with the coffee she had brewing. "I needed to get up anyway. I have to work in a few hours."

"I'm sorry." I slid a hip onto the barstool. "My head is just . . . all over the place."

I had arrived last night, damn near in tears, but the great thing about Adria, she didn't push. She merely opened the door, gave me a hug, and showed me to her office where she kept a futon for sleepovers. I appreciated that, because I wasn't up for talking. But now, it needed to be said.

Adria poured two mugs of coffee and sat one in front of me. "I don't really have much for breakfast except cereal."

I took a sip of the bitter coffee, not bothering with the cream and sugar. It singed my tongue and scalded my throat as it went down, but I took a healthy gulp anyway. "I'm not really hungry," I said finally.

Adria nodded as she mixed a healthy dose of cream and sugar in her cup until the liquid was a caramel hue. She busied herself with stirring, but it was obvious she was waiting.

"It's Leo," I said quietly. "There was an accident. He died yesterday."

Adria's face registered the sheer shock I was already feeling. "Are you serious? What kind of accident?"

"A hit-and-run." My voice was calm. Very calm. As if I was recounting some dry-ass documentary rather than my husband's death. "He was airlifted to the hospital, and they did surgery, but too much internal bleeding. And his driver—my driver," I corrected, remembering the many times Eddie had chauffeured my spoiled ass around without any type of hesitation or explanation, "he died too. On impact."

"Damn," Adria whispered and shook her head. "That's crazy. Well, are you—I mean y'all . . . now what?"

"Now, we plan another funeral." My mind started clicking details into place. "And I guess call his family in the Ivory Coast. I don't really know how this works. Maybe they'll want his body buried in his home country. I guess I need to talk to Tina and see what we need to do." I suddenly remembered Vincent from last night. "Oh, and I need to go to the police station."

"For what?"

"To collect Leo's things," I answered nonchalantly. "Nothing major."

"Oh." Adria remained quiet as she sipped her drink, reflecting on my words. "I'm just in shock. Is that some ironic shit or what?"

I frowned. "Ironic?"

"Well, weren't you talking about leaving him? And now this? How coincidental is that?"

The thought was nerve-racking and only heightened my guilt.

"I don't want to think of it like that," I murmured. "It's a tragedy, Adria. I mean, damn, he just buried his mom. And, hell, Lena for that matter not too long ago."

"I'm not saying it's not tragic," Adria said. This time her voice was laced with compassion. "I'm just saying . . . hell, things happen for a reason. That's all."

"Really? And what would be this reason?"

Adria shook her head and waved off my question. "I didn't mean anything by it, Kimmy."

She was right, but it still seemed like a cold, heartless thing to say. Or feel, for that matter. I hadn't wanted to focus on the fact that, yes, I was free of that dumbass contract. It was horrible to think of it like that, but fate had managed to intervene and snatch me from the situation I had wondered how I was going to get out of anyway. In a sick and twisted way my problem was solved. Now I was able to date Jahmad because I had fulfilled my obligations. I didn't want to ponder too much on the fact that I had killed the man's baby not even twenty-four hours prior, or what may have been his baby, and now he was gone just as quickly and I was in no way, shape, or form tied to the Owusus any longer. No, I didn't want to relish that fact, because that would be too much like I was happy he was gone. And despite what had happened between us, it was still heartbreaking all around. My guilt outweighed my selfishness and wouldn't allow me to focus on the positives.

"Adria," I said, fiddling with a napkin on the counter. I didn't look at her as the question left my lips. "Do you think I should tell Jahmad?"

Adria sighed. "I really don't know." I expected that honest answer, but I had asked still hoping she could give me some insight into the right direction. "I mean I get why you wouldn't because, frankly, why open up that can of worms? But then, I can see why you would too, because doesn't he have a right to know something like that? Y'all are pretty serious, right?" I nodded and Adria shrugged again. "Just think about it. I mean, wouldn't you want to know? If all this time you found out he was married and his wife died? How would you feel?"

Betrayed. She was right. But then, and here was the selfish part of me again, I didn't want to lose him. It had taken me so long to get him and we were finally where I had dreamed for us to be.

As if on cue, my cell phone's muffled notification tone blared from the bedroom and I went to retrieve it. My lips curved at the text message.

GOOD MORNING BEAUTIFUL. MISS YOU AND WANT TO SEE YOU SOON. DINNER TONIGHT?

My fingers froze over the keys while I thought about the suggestion.

GOOD MORNING AND YES, I WOULD LOVE TO. WHAT TIME?
8:00ISH?
ISH?
YEAH YOU KNOW I HAVE A PROBLEM WITH TIME, LOL. JUST COME TONIGHT AS SOON AS YOU CAN HOW ABOUT THAT?
SOUNDS LIKE A PLAN.

I held the phone long after the message was sent. I still didn't know if I would tell Jahmad but I did want, no, *need*, to see him. He was my comfort zone. My sanity. And the way I was feeling, I needed him to keep me from having a nervous breakdown.

———— ❧ ————

"Sorry to have kept you waiting."

I looked up as Vincent entered the lobby from a back hall and gave me a welcoming nod. Strangely, he didn't seem quite as warm as he did at the hospital the night before. Now he was a little more formal as he gave my hand a brisk shake. Which was fine with me. I wasn't really in the mood for the pleasantries. I'm sure Tina had given him all he needed to know and I was here just to collect his things, per Tina's request.

Vincent led me to an empty room with a single table and two chairs dominating the center. Off to one corner was a water cooler, and a huge mirror covered one entire wall. I had seen enough *Law and Order* episodes to know it was a two-way mirror. What I didn't know, however, was why I was being brought here for something as minimal as retrieving Leo's items.

"Please, have a seat," Vincent said, gesturing toward the table. "Would you like some water?"

"No, thank you," I said, sitting down as instructed. Despite my refusal, Vincent shifted the manila folder in his hand under one arm and used the blue spout to pour water into two Dixie paper cups. He set one down in front of me and took a seat, putting the other one to his lips.

My anxiety kicked in as I tried my best not to seem too eager. But I did notice him taking his time, sipping his water, sifting through the few sheets of paper in his folder. I tapped my foot and crossed my ankles. Then uncrossed them. My eyes darted to the mirror, wishing I could see who was on the other side, but all I saw was my own casual appearance in the reflection. And the rising panic in my eyes the longer he took. Finally, needing something else to do, I picked up the cup and took a sip from the warm liquid.

"So glad you could come down today," Vincent started, but nowhere did I get the impression that he was actually glad. He didn't bother lifting his eyes from the documents. "So I'm just going to get a brief statement from you now if that's okay."

"Sure."

"Is it okay with you if I record this?"

I nodded and watched him reach in the breast pocket of his suit blazer and pull out a small tape recorder. He eyed the device before pushing a button and sitting it down in front of me.

"Please state your full name for the record."

"Kimera . . ." I paused. I had never actually changed my name to Owusu. Not on any official documents. "Davis," I answered, finally.

Vincent frowned, and his eyes scanned another sheet of paper. "And what is your relationship status?"

These questions shouldn't have been this hard, I knew. But, hell, I didn't know the legalities of our marriage. Was I even "officially" married to Leo considering he said polygamy was illegal? "Single, I guess," I said.

"Were you in some sort of relationship with Mr. Leo Owusu?"

"Yes. We were together."

"Even though you knew he had a wife? A Tina Owusu?"

Was he intentionally trying to make me uncomfortable? I nodded.

"I need you to speak your answers please, Ms. Davis."

I swallowed the lump in my throat. "Yes. What do these questions have to do with what happened to Leo?"

"These questions are a part of the investigation."

"How? It was a hit-and-run, remember? He was in a car accident."

"Yes, I am aware. Can you tell me where you were the night of the accident?"

"Sure. I had slept over at my parents' house that night."

"And you were there all night?"

"Yes." His doubtful expression had me adding, "They both can vouch for me. They were there."

"I see. And what about earlier that day? What were you doing?"

Killing my child. The thought was painful enough. Under the table, my hand found its way to my flat belly. "Just hanging out with my friend, Adria."

"And what is her full name?"

"Adria Morrison."

Vincent scribbled some information on one of the papers. "And what did y'all do that day?"

"Just hung out," I repeated. "Excuse me, but why is all of this necessary? I feel like I'm being interrogated."

"Is there anything else you feel we need to know to assist us with this investigation?" Vincent asked, clasping his hands together. "Anyone you know who may have wanted to hurt Mr. Owusu?"

"No," I snapped. He hadn't even bothered to address my question. He just simply turned off the recorder and stood.

"Thank you for the information, Ms. Davis," he said. "We will be in touch."

I was still confused as I stood also and made my way to the door. What the hell had happened? Remembering, I turned around. "Wait. Tina asked me to come down to get Leo's things."

"His wife left with those this morning."

I shook my head. Then what was I here for?

I made it to the door before Vincent's words stopped me in my tracks. "If I were you, I wouldn't leave town."

Chapter 21

A person of interest. That's how I was being described. How did I go from a side chick, to a wife, to a person of interest in Leo's murder?

My mind struggled to wrap itself around the insanity as I drove from the station. Funny how the good things going on didn't seem to matter anymore. Suddenly the sun didn't seem as bright, the Porsche didn't seem as luxurious. And me, well, according to Vincent I didn't seem quite as innocent.

I hit the expressway and took out my phone. I had to tell Adria about this. Though I knew I was innocent, this new revelation had me scared shitless.

"Shit," I hissed when her phone went to voicemail. Then I remembered she was at work and wouldn't be able to get to her phone until her break. I steered the car in the direction of Leo's house. Tina was the only other person who I could talk to about this. Hopefully, she would be able to give me some information about what the hell was going on.

I was surprised to see the twenty-foot moving truck parked in the driveway when I pulled up. Movers hauled boxes up and down the ramp before grabbing more from the stacks by the front door.

I parked out of the way and walked toward the truck. It appeared to be Tina and the baby's things. Leo Jr.'s crib had been disassembled and propped up against one of the walls of the truck along with Tina's dressers and a few of the large-screen TVs from the house. I nodded a greeting to the two young movers who looked my way before leaving them alone and going in search of Tina.

I found Ayana in the living room along with two other men taping down boxes. Most of the furniture had already been cleared away, and now the room looked even more massive.

"Hey, Ayana," I greeted. "What's going on?"

For once, the maid was not in her usual work attire of black slacks and a black blouse. She looked like a completely different person in her jeans and t-shirt, her hair in a messy ponytail rather than its usual neat bun.

"Mrs. Owusu said she can't stay here," Ayana said, taking a breath and wiping a bit of sweat from her forehead. "Too many memories."

I could understand that. Just standing in the room now felt uncomfortable and slightly chilling.

"Where is she?"

"In the kitchen."

I thanked her and crossed into the adjoining room. I didn't come in the kitchen much when I lived here, partially because Ayana or someone Tina had hired usually prepped the meals and I couldn't cook worth a damn.

It was a huge gourmet kitchen with white cabinets, brown marble countertops, and stainless steel appliances. Now all of the cabinets were propped open, exposing the empty shelves. Apparently this had already been packed up.

Tina stood next to a pot on the stove, a bottle resting in the boiling water as she bounced Leo Jr. on her hip. Despite the fact that it was obviously moving day, she was decked out in skinny designer jeans and heels, evidence she hadn't planned on doing any manual labor. I heard her cooing lovingly at the baby as I approached, and she immediately stopped when she glanced up and saw me.

"Kimera," she greeted with a friendly smile that I noticed didn't reach her eyes like when she was looking at the baby. "Glad you came by."

"Tina, what's going on?" I asked, cutting right to the chase. "Why didn't you tell me you were thinking about moving? And when were you going to let me know to come get my stuff?"

"First of all, all of this was unexpected," she said. "No, I wasn't planning on moving. But no, I didn't expect Leo to die either."

Hearing the truth voiced out loud certainly hurt. Leo had been killed. Leo was dead. Still too fresh to digest.

"Now with everyone gone, first Lena and now Leo and Eddie." Her voice cracked but she kept talking. "I can't stay here in this big place all alone. Not with all that has happened. I haven't been able to sleep since . . . since the accident. And, hell, it's not like you are staying here either. So what am I supposed to do?" She paused, as if waiting for me to answer, but I just remained quiet. "I tried calling you this morning," she said, turning to take the bottle from the pot. "To let you know what I had decided. You didn't pick up."

Of course. My phone had been on silent from the time I walked into the station. "I've been with the police. That's actually why I stopped by. Why did you tell me to go pick up Leo's things if you were planning to? And what did you tell the detective last night at the hospital?"

"What do you mean, what did I tell him? I told him the last conversation me and Leo had. Why?"

"Because he started . . . I don't know, insinuating some things. He says it wasn't just an accident. Then he started interrogating me like he thought I had something to do with it."

"Oh." Tina waved it off. "That doesn't mean anything. He did me the same way. I think he's reaching. Trying to scare us into saying something incriminating. I was talking to him and he wants to start asking where I was and did I have an alibi and shit like that. Pissed me off so I ended up leaving. I texted you about going to get Leo's things, but then I ended up just going myself since I was on that side of town to put a deposit on a storage unit."

I shook my head, struggling to wrap my mind around it all. "They told us it was an accident and now they're saying it was possibly murder, so why the hell are they looking at us?"

Tina reshifted the baby and stuck the nipple of the bottle in his mouth. He began sucking greedily. "They're just trying to solve a case. I'm not worried about any of that foolishness. I know I didn't do anything and you didn't do anything so we have nothing to be worried about."

I nodded. She was right. But why did I still feel uneasy? "I didn't know you spoke to Leo that night. What did he say?" I didn't know why I felt compelled to ask.

Tina lowered her eyes, and I could've sworn I saw a tear glimmer on her cheek. "Nothing too much," she murmured. "How he missed us, couldn't wait to get home, and he had something to tell us." She shrugged. "He was talking to Eddie for a minute, there was some noise, and the phone went dead."

I shook my head. I couldn't imagine hearing those last few moments. "Do you . . . do you think it was an accident, or . . . ?" I couldn't bring myself to think he had been killed.

Tina's eyes fell back on the baby. "I think it was just an accident," she murmured. "Just a horrible accident. We are just going to have to pick up the pieces and move on, Kimera."

I nodded. If there was such a thing.

"So I guess we need to plan the funeral," I started, but Tina shook her head.

"I made some calls. It's already taken care of."

"Made some calls? For someone to plan Leo's funeral?"

Tina eyed me briefly. "You'd be surprised what money can buy," she said. "It's next Saturday."

"So soon? What about his family? Will they be able to fly in in time?"

Tina shrugged and lowered her eyes. "Damn," she whispered.

"It's only been two days and . . ." I was surprised she didn't bother hiding the tears as they streaked down her face. Her makeup ran, blotting her skin with color from her mascara and eye shadow. I suddenly felt sick. Never had I seen Tina so emotional. She had been a bitch for so long that I hadn't even remembered she had feelings.

"I'm sorry." She turned her back to me and busied herself with rinsing out the now empty bottle. She hiked Leo Jr. on her shoulder and gently patted his back to coax the burp from his belly. He looked at me over Tina's shoulder, his huge, curious eyes fixated on mine. "It's weird, you know," Tina was murmuring almost to herself. "I know he didn't mean much to you and Lena, but I loved that man with everything in me. I just . . . hate this. All of this."

She was right. Here again I was too worried about myself to realize what she had been going through. Especially while she cared for his child, his child that looked more like Leo than he did.

"Tina . . ." I was at a loss for words. "Is there . . . if I can do anything, please let me know. I'm sorry."

The tiny burp erupted, and Leo Jr. giggled from the gassy release. Tina sighed and bent her head. "I am too," she said.

I ended up staying to pack my own things. I hadn't prepared to get my own place, hadn't even looked. So for now I would just put my furniture in storage and move back in with my parents. Great thing was I knew it was going to be temporary. Tina said Leo's lawyer would be by after the funeral to discuss the will. According to Tina, there would be quite a few millions that would need to be divided up between us and his family. And that, coupled with the few thousand I had sitting comfortably in my bank, meant I would be set. So why, then, did I feel like shit?

Ayana and the movers had already packed up a number of my

clothes, and I went through marking everything else for them to take. Bedroom furniture, TVs—both the one in my bedroom and the small one in my bathroom. I called around for a storage unit and found one not too far from my folks' place. I had called my own moving truck and they would be arriving shortly. Now I really was just wasting time, wandering around the huge bedroom that had never really felt like mine, in the house that never really felt like home.

I didn't hear my phone ring, but I did see Adria's name come across my screen. Damn, I forgot to turn the ringer back on after I left the station. No wonder I hadn't heard Tina's phone call. I dog-eared the page of Lena's journal I hadn't completed and closed the notebook before answering the phone.

"Hey, girl, where are you?" Adria spoke as soon as I picked up. I immediately registered the urgency in her voice.

"At Leo's house. Why, what's wrong?"

"Leo's house?"

"Yes, girl, I have to update you on what happened when I went down to the station. I came over here to talk to Tina and pack up my things. She's selling the house."

"When will you be back by? I just got off work and I'm headed back to the house."

"I'm going to my parents' in a little bit and then probably Jahmad's later. Why, what's wrong?"

"Okay, I'll meet you over there to talk to you."

"About what?"

"I found out why you were fired."

I rolled my eyes. She made it sound like she had something important to discuss. "Adria, I told you not to worry about it. It's not that serious."

"I didn't think so either until I asked around. Apparently, someone paid to have you fired."

"What?" I frowned and had to realign the phone to my ear to make sure I had heard her correctly. "Paid to have me fired? Why?"

"I don't know why."

Confusing, sure. But still . . . "Well," I said. "Yeah, that's pretty fucked up, but I don't see why it matters now."

"It was Leo."

Chapter 22

"My thing is,"—Adria leaned against my dresser, her face crinkled in confusion—"why would Leo pay to have you fired?"

I shrugged. Sure, it was puzzling me, but Adria's continued interest in the situation was puzzling me even more. I really didn't want to have any ill feelings about Leo at all. Especially given what happened to him. Plus, it was not like he was here to defend himself.

"How did you get this information?" I asked instead.

"Girl, you know I can't just leave shit alone," Adria said with a chuckle. "If it doesn't sit well with me, I'm going to push the issue. And I just kept asking around, trying to see who could give me proof. Even if I couldn't see it myself, I wanted to know if someone else had laid eyes on these so-called records about you. Come to find out, it was all made up."

"Did you ask Aunt Pam about it?" I couldn't help being a little skeptical. Sure, I knew the story about me stealing money wasn't true at all, but the fact that Aunt Pam would be so deceptive, all for some money, I couldn't wrap my mind around it. There must have been more Adria hadn't found out yet.

"No, not yet," she said. "I wanted to come to you about it first. See what your thoughts were."

I was now lying across the bed, my legs folded between two packing boxes that didn't allow much room for moving around. First thing in the morning, I would be looking for my own place. The truck had taken most of my things to storage, but I had still been left with a few boxes to bring back to my parents, which cluttered up my tiny room. That's what I would rather focus on. Burying my husband, collecting whatever money he had left for me, and getting my life started. Hell, it had felt like up until now, I hadn't been living. Just going through the motions like my body was on some kind of autopilot.

"I'm not sure what I'm supposed to do," I admitted, my eyes on the ceiling. "Does it really matter, Adria?"

"I'm telling you that your husband, or whatever he was, paid to have you fired from your job. What do you mean, does it matter? That doesn't sound fishy to you?"

"Of course it sounds fishy, but Leo is dead, Adria," I said, struggling to keep the exasperation out of my voice. "Maybe two months, hell, two days ago it would've mattered, but it doesn't now. Damn, the man is not even in the ground yet and we're worried about what he was up to." I surprised us both when my voice cracked, and the subsequent silence only heightened the bottled emotion I was already feeling. Tears stung my lids and I let out a heavy breath.

"I'm sorry," Adria murmured, watching me closely. "I didn't really stop to think how all of this was affecting you."

"It shouldn't be," I admitted. I was actually feeling guilty that it was. I was alive. I had Jahmad. What did Leo have? "But I still had feelings for the man. Maybe not the same way he felt about me. But it still hurts."

I didn't know Adria had sat beside me until I felt the bed sink under her weight. The tears were coming on their own now, trickles that ran down my face so silently that I didn't know they were there until my cheeks began to feel wet. Who was I even crying for? The confusion was frustrating, that was for damn sure.

As if on cue, my cell phone chimed, and I glanced at the screen. A text from Jahmad. I swiped to open the message.

CAN'T WAIT TO SEE YOU TONIGHT.

Seeing the text, coupled with everything else, was making me sick. I swallowed the swell of nausea and laid the phone back down beside me, not even bothering to respond.

"Well, what are you going to do about him?" Adria nodded toward the phone. Clearly she had read the message as well.

I shook my head. "I don't want to talk about this anymore," I said. "What about you? What's going on with this new guy you were telling me about?"

Adria's face lit up briefly. Very briefly. "He's a good guy. But . . . I don't know, Kimmy. My heart is not there."

"Because it's with my brother."

Her eyes ballooned in shock. "How long have you known about that?"

I had to chuckle at her response. Mainly because she actually thought none of us knew. "Are you serious, Adria? We've all known you've been with Keon since middle school. And it's so obvious when y'all are around each other."

She seemed to be studying my reaction. "Yeah, I'm sorry I didn't tell you. I just . . . didn't know how you would feel. He is your brother."

"And he's going to always be my brother," I said with a laugh. "And you're my best friend. I just don't want to see you hurt, and you and I both know my brother ain't shit."

She didn't laugh at my joke, only lowered her eyes. "I know," she whispered. "And I still love his 'ain't shit' ass too."

I had no words for her. I knew exactly how it felt to love someone so much and not have those feelings reciprocated. Shit hurt something awful. And now here I was finally having the man I wanted, and I was tangled in enough mess to have him taking his ass right back to Texas. I should tell him. The burden of this secret was eating at me and stressing me all out to the point I couldn't even enjoy being with him like I wanted, knowing what I was doing. I just hoped and prayed that he would respect my honesty and we could move on. Lord knows what I would do if he left me. Again.

Just the thought of not having him in my life anymore had my stomach aching. The pain was sharp, a jagged piercing shock that ran up from my pelvis to my belly. I groaned and sat up, clenching my teeth against the discomfort.

"What's wrong?"

I shook my head against Adria's question. Hell if I knew. I thought back to my last few meals. No, I hadn't been eating much of anything. It was a wonder these hunger pains were just now hitting. I doubled over as another sharp pain felt like it was snatching my insides along with it, apparently hitting harder than usual.

"Do you need to go to the doctor?" Adria sounded as worried as I felt.

I opened my mouth to respond, to reassure her of some lie about me being okay so she didn't panic, but no words came out. Heat flushed my face, and I was feeling warm all over. I couldn't sit up even if I wanted to. Weak, I lay there, staring at the spinning ceiling, as my heart quickened. The last thing I remembered before the world went black was a smiling Leo reaching out to me.

———◆◆◆———

Baby.

The word struggled to pull me to consciousness. But whoever

was speaking sounded so far away. Was it Leo? Jahmad? Were they talking about me?

Hurt. Sick. Dead.

The voice sounded muffled and discombobulated, like whoever it was was talking through water. I caught snatches of words, but my brain was having trouble making sense of the conversation.

I felt like I was floating, the hum of a machine seeming to lull me back to sleep. Or into death, perhaps. I honestly couldn't be sure. But I felt so good, so at peace with this catatonic state that seemed to envelope me. Was this what Leo felt like? Lena?

"Kimmy . . ."

This time, I did recognize that voice so close it was as if she were whispering my name right in my ear. Lips kissed my forehead, the slight tremble on my skin forcing me to lift my heavy lids.

The room was blurry at first, then came into focus like a camera lens. A hospital room.

Adria stood right beside my bed, her hand on my forehead, her worried eyes fixed on my face. "How you feeling?" she asked. I opened my mouth to speak, not surprised when the searing pain in my throat had me shutting it promptly. It felt like my throat was raw.

She reached for a paper cup and held the tip of the bendy straw to my lips. Grateful, I took a sip. The warm water had an aftertaste but felt like heaven going down, so I drank more.

"Where . . ." My own voice sounded foreign to me, hoarse and raspy. I sighed and leaned back against the pillow.

"You just passed out," Adria answered. "Scared the shit out of me. Everyone is here. Your parents, Keon, and even Jahmad."

My lids had begun to drift closed but immediately snapped back open at the mention of his name. I looked around the room, which was empty except for Adria.

"Your dad took your mom home to get a change of clothes," Adria explained. "Keon and Jahmad were literally just here but they ran down to the cafeteria to grab something to eat. Everyone has been by your side for two days."

Damn, two days? A few hours, I would have assumed, but I couldn't believe that much time had passed. Guilt began to gnaw at me as I imagined the anxiety I must have put everyone through in the past forty-eight hours.

Adria turned her back on me, and I watched her hand go to her face to hide something. Tears? Was she crying?

"Dammit, Kimmy, I'm so damn pissed at you," she snapped, her back still to me. "You could've died. Why the hell didn't you take the rest of the medicine for the abortion?"

Piece by painstaking piece clicked into place as I remembered my trip home from the clinic. She was right. I did have one more pill to take. But that had been the night Leo had died, and everything else that had happened since, the cops, the interrogation, the move; honestly, my pregnancy had been one of the last things on my mind.

"What happened?" I forced the words out.

"Some kind of infection," Adria said, finally turning back around to face me. Her eyes were swollen, either from crying or exhaustion. Or a mix of both. "That first pill you took at the clinic was supposed to stop the pregnancy, but remember you were supposed to take that second one a few hours later to miscarry."

I looked toward the IV in my arm, followed the tube up to the pouch of clear fluid of whatever drugs they were sifting through me.

"Am I still pregnant?" I whispered.

Adria glanced toward the door before nodding.

My eyes landed on my stomach, now covered by the crisp hospital sheet. I wasn't really sure how to feel about that, honestly. *Baby.* I probably was supposed to be excited. Or at the very least somewhat fearful or anxious. But all I felt was numb. And it wasn't from the drugs either.

"Baby's healthy," Adria went on at my continued silence. It was obvious she was trying to gauge my reaction as she tiptoed over each word. "They thought you had lost it at first, but they did give you some progesterone, did an ultrasound, everything looks good. And you're going to be okay. They gave you medicine for the infection, plenty of fluids because you were dehydrated. They said once you came to, you could probably leave in less than a week—"

"Does he know?" I interrupted, glancing toward the closed door. I could almost feel Jahmad's presence even though he was nowhere in sight.

Adria's lips bent in sympathy. "Your mom was also in the room when the doctor explained everything to us. I don't know if she told . . ."

It was obvious she was trying to keep my hopes up. But she and I both knew my mother. The holy First Lady had a big-ass mouth. Now the question was, what would Jahmad have to say about it?

I glanced at the door just as it eased open. My brother poked his head in first, looking first to Adria before eyeing me. His grin spread.

"Hey, you're up," he said, opening the door wider. "Your ass was knocked out, sis." His weak attempt at humor had my lips curving. Leave it to my brother.

Jahmad followed Keon, his eyes steady on me. I immediately felt uncomfortable under his scrutiny. I was sure he had so many questions. Questions I didn't necessarily have the answers for. At least not at the moment. I was already dreading being alone with him.

"How you feeling?" Keon asked.

"Weak," I admitted. My entire body felt like it wasn't even mine. I couldn't move anything other than my head if I wanted to.

Adria held the cup of water back to my lips, and I took another grateful sip.

We all waited in awkward silence for a moment. Me, I wasn't even sure what to talk about. I wondered how much they knew.

Finally, Keon rolled his eyes. "So when were you two going to tell me y'all were fucking, Kimmy?"

Embarrassment colored my cheeks and had me lowering my eyes. "That's kind of personal, Keon," I murmured. "Besides, I didn't want y'all two to fall out or anything."

Keon pursed his lips and nodded. "I ain't got to like it," he said. "But ain't shit I can really do about it. But still. I thought we were closer than that. Just like I thought you would've told me you were having his baby."

I'm sure I was already pale, but I felt my skin go cold as the color drained from my face. I knew if I had looked in the mirror my skin would've been sheet white. Suddenly, the Band-Aid around my index finger, probably where they had to prick me for some blood, became very interesting. Again, the room was quiet; thank God Adria came to my rescue.

"First off, that's none of your damn business either," she snapped. "Second, why don't you leave so they can talk about their own business?"

Keon laughed. "Well, hell. You leave too, woman. Matter fact, come with me to one of these empty rooms down the hall so I can bang some of that attitude out of you." He kissed the air, and Adria rolled her eyes, though she couldn't hide the smirk.

"We'll be right outside, girl," she said to me and, leaning down, she planted a reassuring kiss on my cheek. Damn, I loved that girl to no end. Part of me was actually thrilled Keon was taking everything so lightly. Shocked, but thrilled nonetheless. I hadn't been sure how he was going to react to the news about his sister and his best friend. But then again, my folks always mentioned that was his problem anyway. He couldn't take shit seriously. Jahmad, on the other hand, was a different story. And the way he was eyeing me was unnerving the hell out of me.

He remained expressionless, even after Adria dragged Keon from the room and the door had long since closed behind them.

I shifted uncomfortably in the bed, my body suddenly feeling like lead on the stiff mattress. I waited for the anger, for the violent verbal abuse I was sure he was trying his damnedest to restrain. And with each second that ticked by, anxiety had my heart aching as it pounded against my chest. Finally, I spoke first. I felt I needed to. "I'm sorry."

Jahmad's eyes flicked briefly to my stomach. So briefly, I wasn't even sure he had looked at all. But his stoic expression had now been replaced with sadness. And I knew he too was thinking about the unborn baby I still carried.

"So, were you going to tell me?" he asked.

I nodded, unable to force the lie from my lips. Again, I went over Adria's story about what happened. How much did he know? How much had the doctor divulged?

"So is it true?" Jahmad asked, and I frowned in confusion.

"Is what true?"

"You got an infection with some kind of abortion. Is that true?"

Damn. Now how the hell was I going to explain that? Tears flooded my eyes and again I looked down to my hands in my lap. "I'm sorry." My voice cracked and I let the tears fall. "I didn't know what to do."

"Dammit, you could've come to me, Kimmy," he snapped. "We could've talked about this before you tried some shit like that."

I welcomed the anger. I deserved it. But what broke my heart was the pain I heard underneath his words. And that had me crying harder.

"I love you so much. Please. Forgive me." My mind went into overdrive, grasping at something, anything to make him understand. "That's why I couldn't go through with it," I rattled on, not caring about the lie. "I was supposed to take two pills. I just took one. I . . . I couldn't do it, Jahmad. I couldn't do that to us."

It wasn't much, but I could see the slight change in his attitude. His face seemed to soften under that last false admission, and I said a silent prayer that maybe, just maybe this was still salvageable. I hadn't given any thought to being without Jahmad or being a single mother at that. Without him, I wasn't even sure that last part was an option.

Jahmad pulled a chair closer so he could sit right beside my hospital bed. He was still staring at me, like he had so many things to say and really didn't know how or where to start. Finally, he rested a hand on my stomach, and I felt my heart flutter.

"How are you feeling?" he asked quietly.

I looked at his hand and carefully covered his with mine.

"Better," I admitted and chanced a small smile.

"You know I love you, right?" He studied my face as I nodded. I hated not being able to read him, and my grip on his hand tightened. That one question felt like a setup for some news I was certainly not prepared for. And I was scared.

"I love you too," I said. "With everything in me, Jahmad. You know that."

"Forgive me, because this was sure as hell not what I had in mind." He chuckled as he reached into his pocket.

My eyes rounded as they caught the velvet box. I screamed just as the beeping of my heart monitor spiked.

I didn't even register that Keon and Adria, plus a few hospital staff, had burst into the room probably wondering if I was dying. But I kept screaming, I kept crying, and Jahmad's ass had the nerve to be laughing. It seemed like he was moving in slow motion as he removed the princess-cut diamond ring from the folds of the pillow inside. It was nowhere near as expensive as the one from Leo I kept stuffed in my purse. But this one I would wear proudly. Little did I know this was only the beginning. But instead of getting better, things were about to get worse.

Chapter 23

"We need to talk."

I caught my mother's eye in the mirror, as she leaned against the doorway of my bedroom. She was looking at my simple black knee-length dress, black tights, and low-heeled pumps, probably wondering where the hell I was going.

She waited patiently as I finished clasping the pearl necklace behind my neck and turned to view my side silhouette. It really had become habit, looking at myself from the side and watching my tiny belly beginning to firm and round with the life growing inside. It still didn't look like too much of anything, but I was anxious to see the first visual signs of this pregnancy.

My engagement ring winked from my finger and my lips curved. Yes, I was headed to Leo's funeral, but I couldn't have been more happy at that very moment. I should've felt guilty for being in such a good mood, but I couldn't come off this cloud nine.

On a sigh, I turned and faced my mom, trying to mentally prepare for this conversation. It was bound to come up, I knew. Hell, I was surprised it hadn't come up sooner. But three days home from the hospital, and both she and my father had managed to leave me to myself. Now here she was, and I still wasn't ready.

"Why didn't you tell me all of this was going on?" she started, crossing her arms over her chest.

I shrugged. "Mama, it's a lot, I know. I was trying to handle it all."

"By almost killing yourself? That's you handling it?"

I didn't bother responding to the rhetorical question. Her tone, though snappy, was laced with hurt. And disappointment.

"I can't believe something like an abortion would even cross your mind," she fumed, narrowing her eyes. "Haven't you been in church enough to know better? Why would you do something like that?"

"Mama." I sank to the bed, the conversation already exhausting me. "I know it was wrong. I know and I'm sorry. But I didn't go through with it. Doesn't that count for something?" I left off the part about me forgetting to go through with it. The way I saw it, that didn't even matter anymore.

She shook her head. Like it did not matter. I felt bad. Not sure if it was stress or what, but my mother suddenly looked old. Like the topic was aging her past the point of tolerance.

"What's done in the dark always comes to the light." She quoted the familiar phrase with a pointed stare, almost accusatory. I shifted under her gaze. God, I hoped for once, just once, my mother was wrong about that.

<hr />

I had thought Lena's funeral would be the last one I would attend for a while. I was even praying for that. I don't know, but it's something about looking at a dead body, knowing that not even a week prior they were flushed with life and laughter, made my skin crawl. I could see why people got so emotional at funerals. But for some reason, the whole ordeal just made me numb. Like an out-of-body experience. Like I was drifting away, watching my body move zombielike down the side aisle, inching along behind Tina

and Leo Jr. and a trail of other so-called friends I had never seen before in my life.

A few sobs were muffled by the notes of Yolanda Adams's song "I'm Gonna Be Ready," which hummed through the church speakers. I wondered if any of the visitors scattered in the pews knew who I was. Or did I just so happen to blend in with everyone else? Tina had taken care of all the arrangements, so I had no idea whom she had invited, no say in the song selection, or even the crisp bronze coffin he now rested in. I probably should have felt bad. Contractually, he was my husband too. But she had offered and I hadn't objected. I saw no reason to stake whatever claim in this matter now. I would be the submissive "wife number three," well, widow rather, and make an appearance. It was like the script of a well-rehearsed movie. Now it was time to roll the cameras.

It felt surreal, looking down on Leo lying in the baby blue cushions of his coffin. I watched my hand extend to caress his face, now neatly shaven to expose his dark complexion in all its African glory. His locs had been retwisted, and he lay on a single braid that pulled the style back from his face. Tina had chosen a navy blue suit with a lavender silk shirt. The scratches on his face from the crash were now completely hidden under layers of foundation and soft mortuary makeup that made him look almost like a sleeping wax figure.

Tina didn't bother to stop long, just enough to lean over and plant a single kiss on Leo's forehead before she breezed on. So I did the same.

Before I knew it, I was seated back in the front row as she bounced Leo Jr. in her lap, struggling to distract him from his boredom at the ceremony. A few words from the pastor, some songs, and Tina was handing the baby in my direction and making her way to the pulpit. I hadn't even known she was going to say anything. I glanced down at the program with Leo's grinning face on the front.

I should be crying right now. Listening to the sniffles echoing throughout the sanctuary, I felt out of place for maintaining my composure. For feeling so . . . detached. As if on cue, Leo Jr. giggled in my lap, and I couldn't help but see the similarity in each of his boyish features. What would we tell him about his father? Hell, I said "we," but would I even have a relationship with him? Would I want to?

"My husband . . ." Tina started, her hands gripping the sides of the lectern. She took a shaky breath. Her eyes flicked to the open casket, to Leo's enlarged picture sitting on the nearby canvas, before looking out at the crowd. She appeared to be focusing intently on something in the back of the room. Anything to keep from making eye contact with any of us.

"I'm sorry," she whispered and cleared her throat. "My husband, Leo Owusu, was a very special man. A man nobody can replace. At least not in my heart. We were married for eight years. Eight rocky, but very loving, years.

"As most of you know, my marriage to Leo was arranged. Our families got together and decided we would grow, prosper, and be very compatible. I must admit, I wasn't completely sold on the idea." She chuckled to herself. "But I went along anyway. I actually didn't officially meet Leo until I was walking down the aisle at our wedding. All I can say is, I thank God for that day. Our marriage wasn't perfect, but our families were right. We were perfect for each other.

"With our union, we gave life to our son, Leo Jr." She gestured in my direction as I held on to the baby. "Unfortunately, we weren't able to have more children, but we were blessed tremendously when our surrogate had him for us. And now, Leo will live on through his son, and through me." Tina placed a hand over her heart and looked up to the ceiling. Her tears glistened on her cheeks as she took another shaky breath. "Leo, I love you with everything in me and I would give anything in this world to see you again. To feel your warm embrace. But I know our souls will

202 / BRIANA COLE

unite for an eternity together in Heaven. In the meantime, please guide us as we try to move forward here on earth. Watch our child. Protect him. Give him strength. I will make sure he knows what a loving, generous, and kind man you are. You will be remembered, my one true love, and you will live in my heart forever. I love you."

I didn't realize I was holding my breath until I felt my chest tighten. I let it out quietly. She made her way back to me among the silence that followed as her words obviously resonated with every listening ear. Since when had Lena become a surrogate? I guess it was a good thing she didn't mention me. The whole "love partners" thing was a tough pill to swallow as it was. I sure as hell didn't want to be mentioned for fear of the subsequent tension or confusion. I had had enough of that with the newspaper article.

Tina grabbed Leo from my hands as she took her seat and held him tightly to her breast. The gesture was familiar enough to have him snuggle against her, his chubby fingers grabbing for the dangling earrings dripping from her ears, a stark contrast to how he had sat uncomfortably with me just moments before.

The funeral continued, but still, I couldn't help but glance at Tina out of the corner of my eye as she finished the rest of the ceremony as the typical grieving widow.

———◆◆◆———

I was hating this whole thing.

So when the last guest, who happened to be one of Leo's great aunts, kissed my cheeks and folded me in a plump hug that had the underlying smell of Virginia Slims, I breathed a sigh of relief.

After the funeral, we had taken limos out to the burial site and stood in the drizzle and mist while Leo's casket had been lowered into the soil. Final goodbyes, more singing, and then it was over. Or so I thought.

Tina had apparently invited everyone back to the house after-

ward. Cars lined the drive as we pulled up, and a slew of mourn-ers cluttered the living room and spilled into the kitchen. She had arranged for some catered food, which had aluminum pans and foil littering the marble countertops.

Someone had offered to fix me a plate but I politely declined. I'm sure my fetus would have a problem with that objection later. But for now, I didn't have an appetite. I would have left had I known she was going to do this, truth be told. I was waiting for afterward, when she said the lawyer would be there for the read-ing of the will. Part of me thought I was really waiting around not to be rude but, hell, none of these people would have missed me, that's for sure.

Soft music had been playing over the speakers and everyone stood around awkwardly, eating, sipping wine, and whispering among themselves over the "terrible tragedy." That's what every-one called it. A "terrible tragedy." Meanwhile, I had found a cor-ner to disappear to, busying myself with playing on my phone and texting Jahmad. I felt bad for that, but Tina was doing enough en-tertaining for the both of us, breezing from room to room making small talk, offering food and drinks, shuffling the baby from rela-tive to relative so they could gloat over each giggle and coo. And that was sufficient for me. I mean, she was the "real wife." I was just the bonus.

Of course, I hadn't told Jahmad anything about Leo. I had merely stated I was going to the funeral of an old friend. He wanted to accompany me but that would have been a disaster in and of itself. Now, part of me wished he had come so this whole thing wouldn't have been so awkward and drawn out.

"You call Auntie Minnie if you need anything," Leo's aunt was saying as she pulled back from the hug while keeping her hands on my shoulders. I couldn't even see her eyes for the creases in her fat cheeks, but she made no move to wipe away the tears that trickled from the thin slits.

I nodded, and she turned and popped open her umbrella before disappearing out into the rain. I closed the door behind her and turned, surveying the room.

With the exception of a few folding chairs and tables, it was completely empty. Tina wasn't playing when she said she was moving. I wasn't even sure where to, but she claimed to have found a place for her, the baby, and Ayana. It felt different. Even while it had been so crowded a moment ago, the place still felt empty. And cold.

I passed Ayana busying herself with cleaning up from the gathering and found Tina in Leo's office. She had positioned Leo Jr. in a blue swing near the large oak desk and now the instrumental version of some nursery rhyme broke the silence in the room.

I leaned against the door as Tina sat with a hip on the desktop, thumbing through papers in a manila folder. "I figured you would have packed his stuff up too," I said, noticing the office had been pretty much left alone.

Tina flipped the folder closed and gave a half shrug, glancing around as if in agreement. "The movers are going to come get the last of it tomorrow," she said. "In here and in Leo's bedroom. Take it to a local shelter."

I nodded. "Listen, I had a question about your eulogy. Just curious. Since when was Lena a surrogate?"

Tina's face wrinkled in confusion. "Listen, Kimmy. You can't be worried about anyone but yourself. Lena was a surrogate. She knew as well as us. That was her role when she was invited into this marriage. Trust me, she was made very aware. But at this point, why does any of this matter to you?"

"Just seemed weird," I admitted, before pushing the thought from my head. She was right.

"I know things haven't been the best with us," Tina said with a comforting smile. "I wasn't a fan of you any more than you were a fan of me. But we got through it. We made it work. And, I hope after all this, we can still maintain some kind of friendship. For Leo's sake. And the baby's."

Not knowing what to say, I simply returned her smile. The odds were highly unlikely that shit would happen, but I dipped my head in a brief nod anyway.

The doorbell rang, and moments later, Ayana led the way into the office with a short, aging white man fast on her heels. He was dressed in an expensive Italian suit, with cuff links and a sharp tan tie. Very neat, I could tell. He didn't have so much as a hair on his beard out of place.

Ayana politely stepped to the side to allow him to enter before shutting the door behind him.

"Mrs. Owusu," the man greeted and nodded toward Tina before turning to me. "And the other Mrs. Owusu, I am to presume."

I nodded.

"Paul, thanks for coming by. Please have a seat."

The man obliged and sat down in one of the chairs facing the desk, setting his briefcase in his lap. "Kimera, as I mentioned, Paul Morton is Leo's attorney."

"And a very dear friend," Paul added, placing a hand to his chest. "Let me just say I am terribly sorry for your loss, ladies. Mr. Owusu loved you both very much."

It sounded rehearsed, but I nodded along anyway. Just as long as we could go ahead and get this over with. I took the seat next to him, and Tina made herself comfortable in Leo's executive chair.

"Now, I won't hold you two up. I just wanted to bring by a copy of Mr. Owusu's will for each of you to review. We've already initiated probate and the court has determined this will is valid and legally binding."

I skimmed the thin stack of papers he handed to me. Lots of legal jargon. From what I could piece together, Leo had a great deal of assets and family money tied up in stocks and real estate. Homes I knew nothing about scattered all over the U.S., a number of bonds and mutual funds as well. We were to liquidate everything and divide it between us, leaving a few things in the baby's name for when he became of age. That's when I noticed how recently he must have drawn up this document, because he mentioned Leo Jr. and nowhere did he speak of Lena.

"As you can see," Paul spoke up again, "between Mr. Owusu's assets and his money in various bank accounts, everything totals about $186 million. And as he requested, a fifty/twenty-five/twenty-five split, with the bulk of the portion going to his son, Leo Jr."

My jaw dropped as the numbers ran through my mind. Sure, he would give the most to his child; that was expected. So that left Tina and me to split about $93 million equally.

"So wait." The figure danced around in my head and damn near made my mouth water and my heart stop. "Are you saying Leo left me with almost $50 million?"

Paul nodded, Tina looked on, and me, I was stunned silent. Never had I thought he would leave me so much money. Never had I even touched so much damn money. I didn't have to work another day in my life. Leo had said this would be the best investment I ever made and damn if he wasn't right.

Tina appeared to keep her composure and began asking questions that I didn't even care about. His debts, being the executor, but none of that mattered to me. All I knew was I was walking out of that room that day with a shit ton of money. Never mind how I would explain that to anyone. My parents, Jahmad. I would have to worry about all of that later.

". . . checks drawn up in a week," Paul was saying, and I struggled to tune back into his words. I couldn't appear too eager, well, more eager than I already did, so I just nodded right along with Tina. Like it was no big deal. Like I could wait. Like I wouldn't be driving myself crazy counting down each second for the next seven days.

We signed some forms so Paul would be authorized to handle everything on our behalf and both of us stood to walk him to the front door. Tina had picked up a sleeping Leo Jr. and nuzzled him against her breast as we left the office.

"I want to thank you again for coming by on such short notice, Paul," she was saying. "I'm sorry we had to deal with all of this now, but it really needed to get done. Kimera and I are trying to move on from this as best we can."

"I completely understand. And hey,"—he turned with a hand on the doorknob—"if either one of you needs anything. Anytime. Please don't hesitate to call me. Like I said, Leo was more than a client. And I want to look out for his wives and baby."

He opened the door, and my eyes landed on the two police officers standing on the other side. The rain was coming down in sheets now, and it seemed to silhouette them as they stood outlining the door in uniforms wet from the downpour. I frowned as they stepped into the foyer without being invited, followed by Vincent brushing the rain droplets from his own blazer.

"Officers." Tina spoke first when no one made a move to speak. "What seems to be the problem?"

"We seem to have some more information about Mr. Owusu's death," Vincent said, before turning his eyes to me.

I shuddered under his stare, even as my peripheral vision caught each officer circling around to me. "Kimera Davis," Vincent said, the corners of his lips turning up into a satisfied smirk, "you are under arrest for the murder of Leo Owusu."

Chapter 24

Interesting how I had held my tears up until this point. Through Lena's funeral and Leo's death. Through identifying the body and even today, through all of Leo's funeral and post-funeral gathering. Not one apology or condolence could prompt me to cry. All I had felt was numbness. Interesting how I had managed to keep my composure.

But now, as I sat huddled on the stiff cot of my holding cell, my arms hugging my stomach to keep from vomiting all up and down these cinder blocks, I couldn't seem to stop crying.

I heard once that some people didn't like having their picture taken because the camera snapshot captures the soul. That was probably one of those rare occurrences when I was actually paying attention in psychology in college, but right now the shit sounded legit. Because when that camera flashed to snap my mug shot, it felt set in stone. Like a permanent stain on my life that would leave a lasting impression on society. I had been fingerprinted and booked and shuffled alongside every other pedophile, murder, robber, and the like. Never in a million years had I thought I would be associated with any of those criminal labels. Let alone hold a murder title of my own. How in the hell had they gotten that?

DNA. Vincent had smiled so smugly as they cuffed me and

read me my rights. They had identified the vehicle that had caused the accident that night of Leo's death. The hit-and-run. An abandoned truck had been found some miles down the road, the front bumper smashed and windshield shattered from an obvious crash. I hadn't listened when Vincent had gone into detail about how they were able to match the car to the accident. I hadn't really cared. No, what made me shit a brick was when they said they had found my blood all over that 2012 Jeep Cherokee. A truck I had never been in, never in my life.

"That doesn't make sense," I was damn near screaming as the metal of the cuffs tightened against my wrist. "I don't even drive a truck. I was nowhere near that street where you found it."

"I think that's what you're going to have to convince a judge and jury," Vincent had said with a nonchalant shrug. "My job is to collect evidence and catch the bad guy."

"But that's not possible. I didn't do it!"

"Your DNA says otherwise. Plus, you never did have that alibi, remember?"

"I was at home." I strained against the officers struggling to lead me to the police car. "Please, just call my parents. They know I came over that night. And my best friend, Adria. She dropped me off."

Vincent dismissed my pleas with a wave of his hand. I could tell he was the kind of man who thrived on success. He thought he had solved a case and put a bad person behind bars. How wrong he was but clearly that's all that mattered to him. At this point, I was sobbing as they maneuvered me into the back of the car. I was soaked from the rain, or from tears—I didn't even know which anymore. I just kept thinking this shit couldn't be real.

I turned my desperate eyes to Tina as she stood near Paul in the doorway. "Call me when you can," she mouthed as the cop slammed the door shut in my face.

That had been a while ago, but hell, I didn't even know while huddled in that shitty cell if hours had actually passed or mere minutes that seemed like hours. What would my parents say? What would Jahmad say? I had begged for a phone call, I know, when I came in because, well, that seemed like shit you were supposed to do. But honestly, if given the opportunity, who the hell would I call? How could I explain the shit I was in now?

"Kimera Davis."

I glanced up as the officer stopped in front of my cell. I know my face was tear-streaked and a migraine was pounding at my temples so much that I couldn't do anything but lay back on the stiff cot and count the minutes as they ticked by. I counted 337.

The officer, a plump woman with a voice raspy from too many cigarettes, used her key to open my cell. "Time for your phone call."

I nodded and allowed myself to be led down the hall to the pay phone situated near the guard's desk.

I held the dirty receiver in my hand for about five minutes before I got up the nerve to actually dial a number. When prompted by the collect call operator, I stated my name and waited, hoping she would answer. Adria picked up, her voice groggy with sleep.

"Kimmy?"

"Yeah, it's me," I said, already feeling a fresh set of tears threatening to erupt. My breath caught in my throat. "I'm in trouble, Adria. I need your help."

"What happened?" Her voice was clear now and I could hear shuffling in the background as if she were moving around. "Where are you? I'm on my way."

"It's Leo. They think I killed him."

"What?"

"They came and arrested me a few hours ago after his funeral."

"They can't do that."

I was full-on sobbing now, because she sounded just as helpless as I did. Of course they couldn't do that because I hadn't killed anybody. But they did and that meant they had some shit on me. I didn't know why or how, but murder? That meant serious jail time or, worse, the death penalty. I watched enough criminal shows to know how this worked and that alone had my chest tightening and me gasping for air. The room spun, and I braced against the wall to keep my balance. This must be a panic attack. I had never had one, but I knew what the hell panicked felt like.

"Okay, calm down and take a breath." Adria demonstrated and I mimicked her technique. It didn't help the nerves but at least my breathing was returning to normal.

"I'm going to call your parents."

"Adria, no! Please."

"Kimera, it's time to stop this sneaky shit. You're in trouble and you need support. Plus a damn good lawyer. You really think you can handle this alone? Look at where you are."

She was right. I didn't have to look around. I knew the pale yellow walls with the peeling paint, the dingy ceiling fan that creaked as it spun right above the guard's desk. The ugly acrylic floor had been scuffed and stained, and there was a lingering must smell that hung like a rank coat, and thanks to my pregnancy sensitivity of smell, it made me want to throw up every piece of residue in my body.

"Please hurry," I whispered.

"I love you, girl. Don't stress. It's not good for my godchild." I rubbed my stomach, somewhat comforted by the tiny jumps underneath my palm. If we were both going to get through this, I had to stay strong. For me and the baby.

<hr>

My lawyer reminded me of Eddie. He was an older black gentleman, tall and lanky with soft eyes and a kind smile. I was on edge after spending the night in jail and not getting a shred of sleep. I knew I looked a mess and I felt even worse. But he came in and sat his briefcase on the table and, despite the no-contact policy, he enveloped me in a comforting hug. I relaxed and wanted to break out in tears all over again.

They had us in some kind of tiny interview room, void of anything except for a huge table dominating the room and two wooden chairs. Along one side, what I assumed was a two-way mirror took up half of a wall, and my disheveled reflection shone back at me. I was reminded of the interrogation room when Vincent told me not to leave town. I should've taken his request a little more seriously.

"Kimera, I'm Larry Barnes," he introduced himself as we took seats on opposite sides of the table. "I'm a member of your father's church and he's a very good friend of mine."

I probably should have known this man, and I felt guilty I didn't. "Thank you for taking this on," I said. I trusted my father's judgment. And at this point, I had no connections of my own.

"My pleasure," Larry said, patting my hand. He produced two bottles of water and sat one in front of me. Grateful, I accepted it. The liquid was a welcome refreshment after the lukewarm sewer water they were serving in here.

"I just want to go over some things with you so you know what to expect." I nodded for him to continue. "You have a bail hearing tomorrow morning. Basically the judge is going to decide if you're okay to have bail and have someone pay it so you can get out of jail until your court date. If he denies it, you'll have to remain in jail until your court date."

"Please get me out," I pleaded. The thought of spending yet another night in jail was too much to handle, let alone until my court date.

"I'm certainly going to try my best," Larry reassured me. "At this point, I don't know all the evidence the prosecutor has against you in regards to the murder charges. But for them to arrest you . . ." He trailed off and I nodded in understanding.

"Then they must have something, right?" I finished his thought and his nod was sympathetic. "But I didn't do it. I was nowhere near that area when it happened. I was at my parents' house asleep. You can ask my best friend, Adria. She was the one who dropped me off after . . ." The abortion clinic was what I wanted to reveal but instead, I just closed my mouth on that part. I knew we had some kind of attorney-client privilege, but still. This was a friend of my dad's, which made him a father figure in my eyes as well.

"I'm going to try to find out as much as possible," Larry said. "Just bear with me because I'm going to do all I can for you." I nodded, still feeling uneasy. No "you're going to get off." No promises and guarantees. I guess he didn't want to give me any false hope. I guess that was good just in case he couldn't deliver. But then I was left with this questioning uncertainty. I didn't know what was going to happen but my fate was in this man's hands.

<hr />

"Have you talked to Jahmad?" Adria asked.

My grip tightened on the phone at the mention of his name. Whether through Keon or my parents, I'm sure he had gotten the news by now.

"I can't call him, Adria," I murmured, my heart breaking at the admission. "He probably wants nothing to do with me anymore anyway."

"You don't know that."

"Can you do me a favor? Can you just please tell him I love him. And . . . I'm sorry. For what it's worth."

"Sure. I'll let him know."

The operator signaled only a minute left on the call. I always hated this part. Being cut off again from the real world and required to go back into my little cell. Now I regretted each and every time I had compared Leo's house to a prison.

"I'll see you at the hearing tomorrow," Adria promised, and I thanked her and disconnected the call. I let the officer take me back to my cell and I just stared at the cinder block wall as she slid the bars shut behind me.

Rather than lie down again, I kneeled down against the side of the cot and did something I hadn't done in a long time. I put my hands together, closed my eyes, and prayed.

Chapter 25

For the second night in a row, I hadn't had but snatches of sleep sprinkled throughout the night. But mostly I had just lain awake and listened to the night jail activity. A snore like a freight train. The jingle of keys on an officer's belt. The occasional static on a walkie-talkie.

The tears wouldn't stop pouring, and my pillow was saturated. In a few hours, I would know if I was getting out of here. That little piece of hope kept me sane.

Someone had slid me a tray of stale breakfast that smelled like rubber, which I hadn't bothered touching. So now it sat lined up across the floor next to yesterday's untouched lunch and dinner trays, attracting a small cluster of flies.

Finally, they came to take me to court. It was the same plump officer, I think they called her Harriet, and I had decided she was the only one who actually worked. She was silent as she ushered me to the shower room and stood against the door, waiting. I figured she would leave, but when she made no move from her post on the wall, I sighed and began undressing.

The water was cold, and I shivered underneath the spray. Well, I couldn't even call it an actual spray because the water pressure was so low, it did more of this staggered stream kind of thing where I had to use my hand to cup underneath and pour over the parts of my body the water was missing. I had been given a disposable wash towel and a thin bar of soap, neither one effective at its job, but I silently did the best I could as quickly as I could. If today went well, I wouldn't have to worry about these half-assed showers anymore.

I wasn't sure whether it was my lawyer, my parents, or Adria, but someone had brought a charcoal gray suit and cream blouse up to the jail for me to wear. No, it wasn't one of my designer outfits, and sure, my little pregnancy weight had the material too snug on my waist, thighs, and arms, but I was appreciative just the same. I didn't have any makeup, my hair was slick and damp from the shower, and I didn't have any kind of comb or curlers to bring it back to life. So I ran my fingers through it, slipped on my black baby-doll flats, and announced I was ready.

Cuffed, I was led outside, and I immediately took a greedy inhale of the fresh morning air. The air outside of the confines of the jail smelled and even felt different. Like inside, it had become stale and everyone was just sucking and breathing on recycled oxygen that felt entirely too thick and suffocating.

I boarded a white bus with what looked like chicken wire running across the windows. Apparently, I was the only one being transported, so Harriet sat me in the front row and closed the door that separated the seating area from the driver. She mumbled something to him, and he nodded his understanding before we were on our way.

Adria said she would be here, and I was glad. Seeing a familiar face was what I needed now more than anything. That support would give me strength. As far as my parents, I hadn't spoken to them directly. I really doubted they would come. And Jahmad. I let out a wistful sigh and glanced down at the silver cuffs binding my wrists. Part of me wanted him to come. Part of me was too embarrassed for him to see me like this.

The courthouse wasn't busy. Just officers and lawyers, and a few prisoners like myself. I kept my eyes focused ahead as we piled onto an elevator and rode it up.

As soon as the doors slid open on the third floor, my legs went slack. Adria stood with my parents and Keon talking to my lawyer. As much as my parents loved me, I sure hadn't wanted to expect their appearance today. Not after what had happened. I didn't want to get my hopes up. But sure enough, here they were, and I couldn't have needed or wanted them more.

Everyone turned as I walked down the hall, and to my amazement, my mom burst into tears. She took a step in my direction, but Larry placed a gentle hand on her shoulder to halt her movements. I wanted nothing more than to run into her arms and sob like a baby, but I just forced my lips into a thin smile and nodded my appreciation, even as the silent tears slid from the corners of my eyes.

Adria blew me a kiss, and Keon flipped me his middle finger, which was supposed to lighten the mood. It worked. A little. My smile spread and I stuck out my tongue at him. God, I loved them so much, and my heart swelled to see them standing there on my behalf. For a moment, a brief moment, my mind was distracted from the situation.

But then the officers opened the door to courtroom C3 and all of the emotions came flooding back. My hands began to sweat, and suddenly the metal of the cuffs felt too tight and began digging into my flesh.

I was led down the center aisle and took a seat behind the defendant's table as an officer removed the handcuffs. Grateful for the relief, I massaged my sore wrists. To my right, Detective Vincent Wright was giving me some kind of evil eye/smug smirk expression that heightened my anxiety. What if? What if? Larry sat down directly next to me and popped open his briefcase on the table.

"You okay?" he asked, though we both knew the answer to that.

"As well as can be expected," I said.

"You want some water?" He didn't wait for a response as he poured some into a glass from the pitcher on the table and I gingerly took a sip. It didn't taste the best, but then again I think everything left a bad taste in my mouth. I sat the cup back down on the table.

"Anything new?" I asked.

"I'm working on it," Larry assured me. "I know it's hard but please just be strong, Kimera." He then glanced down at my stomach. "You're pregnant?" I nodded. "How far along are you?"

Good question. I really had no idea. I thought back to when I first discovered I was pregnant and then the significant milestone after that. Though I'm sure it was on some file at the abortion clinic and at the hospital when I'd been admitted, both times I had been so spaced out I couldn't seem to remember what, if anything, anyone told me about my pregnancy progression. "I guess about three or four months," I estimated, though I had no idea how accurate that was. I looked and felt like I had already been carrying the baby for a year.

Larry nodded and scribbled on a sheet of paper.

"We are going to have faith," he assured me. "God will work this out." I certainly hoped so. Lord knows I had been talking to him more in these past forty-eight hours than I probably had all my life.

I glanced back to the rows of courtroom benches behind me. Adria, my brother, and my parents sat in one row. I wouldn't admit it but I was actually looking for Jahmad. I guess he really had washed his hands of me.

The doors swung open, and my eyes widened in surprise when I saw Tina breeze in. Of course she was primped and glossed like a new magazine cover as she took a seat toward the back and lifted a hesitant hand in greeting when our eyes met. I smiled and waved back. Tina, of all people, was the absolute last person I expected to see. But I was grateful for her presence just the same.

Adria followed my gaze and looked back, only to roll her eyes and turn back around with a frown. No, she had never met Tina but I was positive she knew exactly who she was.

"All rise for the Honorable Judge Edward Brown presiding."

Larry helped me to my feet as a short, balding, white judge entered from his chambers. He took his seat and we all followed suit.

I listened intently as my charges were read. First-degree murder. If I hadn't already been sitting, I would have crumpled to the floor. I concentrated on taking slow breaths like Adria had said. I concentrated on my baby.

"Your Honor, we propose to deny bail." The district attorney had identified herself as Pamela Mays. Apparently a real hardass. "Ms. Davis has been arrested for murder and poses a flight risk."

"Your Honor, my client poses no flight risk," Larry jumped in, gesturing in my direction. "Not only is she pregnant but she has no resources at her disposal to even attempt to flee."

"Ms. Davis has plenty of money in accounts—"

"That have all been frozen," Larry interrupted. "Your Honor. My client is pregnant and needs access to quality prenatal care. She has no liquid assets at this time because everything is tied up in this litigation. Plus her father is a pastor at a prominent church here in the city. She comes from a good, stable environment and that is where she needs to be, given the severity of these allegations. For her health and the health of her baby."

The prosecutor didn't seem to have any comeback for that, and I looked to the judge, praying that he agreed. He seemed to be pondering Larry's words and finally he sighed.

"I concur. I don't believe Ms. Davis presents any kind of flight risk, and given her delicate state, I'm granting your request, counselor. Bail is set at six hundred thousand dollars." My mouth dropped open as he brought down the gavel.

I didn't know whether I should be happy about the bail or pissed at the amount. Six hundred thousand dollars would've been nothing for me had I had access to all of my money. But much to my surprise, Larry had informed me that they were conducting a thorough investigation into my financials, given Leo's wealth and my inheritance.

Larry turned with an accomplished smile, his eyebrows drawing together at my stunned expression. "Hey, you've been granted bail. That's great news."

"Great?" I felt sick to my stomach. "Six hundred thousand dollars is not great news. I don't have that kind of money right now."

Larry glanced behind me, and I turned to follow his look.

My dad reached out and to my surprise, he pulled me in for a hug. I immediately relaxed in his arms. "It's okay, baby girl," he murmured, his voice muffled against my hair. "We got you. We all got you."

I released the breath that had settled into my chest and just let the tears flow. It felt good. It felt safe. I still had a long road to go to prove my innocence, but for now, I felt like I was okay in this very moment. And I was grateful.

I sniffed and glanced up with a watery smile. Tears blurred my vision but I was still able to make out Jahmad's back as he retreated from the courtroom.

Chapter 26

I stepped out of the car, struggling to calm my nerves.

It had been three days since I had been bailed out of jail and at first it seemed surreal. Being back in my own bed, eating my mom's food, and I know I was taking three and four showers a day just to scrub the stench of jail off of my skin. I hated that my parents had to refinance the house plus take out a loan using the church as collateral. The guilt still ate at me every time I thought about it. That's why I swore I was going to pay them back every red cent as soon as I beat this charge.

As soon as instead of *if*. I couldn't afford to think negatively. Especially since Larry had helped me get out on bail. Plus, he kept saying that he was "working on a big part of the case." Whatever that meant. But whatever it was, I trusted him whole-heartedly.

I was dressed comfortably today in some leggings and a blue jean shirtdress with my baby-doll flats. The air had a little chill and made me wish I had opted for my jacket as well. But I had been in a rush for this and hadn't bothered. Now, whether it was the wind or my nerves, I felt a slight trembling and had to hug myself as I started across the parking lot.

I saw Jahmad before he saw me. He sat on a bench directly outside of the door, his body slightly shadowed by an overhanging tree.

As soon as he heard me approaching, he took his time unfolding himself from the seat and stood up, shoving his hands in his jacket pockets.

He stared at me, and I knew he wanted to go ahead and get whatever it was off of his chest. But we had agreed to lunch right after the doctor's appointment so he merely greeted me with a stiff "hey" instead.

"How are you?" I asked, the tension making this conversation even more awkward.

"Good. You?"

"Good."

"And the baby?"

Instinctively, my hand flew to my stomach to rub the underside. "Strong."

Jahmad nodded, his face remaining expressionless. When he made no move to speak further, I added, "Thank you, Jahmad. For coming."

He nodded again and gestured toward the door. "Shall we?"

I led the way up the walk, and we entered the ob-gyn building. This was a new doctor Adria had helped me find as soon as I was released from jail. Larry mentioned I needed to get care as soon as possible not only to help strengthen his bail request argument but also because I needed it. I agreed. I hadn't received any kind of medical attention since the hospital when the abortion infection nearly took my ass out. So much had been going on since then, but I knew I couldn't keep getting so wrapped up in my situation I ignored the health and well-being of my child. That's why I set up an appointment with Dr. Asad as soon as I saw she was accepting new patients. And I got up the nerve to ask Jahmad to accompany me.

He didn't say anything else to me up until the point I was lying on the bed in the ultrasound room, the paper gown I had changed into causing the room's draft to chill my body. I shifted uncomfortably as he just sat on the stool across the room, fiddling with something on his phone. I sighed. I was hoping he would be excited to accompany me to see the baby, but he was acting like he wanted to be anywhere but here. I was already dreading the conversation over lunch.

Dr. Asad was a young, petite Indian woman with a long braid that ran the length of her back. She knocked on the door before entering and sailed into the room with a bright smile.

"Ms. Davis, it's a pleasure to meet you." She extended her hand and gave me a firm handshake that I didn't expect for a woman her size.

"Thank you for seeing me on such short notice," I said.

"My pleasure. I'm always excited to meet new patients." She turned to Jahmad. "And is this Daddy?"

Jahmad didn't readily answer, so I quickly jumped in, embarrassed by his silence. "Yes, it is." Of course, I still didn't know for sure but I was holding firm to my faith at this point.

Dr. Asad nodded, no doubt to cover up the sudden awkwardness. "Good to meet you both. Now let's get started."

Dr. Asad lathered up my stomach with the warming gel and began maneuvering the probe on my belly. Just like before, the baby's rapid heartbeat echoed in the room and I angled my head to look at the screen. The baby's figure was distinct, a white mass that outlined the head and body and even the flickering heartbeat on the display.

"Baby looks good," Dr. Asad commented. She started clicking on the keyboard and a whirring sound signaled a printer taking pictures.

"Girl or boy?" I asked anxiously.

Dr. Asad shifted the probe again and looked closer at the image. "The baby doesn't seem to be in the right position for me to tell," she concluded. "But we can try again next visit if you really want to know."

I turned to Jahmad, surprised when he was directly beside me, leaning over the bed to get a good look at the screen. A smile flirted at his lips, and I could see the love overflowing in his eyes. His hand was an inch from mine and, without thinking, I placed mine on top. Thankfully, he didn't move it.

———— ⊳•⊲ ————

Jahmad picked out a local pizza restaurant not far from the doctor's office. It wasn't quite lunchtime so the place hadn't gotten too busy just yet.

I selected a booth in the back while Jahmad placed our orders at the counter. Waiting on him, I pulled out the ultrasound printout and allowed the overwhelming emotions to consume me as I scrutinized the pictures once again. My baby was perfect. How could I have ever wanted to get rid of him? Dr. Asad said it was too soon, but I knew in my heart of hearts it was a boy. Jamaal. I had already decided.

"Think they gave us enough pictures?" Jahmad slid into the booth opposite me and gestured to the roll of pictures I was holding.

"There's no such thing as too many," I said. "We have to start a baby book."

Jahmad didn't respond. He just began unloading the tray of the pizza slices and drinks he had purchased for us.

I'm sure the pizza was good but I surely couldn't taste it. My mind kept wandering to Jahmad. The silence was killing me. I took one bite before I sighed, put down my slice, and pushed my plate away. "Honestly, Jay, I don't have an appetite," I admitted. "Not until we talk about us and where we are going from here."

Jahmad sighed and took a sip of his Coke. "And where do you expect us to go, Kimera? Honestly? How am I supposed to feel?"

I lifted my hand to show him the engagement ring that I still wore proudly. "I want you, Jahmad," I said, looking him dead in the eye. I wanted him to feel every ounce of passion that I felt for him. "I love you with everything in me and I know you still love me too. So I want us to get through this together."

Jahmad stared at me, his face unreadable. "I can't trust you," he said finally. "You were married while you were seeing me. You lied to me, Kimera. I honestly don't know how I feel about you right now, but I don't think we can come back from this."

I squeezed my eyes shut. That certainly was not what I wanted to hear. "Jahmad, please. It's not like that. I've always loved you. The timing was just bad and I got in over my head. I'm sorry."

"You lied to me. That shit was foul."

"But you had CeeCee," I murmured, trying my best to deflect the situation. "You weren't exactly single yourself."

"Hell no, you're not putting this shit on me," Jahmad fumed. "I left her to be with you. Not once was I with her and leading you on. That's the fucked-up part. I kept it straight up with you the entire time."

Shame had me lowering my head. He wasn't yelling or even cursing me out. He was actually a lot calmer than I expected. Calmer than I would have been. And that alone scared me even more. That meant he had thought long and hard about his feelings, and his words were stabbing my heart more than anything. I had hurt him. Bad.

"What can I do, Jahmad?" I looked up at him, pleading. I hadn't noticed I was crying until I felt the first few tears drip down my face and neck.

He looked away then, his face wrinkled in angry disgust. "Don't pull that crying shit," he hissed. "Don't act like you're the victim in all of this."

I used the back of my hand to wipe my face. "Just please. Think about it. Think about our baby."

"Is it even mine, Kimera?" he snapped. His words and tone were suddenly clipped with restrained anger. "I mean you and ole boy were fucking, weren't you?"

The lie fell from my lips before I even had time to process it. "No, that's not what we were doing. He had his wives for that. One just had a baby by him and the other I caught fucking all over the damn house." Always sandwich the lie with the truth. It made it that much more believable. And the image of seeing Tina sucking Leo off in the office still burned in my mind. So at least that much was true.

I hated having to lie to him but I needed this man in my life like I needed air. I had done so much to get and keep him, I couldn't lose him like this.

Jahmad looked doubtful. I waited, praying silently. *Lord God, if you can get me and Jahmad through this I'll never lie to him again about anything else. I swear. Amen.*

"I don't trust you, Kimera." Jahmad said again. "I'll always love you and you know I'll always be here for you. But this. This I can't deal with. You made me look like a damn idiot. And for what?" He waited, as if he really expected me to answer his rhetorical question.

"I love you," I whispered. "I need you. We need you."

Jahmad rose, leaving his meal barely touched. "Is it possible?" he asked. "Any possibility this baby is not mine?"

"It's yours," I emphasized firmly. I needed it to be Jahmad's. It had to be.

Without another word, Jahmad left the restaurant, and the loneliness had me crying all over again.

Chapter 27

Shock couldn't even begin to describe what I was feeling.

My fingers trembled on the page as I looked at the file Larry had just passed across the table to me.

The first-degree murder charges were bad enough, but apparently their main evidence was my blood found in the vehicle that had hit Leo's limo. That part I already knew, though it still didn't make sense. I hadn't been anywhere near the scene of the crime that night. I had been sleeping off the effects of the medication I had received for the abortion.

I looked at the crime scene photos, the close-ups of the damaged cars, the shattered glass, and the dried residue of blood, my blood they said, on the dash and steering wheel of a Jeep Cherokee. The fear had returned. It seemed pretty damn convicting to me.

"The prosecutor's case is that it was intentional," Larry went on, looking at notes. "That you premeditated and intentionally sought out to kill him that night. You ran the vehicle off the road to cause the accident. Then you shot at him with a nine-millimeter revolver."

Larry pointed to a picture of the gun in the brush and leaves on an embankment floor.

"So wait." I frowned at the new information. "Leo was shot?"

"There were no bullet wounds," Larry said. "But the fact that this gun was found with a few shell casings at the crime scene led them to believe perhaps you were trying to shoot at him. Maybe you heard someone coming and drove off."

"I don't even own a gun," I insisted, shutting my eyes against the image. "I've never shot a gun in my life."

"It was found at the scene," Larry said. "With your fingerprints on it."

I sat back and let out a quivering sigh. It just kept getting worse. Larry reached across the kitchen table to give my hand a comforting pat.

I glanced to my parents sitting next to me. As promised, they remained quiet, apparently just taking all of the news in as much in disbelief as I was.

"But why would I do this?" I asked more to myself. "Don't I need some kind of motive or something? Or are they saying I snapped?"

"Of course, money. That's always a go-to motive. You wanted your inheritance as outlined in the will. It didn't help that he had just changed his will to give you a good chunk of money."

"I know. Twenty-five percent."

Leo shook his head. "No, well, more than that. More like seventy-five percent."

I frowned. "No, that's not what the lawyer said before. He changed his will? Why?" And why had the lawyer said otherwise?

"I don't have the answers to any of this," Larry said, running his hands over his face wearily. He looked like this was taking as big a toll on him as it was on me. "So, I think we need to work out some angles. Did Leo ever hit you? Any kind of abuse whatsoever?"

"Wait, wait, wait." Now my mother did speak up, her hand in the air to pause the conversation. "Are you trying to go with self-defense? Wouldn't that mean she did it?"

"Well—"

"Because my daughter didn't kill any damn body, Larry."

I looked to my mother, struggling to contain her rage. And she surely was angry for her to have cursed.

"She's right," I murmured. "I didn't kill Leo or Eddie. Not in self-defense or anything else."

"Did he put his hands on you, baby girl?" my dad asked, worry creasing his brow. "Be honest, if it happened, then it happened."

"It doesn't matter." Frustration had my voice on edge. "Leo could have beat me 'til I was black and blue every night. I still wouldn't have killed him." I turned back to Larry. "Is that my only hope? Is there anything else we can do?"

Larry drummed his fingers on the table. "Someone owes me a favor. I have something else in mind. It's just a theory but maybe there's something there."

"Great. What is it?"

"I'll let you know when I have more information," Larry said. "I would hate to get your hopes up. You went to the doctor the other day, right?"

I sighed at his weak attempt to distract me. Maybe it was for the best to get off this subject. I could feel my blood pressure rising anyway.

"Yes, I went."

"And how was it? How far along are you?"

"Five months."

"Congratulations. Do you have any ultrasound pictures?"

I nodded and stood to retrieve the images from my purse. My phone was vibrating. Eager, I looked to see if it was Jahmad. My face fell at the unknown number. Damn, he hadn't bothered to return my phone calls yet. My hope for us was slowly diminishing.

I brought the pictures back to Larry, whose grin spread.

"Aw, boy or girl?"

"I don't know yet."

"Well, he or she is going to be big. I've got two grandchildren myself."

I nodded absently. I appreciated his small talk but my mind

was running wild from all the information he had just laid out to me. My hope for my freedom was starting to diminish as well.

> *The tickle of a whisper against her ear*
> *The faint caress of his fingertips*
> *The love glittering in his eyes*
> *The urgency on his tongue*
> *She's dreaming while she's awake*
> *He's in pain while his love is strong*
> *Their heart is joined as one*
> *Their love laced with the pain that often comes*
> *The feeling of love*
> *The love of feeling*
> *Apart they grow, yet together at last*
> *The heart's company.*

I looked up from Lena's journal, her words as clear as if she had spoken them aloud. Amazing how someone who knew absolutely nothing about me could describe my own emotions so perfectly.

I really hadn't meant to keep reading through her personal business, but I found solace in Lena's heart. And she did indeed write from her heart. She brought me comfort. Much of which I needed.

In the last month, I'd had a few more conversations with my lawyer, but nothing that eased my fears. Most of the time he called he spoke to my dad, both feeding me words of encouragement so as not to stress me out, I'm sure. But the not knowing was stressing me out even more. I was lapping into six months of pregnancy with my trial date inching closer. Between my mother getting every prayer circle involved and my worry sending me into fits of depressed exhaustion, there wasn't much I could do now except wait. And hope. But mostly wait. Which was one reason why I engrossed myself in Lena's words. She was my escape.

Lena always started her diary entries with a poem before going into her thoughts for the evening. She had written every night up until three days before she died. I was in the last entry.

She had spoken heavily of Tina being a bitch—that part had me laughing out loud—her love for Leo, well, not love in the intimate sense but more deep admiration and appreciation. She talked about Leo and Tina's arguments; apparently they had begun to have them every night. She spoke a lot about her anxiety about the baby because she wanted so badly to be a good mother. And she had mentioned me. Said she liked me. Was concerned for me. I didn't know what I had done to prompt her concern but she obviously had a lot of feelings she kept to herself.

It's raining again. I always love the rain. It calms me and calms the baby. And I really need calming now. Not sure what it is but I've been having terrible nightmares lately. And they are scaring me.

Something feels off between Leo and Tina. They're not even speaking today after arguing about Kimera again all last night. Leo has shut himself off in his office and he's not talking. Not even to Leo Jr. And he's made a habit of talking to the baby and rubbing on my stomach every chance he gets. I think he's planning on going away for a while. He's on the phone all the time making some kind of plans with somebody. I wonder if he has another woman he wants to bring into the relationship. I don't know how many more of them I can take, lol.

Short entry tonight. I got to go. I've been feeling so sick lately so Dr. Lin is coming to see about me in the morning. Good night for now.

I frowned, turning the page as if expecting to see more. But the rest of the pages were completely empty. That was it. That was the last thing Lena wrote. A few things she mentioned did linger in my mind. Arguing about me again? Why were they arguing about me?

My phone startled me from my little reflection. I swiped the screen to view the incoming text message.

KIMERA.

That's all it said. I frowned when I didn't recognize the number. I typed back.

WHO IS THIS?
DR. LIN.

My frown deepened. Dr. Lin?

WHY ARE YOU TEXTING ME?
YOU'RE IN TROUBLE. I THINK I CAN HELP. COME SEE ME TO-
MORROW. 7280 CAMBLETON DR.

I started to type a response but instead I dialed the number. If he thought he could help, why wait until tomorrow when we could talk now?

"The number you have dialed is not accepting calls at this time." I hung up, puzzled. I was not sure what was going on but I guessed I would find out the next day.

Chapter 28

"I think I should come with you," Adria said as she leaned against the doorway of my bedroom. I shook my head as I shoved my legs into a pair of sweats. This belly of mine along with these thighs had me giving up on jeans altogether. They were just too uncomfortable.

"Why do you say that?"

"Because I want to be there for support. We don't know what the hell is going on."

I chuckled and pulled the matching sweatshirt down over my head. The bagginess just barely seemed to hide my stomach. At first glance, folks would think that my ass was just fat. Not six months pregnant. Not that I was trying to hide it or anything. I was actually getting excited about the baby as the days wore on.

The text from Dr. Lin had been strange but this just might be the lifeline I needed to keep me out of jail. He must have known something else about that night. The circumstances surrounding Leo's murder were a mystery, and the uncertainty was making me uneasy. I had not only me to think about. But my family. My baby. Jahmad. I couldn't let anything happen to any of them. It wasn't enough to scare me into leaving or doing anything drastic. But it was enough to have me taking the necessary precautions. And it could be over after this. But for some reason, that thought wasn't as comforting because it hardly seemed possible. But I still held out hope.

"You know this whole situation is freaking me out," I said, my eyes darting around the floor for my shoes. "But what else am I supposed to do, Adria? Really?"

"Have me go with you. Or Jahmad. Keon. Somebody."

"I don't think all of that is necessary." To do all of that seemed like overreacting, and I surely didn't want to make this situation any messier. He might not be so willing to divulge important information if I had Adria with me. And as far as Jahmad or Keon? Completely out of the question.

Adria pursed her lips and instead of watching me struggle, she entered the room and grabbed my shoes from underneath the bed. I was so grateful when she kneeled down in front of me and helped me put them on. Lord knows I was in no condition to lean over and put them on myself.

"Thank you," I said with a smile. "And listen, I appreciate your concern. I want you to go, I do. But I think it's best if I go alone."

Adria nodded. "I'm not going to lie. Part of me just wants to see what this joker has to say. Maybe then I'll be able to understand this foolishness. Maybe it's something you could miss."

"Trust me. I want to, too. And don't worry. If I need to, I'll dial out to you or record it or something."

Adria laughed. "On some *Charlie's Angels*-type shit. Yeah, do that."

"Well it's only two of us, so we'll have to make do," I teased.

Adria stood, fidgeting with her fingers. It was more than obvious she had something else to say. "What?" I prompted.

"Well, Keon and I talked," she started, nerves having her eyes downcast to the floor. "I think—well, *we* think we are going to try to work on something between us."

I nodded, waited for something else, but when she made no move to speak further, I let out a chuckle. "Okay and?"

Adria seemed surprised. "And? What else do you want?"

"Adria, are you really asking me for my blessing? For you and my brother to make it official?"

Her nod was slight and she took a breath. "You're my best friend," she said. "I just don't want anything to come between us. Not even your brother. So if you don't approve—"

"Stop it." I stood now and embraced her in a hug. "If there was any woman my brother deserved, it's you. You just need to put his crazy ass on a leash or something. He already knows if he hurts you, it's on."

Adria relaxed into a laugh. "I'm so glad you're not mad. After everything that has been happening, we just kind of wanted to seize the opportunity, you know. Life is so short."

I nodded at how true that was. I was proud of my girl for going for her happiness. Lord knows she deserved it. I just wished Jahmad and I could get back to our happy place as well.

I tried my best to be discreet in looking at my phone but I was clearly waiting on a notification. Jahmad hadn't called. I wondered if this whole thing was too much for him to handle. Our relationship was strained, which was another reason why I was praying this baby would be our fix. I needed him. Hell, everything I went through was for him. Otherwise, I could have sat back and acted as the dutiful Mrs. Owusu without complicating the situation.

I would have been stupid to think he would have just picked us up where we left off. As if none of this had happened. And it was way too much unfinished business. I still had a trial coming up in a few weeks.

———◆◆———

The GPS directions led me to a quaint subdivision where the houses were small but separated by acreage and lush foliage. I expected more from Dr. Lin. Perhaps something as lavish as the Lake Spivey mansion Leo had purchased. I guess not everyone was into the flash, glitz, and glam that came with long money.

236 / BRIANA COLE

I slowed and wheeled my car into the driveway of one of the one-story homes on the cul-de-sac, right behind a glistening white Range Rover that appeared out of place against the older model homes with aged wood paneling and jutting roofs.

It was beginning to get dark, and the first few pellets of rain dampened my skin as I stepped from my car and made my way up the walk.

To my surprise, the front door was propped open with a box, and I stepped inside to see more packing boxes strewn all over the room.

The house was minimally decorated with just the bare essentials, I noticed. An L-shaped chocolate couch dominated the living room, big-screen TV mounted on a black TV stand, and a coffee table. No decorations, no expensive furnishings.

Not a soul was in sight, so I made my way to the back where the faint noise was coming from.

"Dr. Lin?" I called.

Silence. Then the man peeped his head into the hallway, his eyes large and curious behind his thin frames.

"Kimera." He let out a nervous laugh. "I wasn't expecting you."

"You weren't? You texted me and told me to come by." I gestured toward the boxes littering the floor. "Moving?"

"Um." Dr. Lin walked into the hallway, rubbing his hands on his jeans. "Yeah. It's time for a little change. After Leo, you know . . ." He trailed off and readjusted his glasses.

"What about the practice?"

"I'll be closing that as well." He looked at my pregnant belly and I could've sworn I saw his face pale a few shades. "C-congratulations," he stuttered, nodding toward my stomach. "I didn't know you were . . ." He cleared his throat and said, "So what are you doing here, Kimera? How did you get my address?"

"You texted me," I reminded him. "Last night. Told me to meet you so we can talk."

Dr. Lin's face wrinkled in confusion.

"You said you maybe could help me," I pressed. Was the man crazy?

"I didn't text you, and I certainly don't see how I could help you," he said quickly and turned away.

"Dr. Lin, please," I begged. "I'm about to go on trial for murder. I can't go to jail for something I didn't do."

Dr. Lin sighed but didn't turn around to face me. His shoulders fell and he lowered his head. "Kimera, please just go. There is nothing I can do."

"Then why would you tell me you could help me?" I was damn near in tears. For just a brief moment, I thought Dr. Lin was my answer. My hopes were up. I was banking he would be my saving grace.

Instead of responding, he ignored me and pulled out his cell phone. He disappeared into a room and slammed the door behind him, murmuring inaudibly to someone on the other end of the call.

Dejected, I turned and headed back toward the front door. I was no better off than when I had first gotten tangled in this mess. But if not Dr. Lin, who the hell had sent me the strange text message last night?

My phone rang as soon as I got back to the car. I started not to answer, but immediately changed my mind when I saw who it was. I stayed parked as I swiped the screen to pick up the call.

"Hello?"

"Kimera, it's Larry." His voice was eager. "I've got some news I wanted to share."

I caught the blinds flicker somewhere inside Dr. Lin's house. Was he watching me?

"What kind of news?" I asked, eyeing the window more closely.

"The more I thought about it, the more I started thinking about your blood. You would've been pregnant at the time of the murder. So I had some tests run on the blood found in the truck."

I listened closely, still not understanding. "But we already determined it was my blood in the truck, remember?"

"Yes, it's yours for sure. But the blood didn't contain any hCG. Meaning it was your blood from when you weren't pregnant."

My breath quickened as I put two and two together. "So that doesn't add up."

"Exactly. So that blood was obviously planted. So that now begs the question, who would have ounces of your blood in order to place it in the truck?"

My eyes widened as the final piece clicked into place. I looked again at the house. Dr. Lin was now standing at the door, not at all hiding the fact that he was staring with a gun pointed at me through the windshield.

Chapter 29

I swallowed, frozen in place at the realization. "Larry, can you please come to 7280 Cambleton Drive? I know who did it."

"What? Who? Kimera, are you safe? Get out of there."

Dr. Lin was now walking toward the car. My first thought was to crank it up and flip it into drive but for some reason, I remained still. The only thing on my mind was that damn gun and how, at any moment, I would see a bullet shattering my window before splitting a hole through my chest.

He beckoned me to get out, and I slowly pulled the phone from my ear and slid it into my pocket, still hearing Larry shouting commands through the receiver. Hopefully, they could track me or something.

I opened the door, lifting my hands in the air. "Dr. Lin—"

"Don't speak," he said, his voice shaky. He was obviously as nervous as I felt. Even his hand shook on the gun, and that scared me even more. "Just come inside. You wanted to talk. Let's talk."

The cylinder impression of the gun's barrel bored into the small of my back as we walked toward the house. Once inside, Dr. Lin closed the door and glanced out of the window before ushering me to the couch.

"Why are you doing this?" I asked, already feeling the fearful tears swell in my eyes. My only hope now was to stall until Larry got there. Larry, the police, somebody.

"Who told you to come here?" Dr. Lin asked, still aiming the gun at me. He used his other hand to loosen his shirt, and I saw the first few beads of sweat pepper his forehead.

"You did."

"Stop lying for her."

He was yelling now, and I just pursed my lips, unsure of what he wanted me to say. I kept my eyes on his trigger finger trembling on the gun.

"It's too much of a coincidence that you're here," he rattled on, shaking his head at his own thoughts. "It's not supposed to be like this. Why are you pregnant?"

I doubted if he really wanted me to answer that. Dr. Lin seemed to be in his own world, alternating between mumbling to himself and yelling at me as if I could give better clarity on the situation.

"Why are you framing me?" I whispered, hugging myself to keep from shaking.

Dr. Lin's eyes seemed sorrowful for a moment before he turned away, his arms by his sides. At least he wasn't pointing the gun at me anymore. "I'm sorry," he said. "I didn't want to. I just needed the money. I never meant to hurt you. Or Lena."

Lena? My mind flipped back to the pages of her journal that I had just read. He had come to visit her a few days before she went into labor. "You hurt Lena?" His silence answered my question, and I gasped. "But how? Why?"

"I just gave her a little medicine to induce the labor," he admitted. "It wasn't supposed to kill her, I swear. That wasn't me."

Somewhere far off in the distance, I thought I heard the sound of sirens, though I couldn't be entirely sure. I prayed they were headed this way. *Just keep talking to him, Kimmy,* I instructed myself. *Don't panic.*

"But Leo was your friend," I mumbled, watching him pace the floor. "Your friend. How could you—"

"You don't know what it's like being in my line of work," he snapped, waving the gun for emphasis. "The long hours. The stress. I started drinking and even gambling to take the edge off. It was supposed to be all in fun. Nothing serious. Until it became a problem. Had to borrow money. Pinch and scrimp just to get by. I got in way over my head. I needed the money." He turned to me, his eyes almost begging me for understanding. Or maybe it was forgiveness. I couldn't really tell. "Don't you see? It was never about you. At least not for me. It wasn't personal. But you were my only hope."

"I don't understand. Why me? Why frame me? How was that going to help you while I rot in jail?"

A door slammed right outside the house, and I held my breath, watching Dr. Lin's reaction. He heard it too, because he shook his head as if he was too exhausted to fight anymore. Even his sigh was heavy with regret. And acceptance. He lifted the gun, a single tear trailing down his cheek.

"I'm so sorry, Kimera," he whispered. "Please forgive me." I screamed as his finger pulled back to squeeze the trigger, and a single shot echoed in the air.

Chapter 30

I screamed. I was still screaming when I felt someone's hands on my shoulders, shaking me to calm me down.

"He shot himself," I sputtered. I couldn't help but look at the body angled in the corner between the wall and the front doorway. Blood and brain matter were splattered on the walls behind him and his face, oh God, his face was frozen in horror and held the empty eyes of death. That look would forever be ingrained in my mind. I couldn't stop myself. I fell to my knees and threw up everything but my child.

I was shivering and my throat burned from the stomach acid that was now staining the plush carpet. I heard the water run and a cold compress was put to the back of neck, the shock of the cold water startling a gasp from my lips.

I saw the Gucci sneakers first. Sneakers I didn't recognize but I was pretty certain I knew who they belonged to just because of the brand. My eyes lifted to Tina.

She looked different. Her face was more chiseled, like she had lost some weight. Her hair, though, was just as dramatic as she usually wore it, this time in a bone-straight wig with a razor bang.

"Shit, Kimera, are you okay?"

I was surprised. Never had I heard so much concern directed at me from her. I gave a hesitant nod, my teeth now chattering from either the aftershock or the cold, wet cloth on the back of my neck. "We need to call the police," I stuttered through clenched teeth.

Tina helped me to my feet and onto the couch behind me. "What happened?" she asked, sitting beside me. I could tell she was making a huge effort not to look in the direction of Dr. Lin's corpse.

"He did it," I murmured, still shaking my head in disbelief. "Dr. Lin killed Leo."

She frowned. "Dr. Lin? Where did you get that from?"

"He admitted it to me. Right before he . . ." I gagged, feeling a fresh bout of nausea rising.

Tina's mouth dropped and she shook her head. "That's not true."

"I got a text from him last night," I explained. "He wanted to meet me to talk about everything. Said maybe he could help me. When I got here, he acted like he didn't even send me the text. Then, he just kind of told me that he did it for money because of some gambling problem. And he killed Lena."

Tina leaned her elbows on her knees as she seemed to be pondering my words. "I just don't get it," she murmured, as if to herself. "None of this makes any sense." I watched her eyes glance toward Dr. Lin's body before flicking back to me. "Does any of this make sense to you?"

There was something about the question that sent a shudder up my spine. She didn't seem surprised. Why didn't she seem surprised? I swallowed on a frown and gave a slight shake of my head. For some reason, Tina was no longer looking as perplexed. No, that confusion had been replaced with something else. Something unreadable.

"What else did Dr. Lin say?" she asked, angling her head to one side as if to study my response.

Something wasn't right. Somehow, the tension in the room had heightened. Plus, that strange way Tina was looking at me was

244 / BRIANA COLE

making me wish I had taken Adria up on her offer. Suddenly, being alone with this woman seemed dangerous.

Think, Kimmy, think. A flood of excuses swarmed my mind as I struggled to pick the best one to use as a scapegoat. I rose from the couch, feeling the strain in my back with the gesture. Instinctively, my hand flew to rest underneath the pudge in my stomach. Tina's eyes followed my movement. A frown flickered across her face so fast I had to question if I had even seen it. What the hell was going on?

"I'm going to call the police." I didn't realize I had whispered the statement.

"What?"

"We need to call the police," I reiterated, a little more forceful. My attempt at being calm was weak as hell as I began to back toward the kitchen. "They need to come do a report or something. We just witnessed a suicide." Dr. Lin's body was laid out in front of the door. My only prayer was that there was a back door somewhere. Or a window I could get out of.

"Sit down, Kimera."

I kept moving, this time a little more quickly.

"Kimera." Her tone had lowered, more threatening. Menacing. She continued to stare me down, as if daring me to try something. I did.

I spun around and nearly stumbled over myself as I ran toward the kitchen. Sure enough, a door was on the other side of the galley. I caught a glimpse of the backyard grass through the window.

A single bullet splattered the wood of the door not even five inches from my head. I screamed and ducked, expecting the gunfire to riddle my body. But except for my panting roaring in my ears, there was nothing but silence.

"You may want to have a seat, Kimera." Tina's command had me risking a peek in her direction. She now stood next to Dr. Lin's body, his gun clutched in her fingers.

Chapter 31

Déjà vu was all I could think as I stood still, not moving a muscle. "I asked you nicely." The corners of Tina's lips turned up as she gestured with the gun to the sofa.

I lifted my hands up, palms out, and obediently eased away from the door. Fear gripped my vocal cords as I watched the gun focused intently on me. I squeezed my eyes shut, my mouth already moving in a prayer that this woman didn't feel anxious and pull the trigger. Again. The bullet hole in the door flashed through my mind and I could only think if it had been a few more inches to the left, that would have been my skull. A shuddering sigh seeped from my lips. That made this all the more nerve-racking. Not knowing if and when any second was going to be my last. This was different than with Dr. Lin. I knew Tina, and I knew she wouldn't think twice about shooting me.

"Tina." I didn't even recognize my own voice as it came out in a hesitant whisper. "Please."

"Just shut the hell up," she snapped. Irritation laced her words but her demeanor was calm. Entirely too calm. The only outward display of tension was her visibly tight grip on the gun she still had aimed at me. She was dressed in all black so she almost looked like a shadow as she remained motionless.

I chanced lifting my eyes from the weapon to train them on

her. They say only psychos could shoot someone making eye contact. And despite this whole ordeal, I prayed like hell that this chick wasn't as psycho as she seemed.

"Just put the gun down," I pleaded, my hands up, palms out. "Let's talk about this."

"You should be in jail." Her words were accusatory. She shook her head, her lips peeled down into a frown. "All the evidence points to you."

My breath caught when her finger flinched on the trigger. "Tina," I tried again. "Please just put the gun down."

Tina's eyes narrowed as if she were struggling with something. To my surprise, she tossed her head back and let out a laugh. "You just couldn't leave well enough alone, could you?" she said and shook her head at the rhetorical question. Her obvious amusement only increased my anxiety. "The shit was perfect. Foolproof. And you just had to go fuck it up."

It was her. I should have known. I shook my head, already trying to deny whatever the hell she thought I had done, but she lifted the gun to my head and immediately I froze.

"Can you really be that stupid?" she said. "You haven't caught on to anything yet, Kimmy? Really?"

I kept my mouth shut, not sure if I needed to open it and reveal that yes, I was indeed that stupid because I should have picked up on this a long time ago.

"It was a setup," Tina said. "The whole thing. You, Lena, Leo, all of it."

So she was in on it with Dr. Lin. Damn.

"Exactly," she said as if reading the montage of thoughts that played across my face. "But I really hope you didn't think that Dr. Lin was smart enough to pull this shit off without me. He was just going to get a cut. But I still didn't think anyone else would figure that out. Hell, your blood and prints were all over the vehicle thanks to him. Remember he did all of that blood work and testing on you for no reason other than I asked him to? I needed your DNA at the scene."

I shook my head, still trying to make sense of the revelation. The pieces didn't fit. How could she have been behind the whole thing and I not have known? The swell of nausea rose in my throat and I had to swallow just to keep from throwing all of my stomach's contents on the plush carpet once more.

"So . . ." I paused to take a breath and leaned forward to place my hands on my knees. "So you killed Leo?"

Tina's shoulders lifted in a nonchalant shrug. "I wouldn't say *killed* per se. Arranged, maybe. I definitely don't have the guts to do that myself. I loved Leo. Still do."

"Then how . . . ?" I was near panting now. Passing out wouldn't be good. I needed to stay conscious. I needed answers. I needed to stay alive. At least until . . . hell, when? Someone heard us? Doubtful. Someone came looking for me? Equally doubtful. My panic was rising by degrees. Would I really make it out of this one?

"You know I never liked you, right?" Tina said as if the statement was obvious. "From the time Leo started hanging out with you, I knew I didn't like you. You see, Leo was content with me since our marriage was arranged. But I loved him with every fiber of my being. But you, you he really loved. You were just too dumb to see it or, hell, even appreciate it. And when Leo confessed he was thinking of leaving me, leaving this whole marriage because he was suddenly *unhappy*, changing his will and shit to give you a greater percentage of what he owed me, well, I just knew that wasn't going to happen."

"But you said you loved him."

"That's right. But if I couldn't have him, then you sure as hell weren't going to."

"But I didn't want him," I cried desperately. "You could have had Leo. I never loved him."

Tina's eyes narrowed in apparent doubt. "Doesn't matter," she said. "I wasn't about to let him divorce me and leave my ass high and dry. Not after everything I had done for him. I was his wife. You and Lena, y'all weren't shit but pawns."

The mention of Lena's name chilled my blood.

"I didn't need to split the money with either one of y'all," Tina went on. "So she had to go. And so did you. But remember I told you every wife had a purpose? Well, Lena's was to produce a child for Leo. Well, for me, rather. That way I could get a larger percentage of his money after he was gone. She was getting sick because I was poisoning her, slowly. Not enough to kill her. Just make her a little ill. I had Dr. Lin come over to give her something to induce the labor. I needed that baby out and healthy. And her job was done."

I squeezed my eyes shut. Either the information or the pregnancy had my emotions on high, and my heart broke knowing Tina had really killed Lena too. Well, *arranged* if we were using her terms. But either way, this bitch was responsible for everything. Evil wasn't the word to describe her.

"And you." Tina gestured to me with the gun. "Well, I already told you your purpose. You were supposed to take the fall for his murder. Like I said, it was all foolproof. Lena's dead, Leo's dead, your ass is in jail, and me and Leo Jr. ride off into the sunset on Leo's dime. Well, until the baby suddenly died from SIDS or some shit." She shrugged as if she was talking about the baby's clothes as opposed to his death. "I don't know. I hadn't thought that far yet."

Tina refocused on me and she took a step closer. It was as if she were actually looking at me for the first time. I held my breath as her eyes trailed down to land on my stomach, and I watched the realization strike her face. "Oh, I see." Her voice was light with pleasure at the sight of my little tummy. "Now it makes sense."

"It's not Leo's," I blurted out, immediately wrapping my arm around myself as if it would stop whatever thoughts were playing around in her mind. "It's not. I swear. I was having an affair."

"I knew all about the affair. Tried to tell Leo but his dumb ass really didn't care to listen to me. But it could be Leo's too. So now we seem to have a problem, Mrs. Owusu."

I backed into the corner of the room as Tina lowered the gun to my abdomen. She seemed to be taunting me, purposely taking her sweet time to drag this torture out even longer. *Oh God, please don't let her shoot me in the stomach.*

"See, now you're entitled to more money since you have Leo's seed," Tina said.

"But it's not his. We took a test and everything." I was spitting out lies through tears but I didn't care. Anything to save me and my baby's life. "The father, the *real* father knew I was married so he made me do it as proof. I swear."

For a moment, Tina paused and looked as if she were really considering my words. Then she tightened her finger on the trigger. "Doesn't matter," she said, her voice low and menacing. "You and that baby have no purpose anymore. I can't let you live."

I hit the floor as the first bullet burst through the plaster of the wall beside me. Before I could think, I threw my body in Tina's direction, wincing as I felt the next bullet pierce the flesh in my shoulder. I grabbed at her wrist and angled the gun to the ceiling before she could pull the trigger once more. I didn't know anything about guns, or rounds for that matter, but I knew she had to have more than two bullets in that thing, so my ass was as good as dead if I didn't get out of that room.

The wound in my shoulder was burning like hell as I clutched Tina's wrist. I struggled to knock her off her feet, but she was much stronger than I was in my current state. Before I knew what had happened, she lifted her knee to my stomach, and the impact had me screaming and letting go as I doubled over in pain. It was beyond excruciating, and right then and there, I prayed like I had never prayed before. *Please, God, let my baby be okay.*

I crumbled to the floor, clutching my stomach and grimacing against the agonizing pain that stabbed through my abdomen. The blood from my shoulder poured warm down my arm and the entire room began to sway.

Tina was mumbling something. I didn't know what, but again she had the gun pointed in my direction, so I knew this was the end.

My vision blurred so I couldn't make out the movement at the window. I hoped like hell it was a neighbor or someone who could help me. Surely someone had heard gunshots. Surely someone knew this bitch was about to murder me in this tiny little Pleasantville house. My thoughts lingered for a moment before wandering to Jahmad. And then Leo. I wasn't shit for how I had done them, I knew. They both deserved better. Maybe, just maybe this was my karma. My lids lowered and Jahmad's smiling face entered my mind. I would never get the chance again to tell him how much I loved him.

As I was lulled into unconsciousness, I caught the familiar voice. The accent, the tone, I would always remember it as the darkness enveloped me. Leo?

Chapter 32

She slept, unstirred
She dreamed of Heaven's gate
Her breath a rhythm of silent whispers
Whispers of unspoken promises
Cold, clear, and shaky with death

He watched her with quiet tears
His eyes glittering the pain bursting his heart
His fingers a tremble on her cheek
And there she slept
There she lay
A toneless rest
She'd never wake.

I had memorized Lena's poem because it was my favorite. Not sure why, but that one stuck out to me. I went over the words again and again as I wheeled myself down to NICU.

When I had woken up in the hospital, I was immediately panicked when I saw my flat tummy. The searing pain had me crying and screaming until four nurses had to restrain me and give me a shot to calm me down. Then they let me know that I was okay. My baby was okay. Everything was okay.

Tina's kick to my stomach had ruptured my placenta and had them doing an emergency C-section. My baby boy was alive, albeit with a few medical issues due to his prematurity. I had been only six months along, so of course he would have to spend a while in the hospital but he was strong. God had him. I had faith. After all, my son was the one who had saved my life. And now, well, now I had more than enough hospital and near-death experiences to last a lifetime.

The nursery in NICU was highly secure with rows of incubators where all you could do was stare down through the glass at your precious miracle. Which was fine with me. I would be able to hold and touch him soon enough.

At the registration desk to sign in to the ward, I waited patiently behind a gentleman who stood completing papers. It was when he mentioned my son's name, Jamaal, that I glanced up and met the eyes of a dead man.

He had cut his locs off. That's the first thing I noticed. I wanted to scream, but something about Leo's demeanor settled me. Like I shouldn't be afraid.

"Hi, my love," he said with that charming smile of his. That hadn't changed a bit either.

I wanted to be angry. Or relieved. But my mind wouldn't let me register anything other than shock.

"You were there," I said, suddenly remembering the voice at Tina's house right before I passed out.

"I couldn't let her hurt you, my love," he said. Leo reached for my hand and kissed the inside of my palm as if to affirm it was real. This was real. I wasn't dreaming.

"But you—"

"Come on." He grabbed the handles of my wheelchair and steered me over to a private corner of the lobby. He sat down and maneuvered my wheelchair directly in front of him. "I'm sorry," he said. "I had no idea what they were planning. Tina and Dr. Lin. I knew I just needed to disappear."

"So you faked your death?" I whispered, now feeling the rage bubbling up. How could he be so damn selfish?

"I had to get away," he said again. "As soon as I saw Tina tried to have me killed, I thought it would just be better if I made it seem like she was successful. I needed to get away from it all because it was too much to handle. Especially because I had actually fallen in love with you. Let's just say, not everyone was happy about the news." He reached out to touch my face and I slapped his hand away. Angry tears stung my eyes. When did he become such a coward?

"Don't touch me," I snapped. "I was going down for your murder and you didn't even do shit."

"No, my love, that's not it," he said gently, shaking his head. "I had no idea what they were planning until after your arrest. And when I found out, I knew I had to come back discreetly to help you. That's why I sent you the text. So you could go get information from Dr. Lin."

Wow. So he was the one that sent the text. "And Tina?" I pressed. "You were there when she was about to kill me."

Leo lowered his head to his hands. "I was almost too late," he whispered, his voice quivering. "I had been following her, keeping tabs on her. But don't worry. She'll never bother you again. I promise. "

I wasn't sure what that meant, but I knew I didn't want to know either.

"But your body." I remembered them pulling back the sheet to reveal his dead body. The funeral. I'd seen him with my own eyes.

"A body double," Leo answered. "A little money and a little makeup goes a long way."

I wanted none of this to make sense but at this point, I had no choice but to accept it. All of it. I was too exhausted to do otherwise.

I looked again at the registration desk. "Why are you here?" I asked, though I already knew the answer.

"To see my son."

"He's not your son."

Leo was watching me closely. Much too closely, and I shifted uncomfortably. I wondered if he could tell. Because truth be told, I didn't know who my baby's father was. But I held steadfast to Jahmad being the father so that I wouldn't allow room for any other possibility.

"Are you sure, Kimmy?"

A loaded question. I could tell he was asking was I sure about this decision. Sure about us. Sure about what needed to happen. And I couldn't have been more sure about anything in my entire life.

"Goodbye, Leo," I said. I kept his gaze as he watched me another minute or two before rising. He straightened his slacks, brushing invisible dust off the front.

Without another word, he disappeared down the hall, his shoes squeaking on the linoleum and signaling his retreat.

I waited until I was sure he was gone and let out a shuddering sigh. It was for the best. I had already been cleared of the charges. It was best to keep all ties severed so I wouldn't get pulled back into any more complications.

*

"You have a visitor, baby girl." My dad knocked on my hospital door before peeking his head through.

I lifted the cover up higher to my chin and turned over. I was still sick to my stomach and after not eating for several days, a huge migraine had been pounding at my head to add to my discomfort.

"Please, no visitors," I murmured, squeezing my eyes shut. I had already turned away Keon and Adria, insisting I would see them when I felt better.

"I think you want to see him."

I turned slightly, just making out the man's silhouette behind my dad. He stepped into view and it took everything in me not to spring from the bed and fly into his arms.

"I'll leave you two alone." My dad stepped out of the way and closed the door behind Jahmad.

I could tell he was at a loss for words. I sat up, letting the covers pool around my waist and belly. Jahmad took another step into the room and sank to the edge of the bed.

"How is the baby?" he asked tenderly.

"Good."

"And you? How are you?"

My smile bloomed at his concern. I felt better than I had in the days since I had witnessed the suicide.

"I'm better now," I answered honestly.

"Your dad told me everything was dropped."

I nodded. Thank God.

Larry had updated me that Dr. Lin and Tina's confession he had overheard and recorded on my phone was enough to get me acquitted. Since then I felt like a huge weight had been lifted off my shoulders. Nothing like the possibility of prison to scare the shit out of you.

"That's good." Another awkward moment of silence. Jahmad ran his hands over his face; I could tell he was stressed. It was obvious in the lines that creased his forehead and he carried it in his eyes. My heart ached. I had put him through all of this. "Look," he started before I had a chance to speak. "When I got the call . . . When I thought something had happened I was completely fucked up, Kimera. I'm not going to lie. It was easy to be mad and hurt over what you did. But I would never want anything to happen to you. I love you too much."

I nodded. His words were what brought the first tears of joy to my eyes. Damn, here I was crying again. I felt like that's all I ever did. "I love you too, Jahmad. So much."

Jahmad took the opportunity to scoot closer. He pulled me in for a hug, and I melted in his arms on a sigh. Jahmad hadn't said we were back together but he sure as hell hadn't taken his ring back either. That meant something, and I held on to that possibility. In a minute, I would take him down to see his son. *Our* son. Whether that was biologically the case or not really didn't matter. Maybe with time we could work on repairing us. I was patient. I could wait. Every wife had a purpose, Tina would say, and it wouldn't take long to show Jahmad that I was his.

"Now what?" I murmured against his shoulder.

Now it was his turn to sigh. "Let's take it one day at a time," he said.

I laughed. "Yeah, because after my last relationship, I'm not trying to rush into another commitment."

THE WIVES WE PLAY

Briana Cole

ABOUT THIS GUIDE

The suggested questions are included to enhance your group's reading of Briana Cole's *The Wives We Play*!

DISCUSSION QUESTIONS

1. Consider the character of Kimera Davis. Describe her conflict throughout the story. Do you think she is the victim? If not, who is the victim (if any), and why?

2. Discuss the ways Kimera grows (if she does) during the course of the novel.

3. Who were your favorite and least favorite characters? Why?

4. What were the underlying themes you took away from this story's premise?

5. How do the polyamory themes portrayed in the book relate to the conventional relationships in today's society?

6. What do you think will happen now that the baby is born? Are you rooting for Jahmad and Kimera to work things out?

7. How does the role of family and religion play a positive or negative influence in Kimera's actions?

8. Describe the conflicts with Leo Owusu.

9. Do you think the story was plot-based or character-driven?

10. Tina's main tagline is "Every wife has a purpose." What other quotes stood out to you and why?

11. If the book were being adapted into a movie, who would you want to see play what parts?

12. What scene was the most pivotal in the book? How do you think the story would have changed had that scene not taken place?

13. How did you feel overall about the book?

DON'T MISS
Triple Threat
by Camryn King

A tenacious reporter. A billionaire philanthropist. And all-access secrets that won't leave anyone safe fuel Camryn King's relentless new thriller . . .

Enjoy the following excerpt from *Triple Threat* . . .

1

A year ago today, Mallory Knight's world had changed. She found her best friend dead, sprawled on top of a comforter. The one Leigh had excitedly shown Mallory just days before, another extravagant gift from her friend's secret, obviously rich lover, the cost of which, Mallory had pointed out, could have housed a thousand homeless for a week. Or fed them for two. Leigh had shrugged, laughed, lain back against the ultra-soft fabric. Her deep cocoa skin beautifully contrasted against golden raw silk.

That day, when the earth shifted on its axis, Leigh had lain there again. Putrid. Naked. Grotesquely displayed. Left uncovered so as not to disturb potential evidence, investigators told her. Contaminate the scene. *With what, decency?* She had ignored them, had wrenched a towel from the en suite bath and placed it over her friend and colleague's private parts. Her glare at the four men in the room was an unspoken dare for them to remove it. That would happen only over her dead body.

She'd steeled herself. She looked again, at the bed and around the room. Whoever had killed Leigh had wanted her shamed. The way the body was positioned left no doubt about that. For Mallory, the cause of death wasn't in doubt, either. Murder. Not suicide, as the coroner claimed. But his findings matched what the detectives believed, what the scant evidence showed so . . .

case closed. Even though the half-empty bottle of high-dose opioids found on Leigh's nightstand weren't hers. Even though forensics found a second set of prints on one of two wineglasses next to the pills. Even though Mallory told investigators her friend preferred white wine to red and abhorred drugs of any kind. She suffered through headaches and saw an acupuncturist for menstrual cramps. Even though for Leigh Jackson image was everything. She'd never announce to the world she'd killed herself by leaving the pill bottle out on the table, get buck naked to do the deed, then drift into forever sleep with her legs gaping open. Details like those wouldn't have gotten past a female detective. They didn't get by Mallory, either. Beautiful women like Leigh tended to be self-conscious. What did Mallory see in that god-awful crime scene? Not even a porn star would have chosen that pose for their last close-up.

The adrenaline ran high that fateful morning, Mallory remembered. Early January. As bitterly cold as hell was hot. Back-to-back storms in the forecast. This time last year, New York had been in the grips of a record-breaking winter. Almost a foot of snow had been dumped on the city the night before. Mallory had bundled up in the usual multiple layers of cashmere and wool. She had pulled on knee-high, insulated riding boots and laughed out loud at the sound of Leigh's voice in her head, a replay of the conversation after showing Leigh what she'd bought.

"Those are by far the ugliest boots I've ever seen."

"Warm, though," Mallory had retorted. "I'm going for substance, not style."

"They'd be fine for Iceland. Or Antarctica. Or Alaska. Not Anchorage, though. Too many people. One of those outback places with more bears than humans. Reachable only by boat or plane."

Mallory had offered a side-eye. "So what you're saying is this was a great choice for a record cold winter."

"Absolutely . . . if you lived in an igloo. You live in an apartment in Brooklyn, next door to Manhattan. The fucking fashion capitol of the world, hello?"

Mallory had laughed so hard she snorted, which caused Leigh's lips to tremble until she couldn't hold back and joined her friend in an all-out guffaw. Complete opposites, those ladies. One practicality and comfort, stretch jeans and tees. The other back-breaking stilettos and designer everything. They'd met at an IRE conference, an annual event for investigative reporters and editors, and bonded over the shared position of feeling like family outcasts who used work to fill the void. Leigh was the self-proclaimed heathen in a family of Jehovah's Witnesses, while second marriages and much younger siblings had made Mallory feel like a third wheel in both parents' households. To Mallory, Leigh felt like the little sister she'd imagined having before her parents divorced.

That morning a year ago she'd stopped at the coffee shop for her usual extra-large with an espresso shot, two creams, and three sugars. She crossed the street and headed down into the subway to take the R from her roomy two-bed, two-bath walkup in Brooklyn to a cramped shared office in midtown Manhattan, a five-minute walk from Penn Station in a foot of snow that felt more like fifteen. She'd just grabbed a cab when her phone rang. An informant with a tip. Another single, successful, beautiful female found dead. One of many tips she'd received since beginning the series for which she'd just won a prestigious award. "Why They Disappear. Why They Die." Why did they? Mysteriously. Suspiciously. Most cases remained unsolved. Heart racing, Mallory had redirected the cabbie away from her office down to Water Street and a tony building across from the South Street Seaport. The building where Leigh lived. Where they'd joked and laughed just days before. She'd shut down her thoughts then. Refused to believe it could be her best friend. There were nine other residences in that building. She'd go to any of the condominiums, all of them, except number 10. But that very apartment was where she'd been directed. The apartment teeming with police, marked with crime tape.

"Knight."

Jolted back into the present, Mallory sucked in a breath, turned her eyes away from the memory, and looked at her boss. "Hey, Charlie."

"What are you doing here? It's Friday. I thought I told you to take the rest of the day off and start your weekend early."

"I am."

"Yeah, I see how off you are." He walked over to her corner of the office, moved a stack of books and papers off a chair, and plopped down. He shuffled an ever-present electronic cigarette from one side of his mouth to the other with his tongue. "That wasn't a suggestion. It was an order. Get out of here."

He sounded brusque, but Charlie's frown was worse than his fist. It had taken her almost three years to figure that out. When she started working at *New York News* just over four years ago he was intimidating, forceful, and Mallory didn't shrink easily. Six foot five with a shock of thick salt-and-pepper hair and a paunch that suggested too many hoagies, not enough salad, and no exercise, he'd pushed Mallory to her limit more than once. She'd pushed back. Worked harder. Won his respect.

"I know it's a hard day for you." His voice was softer, gentler now.

"Yep." One she didn't want to talk about. She powered down her laptop, reached for the bag.

"She'd have been proud of you for that."

"What?" He nodded toward her inbox. "Oh, that."

" 'Oh, that,' " he mimicked. "That, Knight, is what investigative journalists work all of their lives for and hope to achieve. Helluva lot of work you put in to get the Prober's Pen. Great work. Exceptional work. Congrats again."

It was true. In this specialized circle of journalism, the Prober's Pen, most often simply called the Pen, was right up there with the Pulitzer for distinctive honor.

"Thanks, Charlie. A lot of work, but not enough. We still don't know who killed her." A lump, sudden and unexpected, clogged her throat. Eyes burned. Mallory yanked the power cord from the wall, stood and shoved it into the computer bag along with her laptop. She reached for her purse. No way would she cry around Charlie. Investigative reporters had no time for tears.

She was two seconds from a clean escape before his big paw clamped her shoulder and halted her gait. She looked back, not at him, in his direction, but not in his eyes. One look at those compassion-filled baby blues and she'd be toast.

"What, Callahan?" Terse. Impatient. A tone you could get away with in New York. Even with your boss. Especially one like Charlie.

"Your column helped solve several cases. You deserved that award. Appreciate it. Appreciate life . . . for Leigh."

"Yeah, yeah, yeah. Out of my way, softie." Mallory pushed past him the way she wished she could push past the pain.

"Got a new assignment when you come back, Knight!"

She waved without turning around.

Later that evening Mallory went for counseling. Her therapists? Friends and colleagues Ava and Sam. The prescription? Alcohol. Lots of it. And laughter. No tears. At first, she'd declined, but they insisted. Had they remembered the anniversary, too? One drink was all she'd promised them. Then home she'd go to mourn her friend and lament her failed attempts to get at the truth. After that she'd go to visit her bestie. Take flowers. Maybe even shed a tear or two. If she dared.

Mallory left her apartment, tightened her scarf against the late-January chill, and walked three short blocks to Newsroom, an aptly named bar and restaurant in Brooklyn, opened by the daughter of a famous national news anchor, frequented by journalists and other creative types. Stiff drinks. Good food. Reasonable prices. Not everyone made six figures like Mallory Knight. In America's priciest city, even a hundred thousand dollars was no guarantee of champagne kisses and caviar dreams.

Bowing her head against the wind, she hurried toward the restaurant door. One yank and a blast of heat greeted her, followed by the drone of conversation and the smell of grilled onions. Her mouth watered. An intestinal growl followed, the clear reminder she hadn't had lunch. She unwrapped the scarf from around her head and neck, tightened the band struggling to hold back a mop of unruly curls, and looked for her friends.

"In the back." The hostess smiled and pointed toward the dining room.

"Thanks."

"Heard you won the Pen. Way to go."

"Gosh, word gets around."

"It's one of the highest honors a reporter can receive, Mallory so, yeah, a few people know."

She turned into the dining room and was met by applause. Those knowing people the hostess described were all standing and cheering. After picking her jaw off the floor, Mallory's narrowed eyes searched the room for her partners in crime. A shock of red hair ducked behind . . . Gary? Special correspondent for NBC? Indeed. And other familiar faces, too. The *Post*, *Times*, *Daily News*, the *Brooklyn Eagle*, *Amsterdam News*, and other local and national news outlets were represented. Highly embarrassed and deeply moved, Mallory made her way across the room, through good-natured barbs, hugs, and high fives, over to Gary, who gave her a hug, inches from the dynamic duo who'd undoubtedly planned the surprise.

"You two." Mallory jabbed an accusatory finger into a still shrinking Sam's shoulder while eyeing Ava, who smiled broadly. "When did you guys have time to do all this?"

"Calm down, girl." Ava shooed the question away. "Group text. Took five seconds."

Ava. Her girl. Keep-it-real Holyfield. "Thanks for making me feel special."

"You're welcome." Ava munched on a fry. "Always happy to help."

Just when Mallory thought she couldn't be shocked further, a voice caused her to whip her head clean around.

"Can I have everyone's attention, please?"

There stood Charlie, red-faced and grinning, holding up a shot glass as two tray-carrying waiters gave a glass to everyone in the room. Her boss, was in on it, too? All that insistence that she get out of the office? Damn, he was trying hard to make her cry.

"She doesn't like the spotlight, so next week I'll pay for this. But I was thrilled to learn that a celebration was being planned for one of the best reporters I've ever had the pleasure of working with, Mallory Knight." He paused for claps and cheers. "Most of you know this, though some may not. The hard work done on the Why series has resulted in three women being found and reunited with their families and two arrests, one of which was a cold case that had remained unsolved for fifteen years. Good job, kiddo."

Mallory accepted his hug. "Thanks, Charlie."

"Speech! Speech!" echoed around the room.

"As most of you know, I'm a much better writer than I am a speaker. At least without a lot more of these, so . . ." Mallory held up a shot glass holding pricey liquor. "Hear, hear."

She downed the drink, swallowed the liquid along with the burn that accompanied its journey down the hatch. Holding up a hand quieted the crowd.

"Okay, I . . . um . . . thank you guys for coming. The Pen means a lot. But your support means a lot more. Um . . . that first toast was for me. Let's do one more for another IR, Leigh Jackson. Everybody here who knew her knew she was . . . pretty amazing."

Mallory blinked back tears. "She was the inspiration behind the series and why I have this award. She held up a second shot glass. "To Leigh!"

For the next half hour Mallory accepted congrats and well wishes from her colleagues, accompanied by a medium-rare steak dinner and more vodka. The crowd thinned. Mallory grew quieter.

Sam squeezed her shoulder. "You okay?"

Seconds passed as she pondered the question. A slow nod followed. "As of a few seconds ago, I feel a lot better."

"Why?" Ava asked.

"I just made a decision." Mallory looked from Ava to Sam. "I know I said I'd let it go. But I can't. Whoever killed Leigh is not going to get away with it. I'm going to find out who did it, and make sure they pay for her murder."

Sam's expression morphed into one of true concern. "Oh, no, Mal. Not that again."

"You think a cold-blooded murderer should walk around free?"

"You know what she means." Ava's response was unbowed by Mallory's clear displeasure. "Or have you forgotten those first couple months after she died, when you were so bent on proving Leigh's suicide was murder that you almost worked yourself into a grave?"

"But I didn't die, did I? Instead, I got the Pen." Mallory's voice calmed as she slumped against her chair. "I'd much rather get Leigh's killer."

"I know you loved Leigh," Ava said, her voice now as soft as the look in her eyes. "And while Sam and I didn't know her as well as you did, we both liked her a lot and respected the hell out of her work as a journalist. You did everything you could right after it happened. Let the police continue to handle it from here on out."

"That's just it. They think it's already handled. The death was ruled a suicide. Case closed."

There wasn't a comeback for that harsh truth. Mallory held up a finger for another shot. Ava's brow arched in amazement.

"How many of those can you hold, Mal? You're taller than me, but I've got you by at least thirty pounds."

Mallory looked up to see Charlie wave and head to the door. Ignoring Ava, she called out to him. "Charlie!"

He waited by the hostess stand, the area now cold and crowded from the rush of dinner guests and a constantly opening door.

"What is it, kiddo?"

"Can't believe you knew about this and didn't tell me."

"Had you known, you wouldn't have shown up."

"That's probably true. I appreciate what you said up there. Thanks."

"Think nothing of it." He looked at his watch. "I gotta run. See you next week."

"One more thing. The new assignment you mentioned earlier. What's it about?"

Charlie hesitated.

Mallory's eyes narrowed. "Charlie . . ."

"Change of pace. You're going to love it."

"What's the topic?"

"Basketball."

"You want me to cover sports?" Incredulity raised Mallory's voice an octave.

"Told you that you'd love it," Charlie threw over his shoulder as he caught the door a customer just opened and hurried out.

"Charlie!"

Mallory frowned as she watched her boss's hurried steps, his head bowed against the wind and swirling snow. His answer to her question only raised several more. *Why would Charlie want an investigative reporter on a sports story? Why wasn't the sports editor handling it? Freelance writers clamored for free tickets to sports events. Why couldn't he give the assignment to one of them?* She wanted to continue doing stories that mattered, like those on missing women and unsolved murders that had won her the Pen. And Charlie wanted her to write about grown men playing games? Her mood darkening and shivering at the blast of cold wind accompanying the next customer through the front door, Mallory walked back to the table, hugged her friends goodbye, and began the short walk home. She lived less than ten minutes from the restaurant, and, although the temperature had dropped and snow was falling, she barely noticed. Mallory's thoughts were on her dead best friend, the botched closed case, and how to regenerate interest in catching a killer. Because whether officially or not, for work or not, Mallory would never stop trying to find out who killed Leigh Jackson. Never. Ever. No fucking way.

Connect with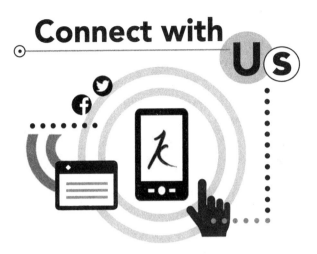

U S

Visit us online at
KensingtonBooks.com
to read more from your favorite authors, see books
by series, view reading group guides, and more.

Join us on social media
for sneak peeks, chances to win books and prize packs,
and to share your thoughts with other readers.

facebook.com/kensingtonpublishing
twitter.com/kensingtonbooks

Tell us what you think!

To share your thoughts, submit a review,
or sign up for our eNewsletters, please visit:
KensingtonBooks.com/TellUs.